BRAINS

DANIEL BREEZE

McNeil & Richards

Published by McNeil & Richards
www.mcneilandrichards.com

Printed in the U.S.A.

ISBN 13   978-0-9825602-4--2
ISBN   0-9825602-4-9

ALMOST ANY MAN WORTHY OF HIS SALT
WOULD FIGHT TO DEFEND HIS HOME,
BUT NO ONE EVER HEARD OF A MAN GOING
TO WAR FOR HIS BOARDING HOUSE.

MARK TWAIN
Mark Twain in Eruption

FOR MY BROTHER,
JERRY,
WHO WOULD HAVE LIKED
THIS BOOK

CONTENTS

I

The Recruit

Sunday, December 7 - Sunday, December 14

1

ON A COLD AND BLUSTERY evening in early December, an eerie calm settled over Chicago. Only the occasional screeching of an el train or the blaring of an ambulance siren shattered the stillness. Throughout the city and its sprawling suburbs, a million nervous people huddled in front of television sets.

In the Windy City Dome, most of the seventy-two thousand fans groaned in unison as the Chicago Philosophers, a team of weary and eccentric geniuses and pseudo-intellectuals, fell four points behind the Dallas Capitalists with a minute and twenty-four seconds remaining in the last game of the season. If the Phils won, they would land in the Brains playoffs for the first time. If they lost, their season would be over.

Philosopher Coach Rock Nelson, a short and intense man with thinning hair and a beer belly, signaled for a time-out. As Rock paced the sidelines mopping his brow with a sweat-soaked towel, he could have been mistaken for an old-time football coach, a Vince Lombardi in a time warp. Rock's exhausted troops gathered around him.

The crowd's deafening cheers and frantic screams played havoc with Rock's shattered nerves. He wanted to win the Brains championship—the Brains Bowl—more than anything in the world. Well, almost anything. He actually wanted to win professional football's Super Bowl more than anything in the world, but since the popularity of Brains was on the upswing and pro football was slowly being flushed down the proverbial toilet, Rock had readjusted his goals and set out in pursuit of the Brains Bowl championship. Now his chances of making the playoffs hinged on the closing eighty-four seconds of the Phils' last game of the season.

Rock faced his weary crew.

"I believe in incentives," he declared in a voice rapidly becoming hoarse after a day of yelling his lungs out. "So I've got a big one for you. Think of all the things you dread most. Think of all the terrible things that could happen to you. Well, if you don't win this game, *they're all going to happen!* It will make the Texas Chainsaw Massacre look like a Sunday school picnic!"

Amos "Freud" Lawton, forty-six-year-old team psychiatrist and assistant coach, pulled Rock aside. Freud wore metal-rimmed glasses and stood a half-foot taller than Rock. His unruly brown hair looked as though it had been trimmed with a lawn mower. His gaze was piercing, his mind sharp. Freud had problems of his own, but next to Rock's they seemed inconsequential.

"Rock, you can't threaten the players at a time like this! The pressure has made basket cases out of them. Do you want them to freeze up completely? Do you want to screw up everything you've worked for?"

Rock took a deep breath. "All right, Freud. All right." He faced the harried players again. "Maybe I was out of line. Let me put it another way: This is what we worked for. We still have time. Try to forget this game means everything, and that millions of fans are counting on you. Do your job and we'll come out of this all right. We're out of timeouts so I won't talk to you again until after the game, unless Dallas calls a timeout. So I want you to know one thing." He paused. *"I know who you are, I know where you live. If you blow this, I'm going to hunt down every one of you, and—"*

Freud restrained Rock as the Phils returned to their seats on the side of the playing court. Enough time remained for the Phils to regain the lead, but Rock couldn't shake the feeling that another disaster was about to befall the team.

Play-by-play announcer Moose Harrison described the scene for millions of fans viewing the game on television:

"THE DALLAS CAPITALISTS LEAD THE CHICAGO PHILOSOPHERS BY FOUR POINTS, 77 TO 73. THERE IS NO TOMORROW FOR THE PHILS IF THEY LOSE. IF THEY WIN, THEY WILL HOST THE FIRST PLAYOFF GAME IN FRANCHISE HISTORY NEXT WEEKEND. ALL THEIR HOPES ARE RIDING ON THE FINAL EIGHTY-FOUR SECONDS OF PLAY. THE SPECIALISTS IN POPULAR ARTS—BRIAN MARSHALL OF THE PHILS AND MARYANN PANTHER OF THE CAPS—ARE HEADING FOR CENTERCOURT TO FACE OFF ON A THREE POINTER."

Noise in the stadium swelled as Brian, the Philosophers' twenty-nine-year-old superstar from California, reached the Hot Zone, as centercourt was called. Brian was six-foot-two, muscular and handsome. He often was mistaken for a movie star or a surfer. Pressure was nothing new to him. Before joining the Phils he had worked for a Los Angeles advertising agency, and in advertising there was always pressure. But he had never faced pressure like this, with thousands of fans screaming their lungs out, ready to kill him if he screwed up.

Perspiration formed on Brian's forehead, but his blond

hair remained in place. He would look good to those watching on television.

The referee signaled for quiet. The clamor subsided to a dull roar.

"For three points ..." the referee said, his voice booming over the loudspeakers. "In 1969, *Midnight Cowboy* won the Academy Award for best picture." A clip from a movie suddenly flashed on the giant Brains Board behind the referee. "Which film won the Canadian Film Awards citation as best picture that year?"

MaryAnn, the fastest button pusher on the Dallas team, swatted her buzzer.

"A Place to Stand?" she blurted out, more as a question than an answer.

Behind her, the giant Brains Board flashed "OOPS!" Chicago fans cheered.

"That is incorrect," said the referee. "Do you want to try it, Chicago?"

These were the moments Brian lived for. All eyes were riveted on him. He seemed cool and confident. He smiled slightly as he said, *"The Best Damn Fiddler From Calabogie to Kaladar."*

"That is correct!" the referee proclaimed. The crowd roared as fireworks exploded on the Brains Board. Brian and a shattered MaryAnn returned to the sidelines. The Phils had closed the gap to one point with 1:06 remaining in the game.

Brian's seat was transported back to the sidelines, where he was parked beside Margaret Kramer, the Phils' seventy-two-year-old Renaissance Woman. (On Brains teams, the Renaissance Woman or Man was expected to have knowledge of many subjects, operating as a modern-day Leonardo da Vinci or Thomas Jefferson.) Margaret, who had been passing her golden years irritating the staff at a Phoenix nursing home when Rock signed her up, appeared slight and frail, but she didn't take guff from anybody—except Rock. Her hair was silver and her face was locked in a perpetual frown, partially the result of decaying teeth and partially the result of being constantly at odds with the rest of the world. But as Brian returned to the sidelines, Margaret was duly impressed he had come up with the title of the Canadian film. Perhaps she had misjudged him. Perhaps he was not a playboy who had wandered into the Phils' locker room by mistake.

"How on earth did you know the answer?" she shouted at Brian as the crowd cheered their hero.

"The flick aired on a cable channel a couple years ago when I was entertaining a girlfriend. I remember because we were making love on the sofa, and—"

"You're a disgusting pig," Margaret snapped.

"That's what she said."

The history experts—Tina Meredith of the Phils and the Capitalists' Bart Unger—moved onto the playing floor. Tina, a former corporate research director in her mid-forties, was a brunette who had been efficient, cheerful and relatively sane when the season began. As it progressed, she became increasingly nervous and distraught.

Tina surveyed the frenzied crowd. Most of the spectators were cheering her on. These were Chicago fans. But somehow, in the heat of battle, it was difficult to distinguish between friendly madness and unfriendly madness. Tina felt weak. Her face was flushed. She took a deep breath—and collapsed.

The crowd's frenzy slowed to a low rumbling. On the sidelines, Rock watched in horror. His dream of sailing into the playoffs and capturing the fabulous Brains Bowl trophy had just suffered a monumental setback.

Freud and Archie Bolton, the team physician, rushed to the playing floor to examine Tina. Bolton checked for a pulse, found it was weak, and held one of Tina's eyelids open to examine the eye.

"Let's get her to the hospital," Bolton said. "She can't go on."

Tina's teammates looked on in shock as she was loaded onto a stretcher and carried through the subdued crowd to exits at the rear of the stadium. Television cameras followed the path of the stretcher. In the distance the massive scoreboard told the story—Dallas 77, Chicago 76 with fifty-two seconds remaining in the game.

THE SIREN WAILED INCESSANTLY as the ambulance weaved along Chicago's Lake Shore Drive, then turned onto Michigan Avenue, where Christmas decorations graced the windows of Lord and Taylor, Neiman Marcus and other glamorous stores along the Magnificent Mile. The ambulance driver radioed ahead to tell Emergency Room personnel he was bringing in the Phils player who had collapsed.

The ambulance slowed for a turn onto Chicago Avenue and two minutes later pulled into the receiving area at Northwestern Memorial Hospital.

In the Emergency Room, Bolton gave an admitting clerk information about Tina while the Phils starter was loaded onto a table.

"Another one," a young doctor grumbled. "What do they do to these people—torture them?"

Tina's blood pressure was high, her pulse erratic. "She'll be here awhile," the doctor said. "Looks like she probably had a breakdown."

In the waiting area, a pregnant Hispanic woman and a cop who had been shot in the arm watched the Philosophers game on television. Moose Harrison sounded excited:

"THE PHILS DID IT! THE PHILS DID IT! JULIE HOWARD'S FOUR POINTS AT THE BUZZER BURY DALLAS, 80 TO 77, AND PROPEL THE PHILS INTO THE PLAYOFFS FOR THE FIRST TIME IN FRANCHISE HISTORY!"

The crowd could be seen surging to the playing area hoisting their reluctant heroes—these weary, triumphant intellectuals—onto their shoulders.

"BUT CHICAGO'S VICTORY CAME AT A BIG PRICE. THE PHILS MAY BE WITHOUT THE SERVICES OF THEIR HISTORY ACE, TINA MEREDITH, WHEN THEY HOST THE POWERFUL CLEVELAND MIDDLE AMERICANS IN NEXT SUNDAY'S PLAYOFF GAME THAT WILL DECIDE THE MIDWEST DIVISION CHAMPION. CLEVELAND DRUBBED THE PITTSBURGH BOOKERS 96 TO 60 THIS AFTERNOON.

"ROCK WANTS TO WIN THE BRAINS BOWL MORE THAN LIFE ITSELF, BUT HE HAS HIS WORK CUT OUT FOR HIM IF HIS TEAM IS TO CONTINUE ITS STORYBOOK QUEST FOR THE TITLE."

2

THE NEXT MORNING, FREUD AND Ben Sloan, the owner of the Chicago Philosophers, boarded a private jet at Midway Airport. Their destination: Indianapolis. Final destination: Franklin, Indiana. Their mission: to sign a replacement for the team's history expert, Tina Meredith, as quickly as possible. The rest of the team was in Chicago preparing for Sunday's playoff game.

As the small plane climbed into the clouds, Ben gazed at the sprawling city below. His thoughts turned to how he and Philadelphia millionaire Blackie Thornton had founded the Brains League four years earlier.

Ben and Blackie already owned professional football teams, but they were disgusted because salaries, bonuses and ticket prices had spiraled to ridiculous heights. Abandoning football for a new kind of league was Ben's idea.

"Think of it," he told Blackie, as they carved up steaks at Michael Jordan's Restaurant on LaSalle Street in Chicago. "Teams of professional know-it-alls, based in cities across the country, competing to get into the playoffs and ultimately slug it out in the biggest game of all—the Brains Bowl!"

Blackie was slow to see the possibilities. "Have you lost

your mind? Who would pay to see teams of nerds answer questions nobody cares about?"

"We're not talking about nerds, Blackie. You're missing the big picture. We'll sign up people from many walks of life. Some will specialize in popular subjects like movies, television, games and sports. Others will be experts in literature and history. Remember how popular 'The $64,000 Question' and 'Twenty One' were years ago?"

Blackie grimaced. "I remember. I also remember the scandal that erupted because some of the shows were rigged."

"But this won't be rigged. Why, if we hype this thing right, we could make millions!"

Blackie finally agreed to go along with Ben—what the hell, if he put a few million into the stock market he'd probably blow it anyway—and the next year the Brains League was launched. Ben's Chicago franchise finished dead last in the Midwest Division. Blackie's Founding Fathers finished in the cellar in the Eastern Division. Not only that, it wasn't long before Brains players and their agents demanded a bigger piece of the action. Now, in the fourth season, salaries and bonuses were nearly on a par with the huge professional football payouts. Ben shelled out millions to players and barely broke even. If Rock could, by some miracle, win the Brains Bowl, it would bring in a truckload of additional revenue and dozens of opportunities to exploit the team nationally, but few people thought Rock and the Phils had more than a snowball's chance in hell of winning it all. The talented and intimidating San Francisco Hackers had won the last two Brains Bowls and most people figured they would win the championship again. For now, however, Ben could bask in the knowledge that he was the owner of a playoff team. His mother had been right. There was a God.

IN A SMALL WOODEN HOUSE on Harbon Drive in Franklin, Indiana, Sam Winslow sprawled in a bed, embroiled in a deep sleep.

He dreamed he was sitting in an uncomfortable wooden chair in a small conference room on a university campus and he was sweating profusely.

He did not want to be there.

Through open windows he could see bright sunlight. Leaves on maple trees swayed in a gentle breeze.

He faced the three professors who had just heard him go over the highlights of his doctoral dissertation. Now it was the committee's turn to respond.

The balding professor with the bow tie and horn-rimmed glasses commented first. "Poorly researched. What on earth made you think you could write about Oxford in the Middle Ages? You've never visited England and you know little about the Middle Ages."

Sam squirmed. "On the surface, that is true. But I have done a lot of research."

The other male professor, who had long hair and beady eyes, grimaced. "Comic books don't count."

"Do movies?"

"I must agree with my colleague," he said. "Very poorly executed."

"But—"

The third professor, a woman with bad teeth who was dressed in black shirt and pants, nodded. "It does not meet our standards."

Sam was devastated. "I spent a year of my life writing this dissertation. I need a doctorate as the anchor for my future academic career!"

"Too bad, kid," said baldy. "Our verdict is unanimous. Next!"

Sam was on the verge of launching a violent verbal protest when he realized a campus security guard had pointed a gun at his head. "One more word and you won't have any career," the guard said.

Sam abruptly awoke. He was breathing heavily. It took a moment to realize he was in Franklin, his hometown, and not a university conference room. It had all been another intense, frightening dream.

He glanced at his alarm clock. 9:21. He had overslept. He struggled to get out of bed. He threw water on his face, slipped into his clothes and hurriedly fixed a scrambled egg and toast. Then he grabbed his car keys and ran out the door. He had promised Carl Jeffries he would meet him at a gym to shoot a few baskets and he was late.

AT INDIANAPOLIS INTERNATIONAL AIRPORT, the Chicago Philosophers' jet taxied to a stop. A rented Chevy van was waiting for Ben Sloan and Freud Lawton. The driver did not recognize his passengers. All he knew was that the shorter man with big jowls seemed to enjoy ordering people around. The taller man appeared pale and glum.

"How long will it take to get to this burg?" Ben growled, as his cigar polluted the air in the van.

The driver glanced at the rear view mirror. "Franklin? About a half hour."

Ben released a long sigh.

As the van rolled south into the Indiana countryside, Ben noticed light snow was falling. He called his secretary back in Chicago and she ran down a list of people who had left phone messages for him.

Wrapped up in his own thoughts, Ben did not realize

Freud was struggling to avoid going into convulsions triggered by smoke from Ben's cigar. The rational thing for Freud to do would have been to tell Ben the cigar was gagging him, but Freud—despite his training as a psychiatrist—had trouble confronting people in positions of power. Obviously, he had a few issues that had not been resolved by the time he finished his residency in the General Psychiatry Residency Program at the University of North Carolina. Perhaps no one would have noticed his peculiarities if he had opened a private practice in Chapel Hill, as he had intended to do, but he couldn't scrape up the money. When Ben offered him $600,000 a year to join the Phils as shrink and assistant coach, Freud could not refuse, and now his eccentricities were not only noticed, they were reported in news media from coast to coast. Perhaps that was a small inconvenience, however, because Freud socked away as much of the money as he could and one day he would use it to open his private practice. In the meantime, Rock and his team full of misfits offered exceptional opportunities for observing dysfunctional behavior.

The same could be said for the cranky old buzzard who was sitting next to Freud.

Ben closed his cellphone and turned his attention to the countryside. "Look around," he grumbled. "Nothing here but farmland. What the hell are we doing here? I don't see how a hayseed who gave up teaching to 'find himself' in the boondocks will help us in the playoffs."

Freud shrugged. "Our research department analyzed computerized scouting reports going back to the day you started the franchise. This looks like our best option. We don't have a lot of time to think it over."

Ben sighed. "All right. Let's sign up this redneck genius

and get back to civilization. I'm supposed to be on Lennie Framton's radio talk show tonight. He'll ask me how Rock managed to get the Phils into the playoffs. Damned if I know."

I know, Freud thought. Threats and intimidation. That's how he did it.

"It's a mystery to me, too," Freud said diplomatically.

Snow fluttered softly to the ground as the van approached the outskirts of Franklin, a city with about 22,000 residents a few miles south of Indianapolis. Ben noted with dismay there were no luxury hotels, department stores, or Trader Vic's restaurants in sight. A sign revealed Franklin was the home of Franklin College of Indiana. Christmas trees could be seen inside many of the brick and wood frame houses. It was a clean town, but it was no Chicago. Ben became increasingly restless.

The van slowed as the driver checked out the house numbers.

"That must be it," Freud said, nodding in the direction of a small white wooden abode. The paint was peeling and the mailbox hung at an angle.

Freud and Ben climbed out of the van and hiked up the four steps leading to the porch and front door. Freud knocked, softly at first, then more loudly.

"He ain't home!"

The voice came from a neighbor's driveway, where a white-haired man leaned on a snow shovel.

"Is this where Sam Winslow lives?" Freud asked.

"Yep. Only he ain't home."

"Any idea where he is?" asked Ben.

"Left about an hour ago carrying a basketball. My guess

is he's over at the Franklin College campus. Shoots baskets there a lot."

The neighbor gave them directions to the gym.

SAM WINSLOW, LANKY AND AGILE, dressed in shorts, tee shirt and tennis shoes, dribbled a basketball to the left side of the court. His opponent, Carl Jeffries, a lawyer he had known since high school, followed.

"Shoot it, Winslow!" Jeffries said. "You haven't hit from three-point range all day. You're due."

Jeffries was baiting him, but Sam figured Jeffries was right. He was due to hit a three-pointer sooner or later. With his back to the basket, Sam dribbled to his right, pivoted on his left foot and let loose with a hook shot. The ball sailed high into the air … and careened off the rim of the basket.

Jeffries grabbed the rebound and scored on a layup before Sam could recover.

Jeffries tossed Sam the basketball. "That does it for me. Gotta get back to the office. Some of us work for a living."

Sam pivoted again, went to his left and unleashed another hook shot. The ball sailed through the basket.

"Like you said, Carl, I was due."

"Yeah, but I didn't really believe it. That was pure slop."

"What's the old saying—I'd rather be sloppy than good?"

"I think it's 'I'd rather be lucky than good'."

Sam shot a few free throws, then launched a long shot from three-point range on the right side of the basket. He missed by about four feet.

"My grandmother can shoot better than that. She's a hundred and two years old."

Sam hadn't noticed that two strangers in street clothes

had wandered into the gym and were watching him shoot baskets.

"You startled me," Sam said.

Freud decided pleasantries were in order. "I wonder if you could help us. We are looking for Sam Winslow."

"I'm Sam. What do you need?"

"Are you the Sam Winslow who graduated with honors from Indiana University, then received a master's degree and doctorate in history from Harvard?"

"That's right." Sam didn't mention he had not earned the doctorate yet.

"Our records show you are twenty-seven years old and unemployed," Freud said.

"I'm twenty-eight. What's up? Am I being arrested?"

"Should you be?" Ben inquired.

"Not that I know of, but my attorney just left. I can still catch him if I need him."

Ben grimaced. "Let's get this over with," he said.

"Sam, I'm Freud Lawton, the Philosophers' assistant coach and team psychiatrist, and this is Ben Sloan. He owns the team."

Sam was dumbfounded. It *was* Ben and Freud! He had seen them on television. The Philosophers had just landed in the playoffs for the first time ever. What were the owner and assistant coach doing watching him play basketball?

Freud glanced at his watch. "We don't have much time. Sam, you probably know that Tina Meredith cracked under the pressure in last night's game."

"I noticed."

"We need to replace her. Fast. Our scouting reports suggest you have the background we need. We want you to join the team for the playoffs. Actually, we intend to put you in the starting lineup. Our second-stringers aren't strong in history."

Sam's eyes opened wide. "This has got to be a joke. Did Carl or my brother Joe send you here?"

"Let's get out of here," Ben groused. "I've got to get back to Chicago. This burg is so sleepy there's probably a seven o'clock curfew. I expect to see Andy and Opie walking down the street any minute. This was a mistake. Besides, we don't know if the kid knows anything about history. He has a couple degrees. Big deal. You can buy those on the Internet." Ben moved closer to Sam. "Name three of the biggest losers in history, hot shot!"

Sam smiled wryly. "Chevalier De Rohan. He thought he was great at deciphering messages, but he lost his life because he couldn't decipher a simple coded message. Cumberland Gap. They lost to Georgia Tech, 222 to 0, in the most lopsided college football game in history. And Melony."

"Melony who?" demanded Ben.

"Your wife. I recall reading an article in *Sports Illustrated* a few years ago that mentioned your wife's name was Melony. She's a loser because she married you!"

Ben glared at Sam. "You smart aleck punk kid. I ought to—"

Freud restrained Ben. "Take it easy!"

Ben tried to calm himself. "It's easy to spout off a couple insignificant facts when you're piddling around in the boondocks, but what could you possibly know about handling big-time pressure when seventy thousand screaming fans are packed into a stadium and millions more are watching on television?

Sam shrugged. He faced the basket, dribbled the ball a couple times and calmly sank a long shot. Ben was not impressed.

"So you can shoot a basketball. Big deal. Anybody can get lucky. But that's not pressure. Let's make it interesting. I'll bet you a hundred bucks you miss your next shot from at least fifteen feet out. What do you say?"

"A hundred bucks, huh?" Sam looked at the basket. It seemed a hundred feet away. "Okay, old man, you're on."

"My name is Ben. Don't call me old man, you little squirt."

Sam dribbled a few times and let the ball fly. It bounced off the rim.

"Just as I thought," Ben growled. "When the pressure is on, you're lousy. We don't need you. We've got enough players who choke under pressure."

Sam realized his chance at glory, his once-in-a-lifetime opportunity to make it big, was fading fast. He had to do something. Besides, he didn't have the hundred dollars.

"A hundred bucks isn't pressure," he told Ben aggressively. "That's chicken feed. … Double or nothing!"

Ben looked at Sam closely. "Two hundred? You sure you got that much?"

"Don't make me laugh, old man."

"You're on," Ben said, obviously enjoying the challenge.

Sam suddenly realized what was happening—his opportunity to be a Brains player and earn a lot of money hinged on whether he could make one shot with a basketball. Talk about pressure. He wished he had played basketball for his high school team instead of dropping out when the going got rough.

Sam dribbled three times and looked toward the bucket. He dribbled twice more, then let loose with a jump shot from about nineteen feet out. The ball sailed through the net.

"Not bad, kid," Ben said as he pulled two hundred-dollar bills out of his wallet. "But if you're as good as Freud says, how come you don't have a job? Why aren't you teaching at one of the big universities or making megabucks somewhere?"

"I taught at big universities for three years while I worked on my master's and doctorate, as I'm sure your scouting reports already told you. It wasn't for me. I wanted time to think before I decide what to do with the rest of my life, so I came back to Franklin. I'm jobless by choice. I'm working on a book."

"Who isn't." Ben handed the two hundred dollars to Sam. "Sounds to me like you're lazy. Where's your ambition? Aren't you tired of sitting on the sidelines? Do you want to get back in the game? Do you want to get out of this mom and pop burg and see some real action? We're in the playoffs and if it's the last thing Rock does, he's going to win the Brains Bowl. I'll pay you a hundred grand for each playoff game—and two hundred thou for the Brains Bowl, if we make it that far. And you'll get twice that for every game we win. What have you got to lose?"

A little fast math told Sam he could earn up to $800,000 for four weeks' work if the Philosophers went all the way, winning two playoff games and the Brains Bowl. "I'll do it. But I want ten thousand dollars for signing. I always dreamed of getting a bonus for signing a contract."

"All right, kid," Ben said. "We'll expect you at the Palmer House Hilton in Chicago tonight. That's where the team's staying while we prepare for the playoffs. You're going to earn that money. You'll work harder than you ever worked in your life."

"We'll have a contract ready for you to sign tomorrow," Freud said. "You might want to get an agent. You'll be asked to appear in television commercials for everything from jockstraps to aspirin. An agent can save you a lot of time and paperwork."

"Don't tell anyone except your agent how much we're paying you," Ben warned. "And no more cracks about my wife!"

Ben and Freud started back toward the rented van as Sam dribbled the ball and began talking, to no one in particular. "And the pass goes to Sam Winslow, who just signed a huge contract with the pros. Sam fakes, shoots and ... *scores* as time runs out!"

"Just what we need," Ben told Freud as they climbed into the van. "Another Looney Tunes player. Rock is going to kill me. ... Do you think Winslow understands he wasn't signed to play basketball?"

As soon as Sam won two more games in the final seconds (and blew three others) he drove his '82 Buick to his parents' house on the east side of town. He hurried up to the front door and knocked. A few moments later, his father, Fred, opened the door and let him in—somewhat reluctantly, it seemed to Sam, but that was the way his father always behaved. Fred, who was heavy-set with unruly black hair, had celebrated his fiftieth birthday earlier in the year.

Sam glanced at the barren artificial green Christmas tree in the living room. Fred probably would get around to decorating it sometime before Christmas.

"You'll never believe what just happened!" Sam exclaimed, as he slipped off his coat.

"You lost another job," Fred guessed, as he plopped down into his comfortable recliner. "I don't understand it. You're supposed to be a genius, but you can't hang onto a job. Then you come over here, and I give you a few bucks to get you back on your feet, but I never see the money again. Well, forget it. I won't give you any more. What little money I have I'll spend on lottery tickets and pizzas over the next twenty years. When I die you and your brother will inherit old pizza cartons and worthless lottery tickets."

Mona, Sam's mother, hurried in from the kitchen and kissed Sam on the cheek. A petite woman with black hair and a sparkle in her eyes, she wore a white apron over her red cotton dress.

"You haven't been over for Sunday dinner in three weeks," Mona told Sam. "You can't drive across town to come to dinner?"

"I've been busy, mom. I've got great news. I was shooting baskets at the college a half hour ago when a couple guys wandered in. The owner of the Chicago Phils and the team shrink! They're going to pay me a huge amount of money to play for the Phils in the playoffs!"

Fred reached for the *Indianapolis Star*. "That's the craziest thing I ever heard. I don't want to hear any more of your foolishness. You've been drinking the cheap stuff again, haven't you?" He buried himself behind the newspaper, but he was still grumbling. "You wouldn't need to buy the cheap stuff if you had a decent job. Why don't you get a high-pay-ing, white collar job like everyone else and embezzle some money so your mother and I can move out of this rat trap?" He peeked at Sam from behind the newspaper. "It's time to quit wasting your time dreaming up silly fantasies and decide what to do with your life. Figure out how to make a good living with the skills you have and then go for the gold. That's what I did." Fred disappeared behind the news-paper again.

Sam's father had owned a drugstore in Franklin for

twenty-seven years before selling it to a chain and retiring. He hadn't exactly gone for the gold. He had gone for the bronze.

"But, Dad, I'm telling you the truth. I'm going to Chicago and they're going to pay me a lot of money for a few weeks work. We're talking big bucks. Monster dollars!"

Fred peeked over the top of the newspaper. "How much exactly?"

"I can't tell you. But it's enough to buy six or seven houses like this one."

Mona shook her head. "Enough of this nonsense. Everyone I've ever known had to work hard all their lives to make a decent living. You can't get rich quick. It's a pipe dream. It may happen to other people, but not to us."

Sam desperately wanted them to believe him. "I'm not kidding! I'm leaving for Chicago this afternoon. I'll be playing on television!"

His mother shrugged. "Well, be sure to take your gloves and earmuffs, Sam. It gets cold in Chicago in the winter. When your Aunt Mildred went up to Chicago a few years ago she said the wind blew her half way across town and it was so cold Uncle Walter's lips froze to a beer can."

"Again with the lips," Fred mumbled, slamming the newspaper down on a coffee table. "Every time someone mentions Chicago I hear about Walter's Frozen Lips, and the surgery, and the doctor bills."

"I only mention it because there's a lesson to be learned from it," Mona declared.

"There sure is," grumbled Fred. "Sam, your Uncle Walter is a total jerk."

Mona ignored Fred's grousing. "You be careful if you go to Chicago, Sam. Call me after you get there. And don't drink beer when you're outdoors."

It was obvious to Sam he could not convince his parents he had found the pot of gold at the end of the rainbow. "I've got a lot to do before I go," he said, as he grabbed his coat and hurried out the front door.

As HE DROVE THROUGH THE streets of Franklin, Sam wondered how he could break the news to Martha Jean, his live-in girlfriend. Sam always viewed their relationship as casual, but Martha Jean had been fishing for a long-term commitment. Sam had grown increasingly uneasy with the situation. It was the perfect time to cut the cord. He would let her down gently, but he would be firm. It was over.

When he arrived at his bungalow, he found Martha Jean lounging in the overstuffed brown armchair in the living room. She was wearing his bathrobe and browsing through the classified ads.

"You really need to get a job," she said. "We can't go on like this. ... Here's one. Computer Corral is looking for a salesman."

Sam snatched the newspaper out of her hands. "You're right, Martha Jean. We can't go on like this." He helped her out of the chair. "I want to get out of the rut I've been in. I just signed up for a job. And it's time for *you* to move on, too. We won't be seeing each other any more."

"*What?* But, Sam ..."

"It's for the best. You need to get on with your life. Start by finding a job. Call Computer Corral."

"But, Sam. I can't sell computers!"

Sam reached for his cell phone and speed-dialed his brother's number. "Joe? I need a ride to the Indianapolis airport. I'm going to Chicago."

"Chicago? Why?"

"I'll explain in the car."

"Give me a half hour."

Sam headed upstairs. "I've got to pack, Martha Jean. I suggest you do the same."

As JOE DROVE SAM TO INDIANAPOLIS a half hour later, conflicting feelings overwhelmed Sam. He was excited about playing for a playoff team. Relieved that his dead-end relationship with Martha Jean was ending. Worried that he might crash and burn with the Phils.

Sam told Joe about Freud, Ben, the playoff deal and his determination to make a break with the past.

"So you fired Martha Jean?"

"Basically. No severance. She's out on the street."

"Poor kid. ... Would you mind if I call her?"

"What?"

"She's one foxy lady."

"It would be awkward, Joe. I just cut the cord. I don't think keeping her in the family is a good idea."

"I suppose you're right."

They rode in silence for a few moments.

"You're going to call her, aren't you?" Sam said.

"Damn right."

3

DURING THE FLIGHT FROM INDIANAPOLIS that afternoon, Sam argued with an attractive Northwestern University co-ed about whether the Internet and cell phones were turning teenagers into nervous basket cases with IQs of thirty. She assured him this was not happening. She demonstrated how she could do homework, Twitter and watch an online movie simultaneously. He then pointed out that her homework assignment read like it had been written by a first-grader.

"That's how I always write," the co-ed said.

"I don't doubt it," Sam said. "That's the problem."

The co-ed then tweeted her boyfriend about the jerk sitting next to her on the plane while Sam pondered whether he needed to work on his people skills.

Sam hailed a taxi at O'Hare International Airport and settled in for the ride to the Palmer House Hilton. The Sears Tower loomed in the distance as the taxi approached the heavily congested Loop. The screeching brakes of buses and taxis and life-or-death battles for parking spaces contrasted sharply with the pace of life in little Franklin, Indiana.

The cabbie pulled into the entryway at the Palmer House Hilton off a short stretch of Monroe Street that had been renamed Palmer House Hilton Way. After the cabbie unloaded the luggage, Sam slipped him a twenty-dollar bill.

The high school Sam had attended in Indiana could be squeezed into the sprawling French-inspired Palmer House Hilton lobby and there would be space left over. Chandeliers hung from the massive ceiling, which was decorated with twenty-one oil paintings of figures from Greek mythology. Plush furniture and carpeting added to the elegance. For someone who usually stayed at Budget Inns or Motel 6's, this was like heaven.

Sam approached the front desk. As a young man with short blond hair checked in a middle-aged couple from Montana, Sam browsed through a brochure describing the Palmer House Hilton. The hotel opened for business in 1871—and thirteen days later was leveled by the Great Chicago Fire. Over the years, the Palmer House had hosted such renowned guests as Oscar Wilde, Buffalo Bill, Mark Twain, Charles Dickens, Rudyard Kipling, Ulysses S. Grant and Sam Winslow.

Sam did a double take. He scrutinized the list of names. His was not among them. He must have been daydreaming.

The desk clerk turned his attention to Sam.

"May I help you?" the desk clerk asked, in a tone that suggested he had more important things to do.

"I'm Sam Winslow. I believe you have a room for me."

As the desk clerk typed on a computer keyboard, fear overtook Sam. What if someone had played a practical joke on him? What if Sloan and Freud hadn't come to see him at all? What if his friends back in Franklin were laughing themselves silly because Sam had actually *believed* Sloan and

Freud would journey to Franklin to offer him up to $800,000 for a few weeks work?

"Oh, God, am I gullible," Sam mumbled. He looked to see where the nearest exits were in case he needed to make a quick getaway.

The desk clerk rang for a bellboy. "Take Mr. Winslow's luggage to room eleven twelve."

A well-endowed young brunette wearing a gray sweatshirt and bluejeans under a maroon winter coat stepped into the elevator just ahead of Sam and the bellboy. She let out an audible sigh. She was tired. It had been a long and difficult season. She had been trying to keep body and soul together despite all the pressures of playing for the Phils and was barely managing to do it. Everywhere she went, fans recognized her and wanted to talk to her. Male fans wanted to do more than talk. She was at the end of her rope. If one more oversexed fan came up and started feeding her a line, she was sure she would lose control and pass over into the Twilight Zone.

She noticed with annoyance that the young man next to the bellboy had recognized her and was about to say something. She turned her back to him, but he spoke anyway.

"Julie Howard! I've seen you on television! It's terrific what you and the others have done, defying all the odds and landing in the playoffs. I'll never forget the Miami game, when you—"

The young man continued to babble. Julie couldn't take any more. She turned and confronted him.

"Let me ask you something," she snarled. "Why don't people like you do something with your lives instead of hanging around hotels, waiting for our players to show up?

You follow us around like groupies, or parasites, or fleas. Leave us alone and get a life!"

Sam turned four shades of red in succession. "Maybe I should introduce myself—"

"Don't bother. I've seen hangers-on like you in every city we've visited. I don't want to know who you are. My life is complete without knowing you. And if you don't shut up and quit bothering me, I'm going to scream for the cops."

"I think there's been a misunderstanding—"

Julie screamed like a wounded moose as the elevator door opened onto the eleventh floor.

"Oh, God," moaned the bellboy.

Sam watched her navigate down the corridor. This was the floor where Sam and the bellboy intended to get off, but Sam didn't want to take a chance on setting Julie off again.

"Touchy, isn't she?" the bellboy noted.

Sam checked in with the security guard on the floor as a young black man and a young woman watched from the doorways to their rooms. Julie's outburst had attracted their attention.

"Nice going," the young man said. "Julie usually doesn't hit the panic button until the second or third date."

. The bellboy opened the electronic lock to room 1112. Sam noticed the furnishings were elegant and expensive, the bedspread plush, the room spacious. The bellboy opened the curtains.

On a desk sat a laptop computer.

"Do people ever steal the computers?" Sam asked.

"They were placed in the Phils rooms by special arrangement. No one has ever stolen one." The bellboy pocketed the five-dollar tip Sam handed him. "But we'll be watching you."

As the bellboy left, the thin, pale young black man and the curvaceous Hispanic woman knocked on the door and entered. The young man had the glazed look of a college student who had stayed up four nights in a row cramming for final exams—and then slept through them. The woman was a sultry, black-haired beauty.

"I'm T.J. Collins. This is Juanita Lorez. We're second stringers on this team of raving lunatics."

Sam introduced himself.

"I'm from Detroit," T.J. said. "Juanita has a husband and small son in Miami Beach. She writes trashy short stories in her spare time."

Juanita glared at T.J. "My stories are not trashy!"

"Tell him what you're working on now," T.J. insisted.

She blushed. *The Naked Union Soldier.* ... Well, magazines buy my stories and publish them!"

Sam smiled. "I'm surprised they didn't make one of you a starter instead of signing me."

"Don't dwell on it," T.J. said. "It's a sore point with us. I've been with this team two years and average three minutes of playing time a game. Three lousy minutes ... On the other hand, that's about 45 minutes of playing time a year, and for that I rake in more than the President does. Not bad for someone who was working at an automobile plant two years ago. Even so, I sure as hell want to be a starter. That's where the big money is. That's where the perks of celebrity status are."

"You aren't upset with *me* because they hired me, are you?" Sam asked.

"No," Juanita said. "If we were, we'd have Chase pay you a visit."

Sam had heard about Chase Turnbull, a Mississippi native who had a shady reputation as a con man and criminal. He had served fifteen years in a Mississippi prison for killing a woman after a swindle he had concocted spun out of control. In prison, Chase passed a lot of time memorizing sports statistics. After his release, a local newspaper ran a story about him, the Associated Press picked it up, and two weeks later, Rock hired Chase as the team's sports specialist.

"Did Chase really kill that woman?" Sam asked.

"I don't know. Let's go ask Chase," T.J. suggested.

T.J. was ready to lead the way, but Sam grabbed him by the shirt sleeve. "Let's not. I was just curious."

"Chase says he never whacked anyone. I don't know if he did or not. We give Chase his own space and let him do his own thing. He gives us an edge, though, because other teams freak out when they come face-to-face with a convicted murderer. ... He's on the twelfth floor with Rock and Freud. The rest of us are here on the eleventh."

Sam told T.J. and Juanita about his run-in with Julie, the team's quotations specialist.

"Julie is the sanest person on this team," Juanita said. "That's a scary thought, isn't it. Come on, We'll introduce you. I can't wait to see the expression on her face!"

"Maybe we should take Chase along as protection," Sam suggested.

"No, she's a pussycat," T.J. insisted, as he led the way through the hallway. "She's just feeling the pressure. She's got a great bod, doesn't she? Too bad she's engaged to some guy back in her hometown, Philadelphia. Don't waste your time asking her out."

"I'd probably have better luck asking Chase out."

"To each their own," T.J. said.

Juanita knocked on the door to room 1107, then ducked out

of the way. Julie, wearing a large towel wrapped around her, opened the door and came face-to-face with Sam.

"You! What do *you* want? I can't believe you had the nerve to come to my room!"

Juanita smiled. "Julie, meet Sam Winslow, the newest addition to this band of overworked, overpaid basket cases."

"Oh, no." Julie turned pale and seemed on the verge of fainting.

Sam put out a hand for her to shake. Hers was soft and supple.

"I really am sorry," Julie said. "Normally I wouldn't treat anybody like that, except maybe T.J., but things are so tense around here we're all on the verge of losing our minds."

"Julie taught literature at the University of Pennsylvania and played for the Des Moines Fundamentalists before Rock signed her as our quotations specialist," Juanita noted.

"Keep the noise down!" The voice of an older woman drifted in from the hallway. Sam recognized Margaret Kramer. "Some of us are trying to study!"

"Give it a rest, Margaret," T.J. said. He introduced her to Sam. "Margaret's son says she didn't get cranky and mean as she got older. She's always been that way."

"Another recruit for Rock's Whaler," Margaret declared. "Hope you can take the pressure. I'm about to have a breakdown. Chase was in the elevator with me when I went down to supper. Mumbled something about how old women annoy him. Damn near dropped a load in my pants."

"Now you understand why we don't let Margaret talk to the press," Juanita commented.

Sam told Julie not to feel badly about the incident in the elevator—he understood the pressure she was under.

"You had trouble in the elevator, too?" Margaret asked

Julie. "I may stop riding in elevators forever!"

"*I* was attacked," Sam pointed out. "Julie was the attackee."

"Why did you do that?" Margaret asked Julie. "He's not *that* good looking."

As they left Julie's room, Sam asked T.J. what Margaret meant by "Rock's Whaler".

"Rock reminds a lot of us of a certain captain from *Moby Dick* whose pilot light went out. Rock's goal in life is to win the Brains Bowl, and he doesn't care if we all lose our minds in the battle for it."

T.J. decided to introduce Sam to some of the other players. He led the way to room 1109 and knocked loudly.

A tall, distinguished-looking man threw the door open. Dressed in a robe and slippers, he wore reading glasses. In his left hand, he clutched a book of *New York Times* cross-word puzzles. At the far end of the room was a fireplace, though Sam wasn't sure if it was real or fake. It was obvious this player had made himself at home in the hotel. The only thing missing was a collie who could lay by the armchair.

"What the devil is going on? My nerves are so bad I jumped three feet."

"I know," T.J. said. "That's why I did it. Edgar Tolin Woodford, this is Sam Winslow. He's been hired to replace Tina in the playoffs. Edgar is our world specialist.

"Edgar, as I'm sure you know, served as secretary of state in the last Administration. When he retired, Rock offered to pay him more than Washington law firms offered, so we wound up with the arrogant pain-in-the-ass. That's Israel's description of him, not mine."

"Don't judge all of us by T.J.," Edgar cautioned. "Some of us have breeding and manners."

"Yes, and some of us are full of it," T.J. replied, as Edgar closed the door on them.

"I love to bait him," T.J. said. "He gets so annoyed."

Sam couldn't believe T.J. was so disrespectful to Edgar. Was T.J. just having fun, or was he trying to push the starters over the edge so he could have his big chance?

T.J. pounded on room 1106. A black girl about fifteen or sixteen years old came to the door dressed in jeans and a dirty red shirt. Rock 'n roll music blared from a radio.

"I knew it was you, T.J. Someday I'm going to rent a Mack truck and smash *your* door in."

"If you don't turn down the boombox, I'm going to throw it *and* you out the window!" T.J. said.

She turned down the volume.

"Annie Jones, kid genius, this is Sam Winslow, our new history pro. Annie is a typical nerd. She's shy around boys, but she's nuts about computers. She could probably hack her way into Defense Department computers and start World War III if she wanted to. Fortunately, she's too busy reading Spider Woman comic books to do anything that destructive."

"A lot you know," Annie said. "I sent two fighter jets over Russia last night."

"She's joking ... I think," T.J. said. "Annie graduated from Stanford at sixteen and Rock immediately signed her up as a backup player, like me. She's never had an honest job and she has no idea what's happening in the real world."

"Yeah, well, from what I hear, the real world isn't all it's cracked up to be."

"Juanita plays a wicked guitar, but the garbage coming

out of Annie's boombox makes it hard for anyone within ten miles to rest or study."

That got Annie's dander up. "Garbage? You don't know what good music is!"

"It's not 'Throw Me a Bone, I'm Hungry for Love'," T.J. suggested.

"All right, everybody out!" Annie declared. "I've got work to do."

"Studying?" Sam asked.

"No. I'm trying to find out what happened to those fighters I sent over Russia."

T.J. led Sam to Room 1108 where the words from a 1950s hit, "It's the Same Old Song", could be heard loud and clear. T.J. pounded on the door as though he were trying to wake up the dead. *"This is the police. Open up!"* he roared, in a deep voice.

The music dropped to a low level and the door opened slowly. The Phils' most popular player cautiously peeked out from behind the door.

"What are you doing, T.J.? I'm trying to get some work done."

"You were not. You were murdering a Four Tops song. When are you going to learn you can't carry a tune?"

"About the same time you learn you can't play Brains."

T.J. pushed the door open and led Sam inside. Brian wore jeans and a Phils sweatshirt. His room was littered with books, magazines and Coke cans. "Brian Marshall, popular arts specialist, meet Sam Winslow, Tina's replacement. Brian was a movie publicist before he joined the team. He's considered our superstar because his surfer image gets him a lot of press. People like to think a beach-boy type can be a

Brains star. The All-American Boy, and all that. I think he's got them all buffaloed. He's been lucky, but he's not very bright, and one of these days it will catch up with him."

Brian smiled and shook his head. "T.J. is jealous of the attention I receive and my success with women. He baits me because he figures if I maim him, I'll go to jail and he'll finally break into the starting lineup. But it would take more than that to get T.J. into the starting lineup. If all the starters died in a plane crash, Rock might start T.J. in the next game—but I doubt it."

T.J. noticed something new on the desk where Brian worked. "What's that?"

"That, for your information T.J., is a laptop computer. It's useful for calculations and—"

"I know it's a computer, Jerkball. It looks like a new Caronium 800. What is it doing on your desk?'

"I told Freud I needed a new laptop. The old 550s are all right for you and other sub-performers, but I need something that's state-of-the-art. The 4800 megahertz Caronium has twenty megs of RAM and a 3200 gigabyte hard drive."

"Giving you a powerful computer is like giving a Rembrandt to a kid who reads comic books."

Brian shook his head. "Poor T.J. Is there no end to your jealousy? … Have you guys had dinner?"

"I'm starving," Sam said.

"Let's go downstairs. I'll break my rule about never fraternizing with rookies and second-stringers."

"It's the second stringers who came up with that rule," T.J. said.

As they polished off steaks in the Lockwood Restaurant and Bar, T.J. noticed Rock's bulldog-like face on the widescreen television. "Looks like they're running the interview Moose Harrison taped with Rock this morning."

"CONGRATULATIONS ON MAKING IT INTO THE PLAY-OFFS, ROCK. AFTER THE LEAN YEARS, THIS MUST BE QUITE A THRILL."

"YES, IT IS, MOOSE. TO APPRECIATE WINNING, YOU NEED TO KNOW ABOUT LOSING. I KNOW A HELLUVA LOT ABOUT LOSING. VICTORIES TO ME ARE LIKE SEX IS TO A NYM-PHOMANIAC. I WANT TO KEEP COMING BACK FOR MORE."

"I hope my mother doesn't see this interview," Sam said. "She'd book me on the next flight back to Indiana."

"CLEVELAND IS GOING TO BE A TOUGH OPPONENT FOR YOU, COACH."

"YES, EVERY TIME WE PLAY THE MIDDLE AMERICANS, I ASK GOD FOR HELP AND MAKE SURE MY INSURANCE IS PAID UP. IT REMINDS ME OF SOMETHING BUM PHILLIPS, WHO COACHED THE HOUSTON OILERS IN THE NATIONAL FOOTBALL LEAGUE, ONCE SAID AT A NEWS CONFERENCE: 'WHEN I DIE, I WANT YOU TO PUT A P.S. ON MY TOMB-STONE: HE'D HAVE LIVED A HECKUVA LOT LONGER IF HE WOULDN'T HAVE PLAYED PITTSBURGH SIX TIMES IN TWO YEARS.'"

"I'VE HEARD REPORTS THERE IS A LOT OF BICKERING ON THE TEAM, ROCK."

"DON'T BELIEVE EVERYTHING YOU HEAR. THE PLAY-ERS KNOW HOW IMPORTANT THIS IS AND THEY'RE WORKING TOGETHER LIKE A WELL-OILED MACHINE."

T.J. flinched. "Rock must have been a PR man for the Army."

"It took a lot of preparation to get where you are today, Coach. I recall a story you told about Greg Hornbeck. I think our audience would like to hear it."

"Well, three years ago Hornbeck was our seventh-round pick in the college draft. He had a good record at the University of Texas and we decided to give him a try. But I didn't realize he had a problem ... he stuttered. When he had ten seconds to answer a question, he stuttered more than ever. After two weeks he had me stuttering, and I told him, 'G-g-get the h-h-hell out of h-h-here!' We traded him to Atlanta, where the team had so many problems no one seemed to notice his. Atlanta, you know, hasn't had a winning season since the city library burned to the ground in *Gone With the Wind*."

Moose laughed.

Sam noticed that even as Rock told his stories, there was an intensity about him.

"I've had other problems with the college draft. In my first year as Phils coach I drafted Tommy Youngblood out of Fresno State. Tommy was seven-feet tall. I said to myself, 'Are you crazy? This isn't basketball. This is Brains. A seven-footer isn't going to help you win.' So I traded him to San Diego. Well, Tommy was a Rhodes Scholar and very smart. Every time we play San Diego, he scores eighteen or nineteen points against us. So, I had learned my lesson. The next time a seven-footer came up in the draft, I signed him. The kid was dumber than an oak tree. I traded him to Des Moines for Julie Howard.

SOMETIMES *SHE'S* DUMBER THAN AN OAK TREE, TOO."

A terrifying scream erupted in a far corner of the restaurant.

"Julie must be watching this," T.J. suggested.

"THE PLAYERS LOOK EXHAUSTED, ROCK. WILL THEY BE READY FOR SUNDAY'S GAME AGAINST THE MIDDLE AMERICANS?"

"THEY'LL BE READY, COME HELL OR HIGH WATER. I'LL JUST WORK THE TEAM A LITTLE HARDER THE NEXT COUPLE OF DAYS."

"Rock's answer to everything is to turn up the pressure a notch," Brian said. "Playing for Rock is like blowing your brains out with a gun, day after day."

T.J. returned to his room to call his girlfriend Mary in Detroit before the phones went dead. "Rock cuts off the calls at ten-thirty every night," T.J. told Sam. "He doesn't miss a trick."

Sam settled into his room and slipped off his shoes and turned off the lights. As he lay on the bed, he gazed out the window at the bright lights of the city. They were seductive, especially to a single man with unfulfilled dreams who was coming into a lot of money. Chicago had a reputation as a tough, hustling metropolis that could ruin people or bless them with success.

It was happening so fast. Twenty-four hours earlier he had been laying in bed with Martha Jean in Franklin, debating whether he would return to teaching, wondering if he would ever start the book he wanted to write, wondering why Martha Jean liked to do it with her socks on. Now he was a major league Brains player living in the lap of luxury at the Palmer House Hilton.

Doubts beset him. Was he really good enough to be a starter on the Phils, or was he destined to embarrass himself before millions of people?

He heard a noise outside his door. When he opened it, he discovered a tattered copy of *Moby Dick*. Whoever left the book had fled.

Sam made himself comfortable in the armchair in his room and began reading. It had been a dozen years since he had tried to navigate through Herman Melville's long and windy tale about Ahab's quest for the great white whale. Before Sam began the grind of preparing for the Brains play-offs, perhaps he would read a few pages of it.

4

TUESDAY MORNING, A POUNDING at the door aroused Sam from a deep sleep. He staggered to the door. T.J. stood before him, decked out in blue workout sweats and white tennis shoes.

"Why aren't you ready?" T.J. asked.

Sam was still groggy. "Ready for what?"

"I suppose no one mentioned we do calisthenics every morning in the Fitness Center on the eighth floor."

"Calisthenics? Why? This is supposed to be a brains game."

"When you get your contract, read the fine print. It will state that if they ask you to dig ditches, empty latrines, or steal your ninety-one-year-old grandmother's car, that's what you do. Rock insists daily workouts keep us healthy, but the real reason we do it is because Rock feels more like a football coach when he's leading a team in calisthenics. ... You'd better hurry. If we aren't there in ten minutes, Rock will make us jog ten laps around the hotel. And it's cold out there!"

Sam had brought a workout suit along in case he had an opportunity to shoot a few baskets in a gym. He fished the suit out of his suitcase and retreated to the bathroom to wash his face and slip into the workout suit.

"I'm not sure they're paying me enough money to get up this early," Sam said. "What time is it?"

"Five minutes 'til seven. Just how much *are* they paying you, rookie?"

"I can't divulge that."

"That much," T.J. mused. "Hmmm. I may have to lock you in there."

Sam emerged dressed in his Indiana Hoosiers red-and-white warmup suit. Just what had he gotten himself into? Had he been hired for his brains, or would he be playing basketball for the Chicago Bulls on Sunday?

BY THE TIME T.J. AND SAM ARRIVED in the workout room, the other Philosophers were already there, looking weary and disgusted, as well as somewhat disgusting because of flabby muscles and excess pounds around the waist. These were not world-class athletes.

Rock had not shown up yet.

Margaret Kramer seemed frail in her "kiss my ***" sweatshirt. Obviously, Rock expected *all* players to report for calisthenics, regardless of age.

"If they ever hold a sanity hearing for Rock, these morning workouts might be the thing that gets him committed," Margaret grumbled.

"You complain every morning," Brian snapped. "Why don't you shut up and do your exercises?"

Margaret turned on the superstar and started toward him. "You lamebrain. Of course it doesn't bother you. You're young. I'm seventy-two years old. Most people my age are in nursing homes waiting to die. You ought to get down on your flabby knees and pray because it's a miracle I'm here. You're witnessing a miracle, you moron."

"Isn't it great to see a team that works so well together," T.J. told Sam.

A large man with short black hair entered the room. Ignoring everyone, he limbered up his ample muscles. Sam knew this was Chase.

Then Sam spotted Freud, who looked more like a congenial old country doctor than a Brains psychiatrist. Freud waved when he noticed Sam.

Moments later, a paunchy man in his late fifties wearing sweatpants and a Notre Dame sweatshirt entered the workout room. It was Rock. He seemed out of place in a game that depended on brains more than brawn. The stories players and fans told about Rock made him out to be a cross between Frankenstein and Knute Rockne. He was the only person Sam had ever seen who was a legend in his own time. Yet, if Sam hadn't known who he was, he wouldn't have paid any attention to this ordinary-looking man. It was Rock's reputation that commanded admiration.

Rock marched over to Sam. "Who are you?" he demanded, sounding like a drill sergeant interrogating a new recruit.

The rookie gulped. "Sam Winslow. I was hired to play for you."

"Oh. Right. I tried to stop them from signing you, but I was too late. … Welcome aboard. You'll go through hell before this is over, mister, so you'd better be in good physical shape." Rock turned to the motley crew. *"Let's go, you meatballs,"* he roared. Immediately the team followed his lead in doing jumping jacks and pushups.

Even Chase followed Rock's orders without complaint despite being exhausted. It was as though Chase, too, knew that nothing that stood between Rock and the Brains Bowl championship would be tolerated.

As the team fell to the ground for situps, T.J. told Sam to hang in there because it would last only a few minutes longer. Everything occurred according to "The Schedule", Rock's master plan for winning the playoffs. The Schedule called for a workout at 7 A.M., showers at 7:30 and breakfast at 8. At 8:30, the team bus would leave the Palmer House Hilton to take the players to the University of Chicago, where daytime meetings, studying and practice sessions were held. At 5 P.M., the bus would return to the Palmer House Hilton, where players could dine before returning to their rooms to study. All players must be in their hotel rooms by 10:30 P.M., the curfew Rock imposed for the playoffs. Late-night studying was not only allowed, it was expected. During the regular season, players returned to their homes or apartments every night they were in Chicago, but when the Phils landed in the playoffs, Rock decreed that all players would stay at a hotel so they would not be distracted from the task at hand. For those Philosophers who had spouses and families—Freud and Juanita—The Schedule meant being separated from their loved ones for long periods of time.

At precisely 7:25 A.M. Rock dismissed the troops.

AFTER SHOWERING IN HIS ROOM, Sam slipped on a gray sweater and jeans. On his way to the Lockwood Restaurant and Bar, where the team gathered for breakfast, he purchased a copy of the *Chicago Mirror.*

Sam devoured french toast and orange juice as he browsed through the *Mirror.* An investigative report on the "Brains drain" appeared on the front page. Congressmen expressed concern because big salaries shelled out by Brains teams lured the best minds away from government, science, business and education. Research and development suffered at a time when the United States needed those bril-

liant minds to compete more effectively in the world mar-
ketplace. Senator Hershell Mitton of Nebraska complained,
"Our smartest people are playing games while the country
heads for disaster!"

Sam flipped the paper over to the main sports page—the
back page of the tabloid. The banner headline stunned him:
"PHILS SIGN SAM WINSLOW". Such extravagant coverage
usually was reserved for murderers, corrupt politicians and
sports superstars.

Recalling that Freud had suggested he find an agent,
Sam asked T.J. to recommend one.

"My agent will probably take you on," T.J. said. "Morey
Walters. As long as you bring in the bucks, he'll take his cut
out of your hide. When you're washed up, he'll drop you so
fast your head will spin."

T.J. gave Sam the phone number. A few minutes later,
Sam called Walters from a telephone in the lobby. The agent
said he would pick up the contract from Ben and look it over
before Sam signed it.

As Sam talked with Walters, T.J. hurried past.

"Get moving, Winslow. The bus leaves in two minutes!"

AT PRECISELY 8:30 A.M. THE TEAM BUS began its short trek to the
University of Chicago campus, following Michigan Avenue
for a short distance before turning onto Lake Shore Drive.
Sam sat next to Julie, who was wearing a gray coat and
black slacks. She didn't seem particularly pleased that he
had invaded her space.

As the bus passed the imposing Art Institute of Chicago, Sam heard a disgusting noise that suggested Vesuvius
might be erupting.

"That's Margaret snoring," Julie explained. "She complains she can't sleep at night, but she doesn't have any problem sleeping on the bus."

"I heard that," Margaret growled, waking from her brief slumber. "You forget that I'm seventy-two years old. Fragile old people like me need more sleep than you do."

"You're about as fragile as a Sherman tank," suggested Annie.

"Shut up, or I'll throw you off the bus," retorted Margaret.

During the short ride, Julie filled Sam in on Margaret's background—how she had edited the magazine *American Horizons* before retiring and moving into a retirement home in Phoenix. Her life there was uneventful until one spring day when Rock showed up and hired her to be the team's Renaissance Woman. Margaret planned to retire after the current season because the pressures were too much for her, but at least she had dared to do something that most people her age never had the chance to do. She was a symbol of what old, crotchety people could accomplish, said Julie. Thousands of elderly people across the country seemed to feel that every game Margaret won, they won.

Julie looked to see if Margaret was asleep. Satisfied that she was, Julie whispered, "I don't know if they'd be such big fans of Margaret if they knew she had a personality like Stalin's."

As the bus neared the Museum of Science and Industry and turned toward the University of Chicago, Margaret's snoring intensified.

The driver parked the bus in a university parking lot. By 8:50 the Philosophers and their coaches hurried across the University of Chicago campus. It was Sam's first look at the institution which had given birth to sociology, John Dewey's progressive ideas on education, and the nuclear age.

As the team approached the Joseph Regenstein Library, Sam noticed the massive bronze abstract sculpture known as "Nuclear Age" which stood where the first self-sustained nuclear chain reaction had been achieved.

The ragtag Phils crew invaded the Regenstein Library and headed for the second-floor seminar room where the team met every morning. The library, located on the site of the original Stagg Field, was the largest of the University of Chicago's libraries with three and a half million books.

In the seminar room, Rock surveyed the motley crew that was entrusted with the task of winning the Brains Bowl for him. They were divided, confused and weary, but he would show them the way. He had a plan. A simple plan. He would step up the pressure.

"It's been easy until now," he thundered, a statement that was greeted with groans from the players, "but play-time is over. Now we get serious. It's for all the marbles. One loss and we're out of the playoffs. If we win three games we'll be the world champs—and that's what I intend to do! You can't go belly-up on me now. You've got to give it every-thing you've got!"

"We passed that point three weeks ago," Brian sug-gested.

Such dissension in the ranks rankled Rock. "I've had about all I'm going to take from you meatballs. If you don't shape up, I'll be forced to start T.J."

T.J. grimaced. "It annoys me that the worst threat you can make is to put me into the starting lineup."

"It annoys me, too," Rock said. "I ought to be able to think of a better threat than that. ... I don't understand

why there's so much subversion and unrest on this team. By
now, you should be a well-oiled machine. Get your heads
on straight! ... By the way, Tina is resting better today, but
she won't be back for the playoffs. You've probably met Sam
Winslow, her replacement. We have a game scrimmage this
afternoon, Winslow. You'll be thrown into the fire of competition immediately. And you'd better be ready!"

Sam could see why Margaret had called it Rock's Whaler.
He could almost feel the room swaying, rocked by the undu-
lating waves of the ocean, and it seemed as though Ahab
stood before them, giving the crew of the Pequod a pep talk
before they chased after the White Whale ...

> "It was Moby Dick that dismasted me; Moby Dick that
> brought me to this dead stump I stand on now. Aye, aye," he
> shouted with a terrific, loud, animal sob, like that of a heart-
> stricken moose: "Aye, aye! it was that accursed white whale
> that razed me; made a poor peggy lubber of me for ever and a
> day!" Then tossing both arms, with measureless imprecations
> he shouted out: "Aye, aye! and I'll chase him round Good
> Hope, and round the Horn, and round the Norway Mael-
> strom, and round perdition's flames before I give him up."

Substitute Los Angeles, Houston and Philadelphia for
the first three and the upcoming battle against Cleveland for
"perdition's flames" and Herman Melville could have been
writing about Rock's battle to win the Brains Bowl.

> And this is what you have shipped for, men! to chase that
> white whale on both sides of land, and over all sides of earth,
> till he spouts black blood and rolls fin out.

AFTER WHAT SEEMED LIKE an eternity, Rock dismissed the team
to study in the bowels of the Regenstein Library the rest of
the morning. In a small room adjacent to a reading room,

Freud explained to Sam the facts of life of playing in the big leagues. Because Brains officials hoped to encourage fans' interest and participation in the game, some types of questions were predictable—those dealing with presidents, vice presidents, unsuccessful presidential candidates and geography, for instance. Freud suggested that Sam skim books outlining the highlights of world and American history, then focus on books that zeroed in on the kind of detail that most likely would be useful. There simply was not time to cover everything.

Freud summarized the basics of the game to be sure Sam understood them: Every half of every Brains game began with a four-point Shakespearean tipoff question. Any of the six starters on either team could answer that question. After the tipoff, specialists in each of six categories—history, the world, popular arts, quotations, sports and miscellaneous knowledge (the domain of the Renaissance Man or Woman) —would go to centercourt in the order selected by the computer at the start of the game.

Individual players would be asked questions worth two to four points. Each quarter, each team had two chances to "Double It!". Before the question was asked, the player pressed a "Double It!" button. Whoever answered the question correctly received double the points for that question. Once each quarter, the referee called for a "Brain Buster". Three players from each team were transported to centercourt to solve puzzles or problems for four points. And once each game, each team could call for the next question to be a "terminnator". If either player answered the question correctly, the opponent sat out the rest of the game.

Each quarter lasted twelve minutes, with three timeouts allowed each team per half. After the question was read, players had five seconds to push their buzzers.

Players and coaches could be penalized two to five points for unsportsmanlike conduct.

Coaches had several strategic weapons at their disposal. They could substitute players before questions were asked, but no player could re-enter the game more than twice per quarter. They could tell players when to "Double It!" or use a Terminator. They could use timeouts to best advantage, and if time was running out, they could tell a player to push the buzzer quickly even if the player didn't know the answer, because the team could swallow the two-point penalty for not giving any answer at all to preserve a victory rather than giving the other team a chance to answer. And, there were intangibles, too, such as psyching out the other team. Some players were so adept at this that it fell into the category of dirty tricks, and occasionally referees nailed them by assessing penalties for unsportsmanlike conduct.

Sam selected a half dozen books from the history stacks and retreated to an overstuffed imitation leather armchair in a remote corner of the library. He usually enjoyed reading history, but he did not like this cramming-for-finals mentality. He would need to cover a lot of ground in five days. He began by thumbing through Winston Churchill's multi-volume *Outline of World History.*

In other areas of the library, Julie skimmed books listing famous quotations from literary classics, Chase reviewed *World Almanac* statistics on National Basketball Association playoff winners through the years, Annie Jones boned up on the Japanese game of Go, Brian Marshall wrestled with Impressionist painting, Edgar Woodford delved into Medieval politics, Juanita Lorez skimmed through the New Testament, T.J. perused the latest issue of *Playboy,* and Margaret Kramer scrutinized *How to Build a Nuclear Bomb.*

AFTER LUNCH, THE PHILOSOPHERS retreated to an auditorium for a practice session—Sam's first encounter with game-like conditions.

Freud served as the head referee, reading the questions and keeping track of time, as Rock observed and criticized. Early in the first quarter, Sam was called on to compete against Annie Jones. Even though it was only practice, Sam perspired heavily.

Freud delivered the question: "For two points: Name the only Englishman to ascend to the papacy."

Annie pushed the buzzer. "Adrian the Sixth!"

"Wrong," said Freud. "You have five seconds to begin answering, Sam."

Sam had difficulty thinking clearly under the pressure. Perhaps Ben had been right—the most pressure Sam had ever faced was trying to get to work on time ... and Sam rarely arrived on time. Precious seconds ticked away. Sam struggled to come up with an answer.

"Adrian the Fifth," Sam guessed.

"Wrong," said Freud. "It was Adrian the Fourth."

Teammates groaned.

In the first row, Rock slammed his strategy book against an adjoining seat. Then he paced the floor.

"We are in trouble," he lamented. "I was afraid of this, Winslow. You don't seem to understand the situation here. We aren't having a tea party. This isn't a picnic. This is the Big Time! This is *war*! You have only a split-second to beat your opponent to the buzzer. You must be fast, and you must be right. You've got a lot of work to do before Sunday! I expect you to work hard day and night!"

As Chase pondered a question about rowing in the 1952 Olympics, Sam found himself envying Chase. Sports was a trivial pursuit compared to history, but at least it was cut and dried. There were a reasonably limited number of statistics to remember. History was more complicated. You couldn't just say the Allies won World War II by a score of 96-78, with Eisenhower scoring two touchdowns and Patton racking up five hundred yards rushing. There was much more to it.

Julie failed to identify a quotation from *Paradise Lost*, drawing more artillery fire from Rock, and Margaret muffed a question about Einstein's theories, but the Phils managed to get enough answers right to run up a decent score. It had been a struggle. They seemed to be making the extra effort not out of determination or love for the game, but out of fear of Rock. As Margaret commented in the last quarter, "this team's morale sucks."

AFTER THE PRACTICE SESSION and a fifteen-minute break, it was back to the books at the Regenstein Library until 5 P.M., when players boarded the bus for the ride to the Palmer House Hilton.

Darkness descended on Chicago as the bus threaded its way through streets packed with rush hour traffic. A stream of pedestrians bustled along Michigan Avenue, unaware their heroes were a few feet away. Sam felt separated from this sea of humanity by an invisible and impenetrable barrier. It was as though he and his teammates were captives on a devil ship commanded by a cranky and obsessed old sea dog. If the crew hollered for help, the stream of pedestrians would not hear them. There was no hope.

And this was Sam's first day with the team. Would he be a raving madman by the end of the week?

At the Palmer House Hilton, the desk clerk handed Sam a message: his agent, Morey Walters, had dropped off his contract. Sam was to look it over, sign it and leave it at the front desk for Walters. The message also stated Walters had arranged for Bill Jacobs to take Sam's picture in one of the hotel conference rooms at 5:45.

"Who is Bill Jacobs and why is he taking my picture?" Sam asked Juanita.

"Your photo will appear on a Brains collector card. It's part of the sweet 'n sour life of a Brains player."

Sam had never dreamed he would appear on a Brains card. He had imagined that one day his picture might be plastered on a *basketball* card, but that was not to be.

Sam retreated to his room and washed up. At 5:46, he presented himself to Bill Jacobs in the conference room. Jacobs was young and lanky, with unruly hair and a beard.

"What's with the basketball?" Jacobs asked.

"It's a prop for my picture."

"It's a little unorthodox, but why not."

Jacobs fine-tuned his camera settings as Sam seated himself under the lights Jacobs had arranged.

"Other players had unusual requests. Edgar Woodford insisted a photo of the Harry S Truman Building, home of the State Department, appear behind him on his card. Ollie Holcomb of the Kansas City Farmers stood beside an old Ford pickup."

As Sam cradled the basketball, Jacobs shot a dozen pictures.

"That's all we need," Jacobs said.

Sam would appear on a basketball card after all.

TEAM MEMBERS COULD GO ANYWHERE they wished for dinner, but most players patronized the Lockwood Restaurant rather than going out. Sam joined Julie, T.J. and Annie at their table. The Lockwood's menu, which changed frequently, was unlike any Sam had seen before: grilled baby octopus, Hawaiian bass and lobster, muscovy duck breast and Scotish salmon, as well as a kobe burger ($24) and steaks ($48-$52). It was obvious to Sam he wasn't in Franklin any longer. Fortunately, the team would pick up the bill.

After finishing off the salmon, Sam returned to his room to study. Rock had laid down the law, and Sam had a lot of work to do before Sunday's game. If he didn't sleep at all, and crammed every hour until game time, he still wouldn't know everything Rock expected him to know. He was beginning to think the best he could hope for was not to look stupid on Sunday.

5

OVER THE NEXT THREE HOURS, Sam skimmed old history books written by Parkman, Turner, Buckle and McMaster. He was ready to quit for the evening when T.J. dropped by, greeting him with a flourish of Shakespeare:

"The tyrannous and bloody act is done,
The most arch deed of pietous massacre
That ever yet this land was guilty of ..."

"*Henry the Eighth*?" guessed Sam.

"No! It's from *Richard the Third* ... I did it, Sam. I killed Rock. He was sleeping in his room. I crept in and strangled him with the cord to his Mickey Mouse telephone."

"It's not healthy to fantasize about such things. Have you talked to Freud about that?"

"He suggested I use a knife with a nine-inch blade. It's quicker."

"This team has problems coping with pressure."

"That isn't true," T.J. insisted. "If I had actually killed Rock, that would show I can't cope with pressure. Talking about it serves as a healthy release."

"Bull," said Sam.

"That's my story and I'll stick to it. Forget the Shakespeare. There's another quotation you might be familiar with: 'All work and no play makes Jack a dull boy.' Let's grab a beer at the Dumping Ground. It's just down the street."

"Are you kidding? Rock would kill us."

"You won't be any good to the team if you're a basket case like the rest of us. Get your coat!"

"This is my first full day with the team. I shouldn't be goofing off."

"By the time you explain why you shouldn't go, we could be on our second beers. *Grab your coat!*"

A BLAST OF COLD AIR GREETED Sam and T.J. as they hustled out of the Hilton. The temperature hovered around 10 degrees above zero, but a strong wind off Lake Michigan sent the wind chill plummeting to 15 below.

"Maybe Rock will trade me to Miami," Sam grumbled, as they hurried a block and a half down Monroe Street.

"Or Alaska."

"You've got a mean streak, T.J."

"I know. Been playing for Rock too long."

The Dumping Ground was dimly lit. The oak bar and tables were scarred by years of service. As Sam slipped off his coat and surveyed the room, he was surprised to see many of his teammates.

"Most of the players come down here once a week, except for Chase and Rock," T.J. said. "They're here every night."

Sam was gripped by terror. Rock hung out at the Dumping Ground? Sam's eyes drifted to the far corner of the bar. Sure enough, Rock and Freud coddled drinks at a table near a door which was labeled neither "men" nor "women" but simply "da john".

"Let's get outta here!" Sam whispered.

"Relax," T.J. said. "When Rock is here, he's in another world. He doesn't want to remember he's coaching a Brains team. In his mind, he's probably back in 1958, preparing to rumble with Lombardi's Green Bay Packers."

Chase had commandeered a table for himself near the entrance. T.J. and Sam joined Brian and Edgar at a table next to Chase's.

Brian perked up when he realized he had someone to pick on besides Edgar. "Well, it's T.J.—the second-stringer whose presence reminds us how much mediocrity there is in the world."

"I thought your barber did that," T.J. grumbled. "Been here long?"

"Ten minutes. It took me two hours to open my fan mail tonight. Would you believe it—two hundred and six letters, including eight proposals of marriage. How many did you get?"

"So you get more fan mail than the rest of us. Big deal," said T.J.

"Eight proposals?" Sam was stunned. This was an aspect of being a Brains player he hadn't thought about. "Do these women enclose photos?"

"Who said they were women?" mumbled T.J.

Brian glared at T.J. "Of course they're women. … Usually they send photos. If they don't, I give their letters to Chase."

Chase grunted to indicate he had heard what Brian said and was appreciative of the leftovers.

T.J. was unimpressed. "These are desperate women who exhausted the normal dating channels. They came up empty bar-hopping and struck out on blind dates. Computer dating services matched them up with bald, fat truck drivers from

Nicaragua. So they look at Brian and think, 'Hey, he looks gullible. If he'll marry me, I can get my hands on his money'."

"It works for me," noted Brian.

"I received a proposal today," Edgar said thoughtfully. "It was a little disappointing. Came from an eighty-six-year-old woman in Turkey Pass, Wisconsin. And yet, proposals like that don't grow on trees."

"Don't be so sure," T.J. said. "She's probably mimeograhing them and sending them to players all over the league."

"At her age, who could blame her?" suggested Edgar. "Young women don't propose to me because they're afraid to approach a former secretary of state who has a high IQ and a devastating wit."

"Have you lost touch with reality completely?" T.J. asked.

"The secretary of defense once asked me the same thing. The problem I'm faced with now is how to turn down an eighty-six-year-old woman without triggering a fatal heart attack. I can't send her the usual printed rejection form."

Margaret barged into the bar accompanied by Julie and Juanita. They headed for the table where the four men were seated.

"Oh, Lord," Brian moaned. "Must we do everything as a team? Can't the men even drink alone?"

"We ignore him," Margaret explained to Sam, as the women took over a nearby table. "He says the same thing every time we come here."

"That's because I mean it every time, you old fleabag."

Margaret fixed an evil eye on Brian. "If you don't behave, I'll tie your throat in a knot and you'll never drink again, you little turd."

Edgar, who was working on his second beer, sighed.

"Let's try to be more civilized, Margaret. Do you really think a Brains player should use that kind of language?"

Margaret glared at him. "How would you like your legs tied around your neck?"

"I was just asking," Edgar mumbled, as he concentrated on sipping his beer. "In the good old days, I could ask the military to launch a missile attack if someone irritated me. Perhaps my poker buddies in the Pentagon have a spare missile lying around. Wouldn't hurt to inquire."

"I've never been so nervous before a game," Julie said. "I don't know how I'm going to keep body and soul together until the game's over."

"If you can't keep body and soul together," Sam suggested, "I've got dibs on the body."

"You see that babe over there?" Brian asked, nodding in the direction of the bar. "She's got the hots for me."

"You're crazy," Margaret said. "She's not paying any attention to you."

"She's trying to be coy," Brian said.

He picked up his beer and made his way to the bar. Teammates watched as Casanova made his move.

"Hi, beautiful. Can I buy you a drink?"

The buxom young woman looked Brian over. "No."

"Maybe I could buy you a small country, like Panama."

"Don't be silly. What would I do with Panama?"

"You could trade it for Switzerland," Brian suggested.

"You're crazy. Would you mind leaving, in case it's contagious?"

Brian smiled. "Certainly, my lovely."

"Well, what did she say?" asked Edgar.

"She's waiting for her lesbian lover," Brian mumbled.

"I doubt it," Margaret grumbled. "The Strikeout King struck out again."

"They don't make women like they used to," Brian lamented.

"You can say that again," Margaret snapped.

ON THE OTHER SIDE OF THE BAR, Rock and Freud coddled their drinks.

Freud often drank with Rock because he felt he was doing his part for humanity by helping Rock cope with defeats, team problems and, well, life in general. He was more than the team psychiatrist and assistant coach. He was Rock's personal shrink, on-call twenty four hours a day.

"The Cleveland game will be a ball-buster," Rock grumbled, as he motioned to the bar girl for another beer. "The Middle Americans are always tough. We've got to prepare for this game like a whore looking for her next trick—with a lot of determination. You and I will be up most of the night looking at game films after we leave here."

Freud nodded. "Cleveland is no pushover. I thought we'd whip them in October, but ..."

Rock grimaced. It was a painful memory. Edgar Woodford blew the game in the closing seconds when he couldn't define "horse latitudes".

"I'm the only coach who ever lost a game because of the damn horse latitudes," Rock lamented.

The horse latitudes were areas about thirty degrees north and south of the equator which were noted for their light winds. Edgar had tried to define horse latitudes in terms of horse longitudes. Unforgiving Philosopher fans sent Edgar two hundred copies of *The Horse Latitudes*, by H. Allen Smith.

"If Edgar blows this game, I'll murder him," Rock grumbled. "Then, I'll send his body to the horse latitudes."

When he felt reasonably certain Rock would not kill himself or anyone else in the next hour or so, Freud returned to the hotel to set up the Cleveland game films, leaving Rock alone at the table to drown his worries.

The coach had plunged into his third beer when he noticed a drunk at the bar scrutinizing him. The drunk shuffled over to Rock's table, beer in hand.

"It *is* you, Rock. Here I am in the same bar with the Phils coach! What the hell do you know about that! Why don't I sit down and we'll talk. I've got some ideas that will help you on Sunday."

Rock fixed a death-ray glare on the drunk. "I don't know you. We move in different circles. Get out of here."

"Different circles, hell. We're both here, ain't we?" the drunk replied cheerfully.

The bartender collared the drunk and hauled him off.

"Get rid of Edgar Woodford!" the drunk hollered as the bartender shoved him out the door. "He did a lousy job at the State Department and he's doing a lousy job for you!"

Woodford, watching this from afar, muttered, "must be a Democrat."

The drunk was right, Rock mused. For a moment, he considered having the drunk brought back to his table. But no, anybody could make one good coaching move. The mark of a great coach was to make the right move consistently.

Rock slumped in his chair, sipped his beer and sulked over the horse latitudes.

AT 10:15, MOST OF THE Philosophers finished off their beers and slipped on their coats. "Fifteen minutes 'til curfew," Brian noted.

Chase reluctantly rose from his table. "It's degrading, getting thrown out of a bar so early. Next year, Rock and I settle that first. If he cuts off the booze, I don't play."

"I'll be along in a few minutes," Sam told his teammates.

The only Philosophers in the bar were Sam and Rock. Sam summoned up his courage, grabbed his beer and headed for Rock's table. This was his chance to find out what made this obsessed coach tick.

"I've got ten minutes till curfew. Mind if I sit down?"

Rock shrugged and took another swig of beer.

"Did you go to college, Rock?" Sam asked.

Rock eyed him with disdain. "Kid, I'm your coach. A Brains coach. Of course I went to college."

"Where?"

"Michigan State. Three years."

"Wow! You graduated in three years?"

After a lengthy pause, Rock said, "Didn't graduate. There was a problem about one of my final exams."

"You cheated?"

Rock sighed. Where did he find these kids, anyway?

"I never cheat, kid." After a few moments, he muttered, "I missed a passing grade by two points."

Sam looked shell-shocked. "My Brains coach flunked out of Michigan State!"

Rock struggled to control his temper. "I like it better when I tell it."

"Good grief."

"Go back to the hotel, kid. Curfew is in seven minutes. I hired security men to make sure crazy fans don't get too close to the team. One of them will go with you. *Hey, Marty. Come over here!*"

As MARTY AND SAM HEADED for the door, Rock sipped his beer. Several minutes later, a voice drifted over from the bar. Someone was talking about Rock.

Rock noticed the television at the end of the bar was tuned to "Late Night Edition", a sleazy tabloid journalism show. Percy Smathers, the "Late Night Edition" anchor, was introducing a segment titled "The Terror of the Playoffs".

"AS EIGHT TEAMS TAKE THE FLOOR IN THE BRAINS PLAYOFFS THIS WEEKEND, THE BIGGEST QUESTION IS: WHAT IS CHICAGO PHILOSOPHER COACH ROCK NELSON, THAT SWARTHY MASTER OF TERROR, DOING THERE?

"ROCK'S PRESENCE IN POST-SEASON PLAY CASTS A DARK SHADOW OVER THE WHOLE SHOW. HE RULES HIS TEAM NEITHER BY INTELLIGENCE NOR MORAL LEADERSHIP BUT BY THE EXERCISE OF RAW, BRUTAL POWER. IN SHORT, HE TER- RORIZES HIS PLAYERS.

"WHEN THE PHILS TANGLED WITH THE SEATTLE ENGI- NEERS EARLIER THIS SEASON, ROCK BEHAVED RELATIVELY WELL. HE USED FOUL LANGUAGE ONLY EIGHTEEN TIMES AND WASN'T EJECTED BY THE REFEREES UNTIL THE CLOSING MINUTES.

"THE PHILS' GAME AGAINST THE PHILADELPHIA FOUNDING FATHERS WAS MORE TYPICAL. ROCK USED FOUL LANGUAGE TWENTY-TWO TIMES, PUNCHED A FAN IN THE MOUTH AND WAS THROWN OUT OF THE GAME BEFORE THE THIRD QUARTER ENDED."

Rock tightened his grip on his beer. The fan had attacked him. Rock tried to shove the fan out of the way so he could get to the dressing room. The league cleared Rock of any wrongdoing. As for the foul language—what the hell was he supposed to do? In the heat of battle, you don't say "please" or "mother may I?"

"EVEN ROCK'S SUPPORTERS, LIKE PHILS OWNER BEN SLOAN, FIND IT HARD TO PRAISE HIM. WE FOUND SLOAN CELEBRATING THE PHILS' SUCCESS AT A CHICAGO NIGHT-SPOT LAST NIGHT.

"OH, I KNOW EVERY SPORTSWRITER AND TV COMMEN-TATOR DUMPS ON ROCK. HE'S A LOWBROW, A FANATIC. HE SCREAMS AND HOLLERS. HE MAKES COLLEGE COACHES LIKE BOBBY KNIGHT AND GENE KEADY LOOK LIKE CHOIR BOYS. AND ROCK WOULDN'T KNOW AN INTELLECTUAL EVEN IF HE MANAGED TO FIND HIS WAY TO THE LIBRARY. BUT I'LL TELL YOU SOMETHING—ROCK CAN COACH. HE'S A WINNER."

"A WINNER, YES. BUT AT WHAT COST?"

Rock couldn't understand why everyone criticized him for being "obsessed" with winning. Sure, he had a goal in life, a goal he worked hard to achieve—but wasn't that what life was all about? Some businessmen toiled twelve or fourteen hours a day, six or seven days a week, hell-bent on making fortunes. Nobody called them "obsessed". They were "dedicated".

Rock slipped on his coat and took one last swallow of beer to brace himself for the cold walk back to the hotel. He mused that there was one thing he truly was obsessed about: disgracing Percy Smathers and driving him out of the television business. But that must wait till the season was over. Rock could fight only one war at a time.

In Brian's room at the Palmer House Hilton, four of the Phils—Sam, T.J., Julie and Brian—watched as Percy Smathers continued his harangue against Rock:

"AS THIS LAME EXCUSE FOR A COACH SPREADS HIS TERROR ACROSS AMERICA, IT IS FAIR TO ASK HOW ROCK'S OBSESSION WITH WINNING ORIGINATED—IF ONLY SO YOU CAN WARN YOUR CHILDREN NOT TO FOLLOW A SIMILAR PATH IN LIFE.

"AS A YOUNG BOY IN PULASKI, WISCONSIN, ROCK IDOLIZED KNUTE ROCKNE AND VINCE LOMBARDI. THEY WERE TOUGH. THEY WERE WINNERS. ROCK WANTED TO BE LIKE THEM.

"DETERMINED TO BECOME A FOOTBALL COACH, ROCK ATTENDED MICHIGAN STATE UNIVERSITY FOR THREE YEARS BEFORE FLUNKING OUT. BUT FAILING TO EARN A DEGREE DIDN'T STOP ROCK. HE WANGLED A FOOTBALL COACHING ASSIGNMENT AT MISSISSIPPI CENTRAL TECH, A SMALL COLLEGE IN THE BOONDOCKS THAT EITHER DIDN'T KNOW ROCK HADN'T GRADUATED FROM COLLEGE—OR DIDN'T CARE. IN SIX SEASONS, ROCK TURNED THE MUDDERS AROUND, TAKING THEM TO SUN TAN BOWL.

"BY THAT TIME, ROCK HAD MAPPED OUT A CAREER PATH, A PATH DESIGNED TO TAKE HIM TO THE GREATEST COLLEGE FOOTBALL COACHING JOB—AT NOTRE DAME— AND THEN TO THE NFL. OVER THE NEXT TWENTY-FOUR YEARS, ROCK PURSUED HIS DREAM A STEP AT A TIME, TURNING OUT WINNING TEAMS AT BOWLING GREEN, COLORADO STATE AND IOWA STATE. THEN, WHEN NOTRE DAME PASSED HIM OVER, ROCK ACCEPTED THE HEAD COACHING JOB AT PERENNIAL POWERHOUSE NEBRASKA. FOR TWO YEARS, HE ENJOYED SUCCESS AT THE CORNHUSKER HELM, BUT THE SPORTS LANDSCAPE WAS UNDERGOING A DRA-

MATIC CHANGE THAT WOULD SEND ROCK'S CAREER DOWN A DIFFERENT ROAD. BRAINS GAMES PULLED IN MORE FANS THAN FOOTBALL, AND HUNDREDS OF SCHOOLS DROPPED THEIR FOOTBALL PROGRAMS. NEBRASKA WASN'T ABOUT TO GIVE UP FOOTBALL—IT WOULD DROP ACADEMICS BEFORE IT DROPPED FOOTBALL—BUT IT HAD A HARD TIME FINDING TOP-NOTCH OPPONENTS. AFTER ALL, YOU CAN'T PLAY OKLAHOMA EVERY WEEKEND. ROCK'S FUTURE AS A COACH LOOKED BLEAK.

"FORTUNATELY FOR ROCK, BEN SLOAN NEEDED A BRAINS COACH, AND ROCK'S DETERMINATION TO WIN AT ANY COST WON HIM THE PHILS COACHING JOB.

"ROCK STRUGGLED THROUGH THREE LOSING SEASONS BEFORE TURNING IT ALL AROUND THIS YEAR. HE SAT ON THE SIDELINES DURING THE LAST TWO BRAINS BOWLS, EATING HIS HEART OUT AS HIS NEMESIS, BRONCO GRIFFIN, GUIDED THE SAN FRANCISCO HACKERS TO WORLD CHAMPIONSHIPS. NOW, NOTHING LESS THAN WINNING THE BRAINS BOWL AND OUT-COACHING GRIFFIN WILL SATISFY ROCK. SO WHAT IF THE ODDSMAKERS RATE THE PHILS A 100-1 LONGSHOT?

"FOR THE REST OF US, THE BIG MYSTERY IS WHY THE LEAGUE HAS ALLOWED ROCK TO COACH AS LONG AS IT HAS. WE PROMISE YOU THAT, OVER THE COMING DAYS, 'LATE NIGHT EDITION' WILL SCRUTINIZE ROCK AND THE PHILS VERY CLOSELY."

"Why is Smathers out to get Rock?" Sam asked.

Brian smiled. "It's all about a hooker, Rock and a kid called Pebble. A couple years ago, Percy paid an informant ten thousand bucks for a photo of Rock and a hooker together in their underwear, along with a document claiming Rock had fathered the hooker's child. Percy dubbed the kid Pebble. He played the story big. There was just one problem. It wasn't true. Someone had combined two photos; Rock didn't even know the hooker. Percy wouldn't admit he had been duped into running a fabricated story. Rock barred Percy and his 'gang of idiots' from our locker room because they trafficked in 'lies, scandal and garbage.' That pissed off Percy, and he's been out to get Rock and our team ever since."

"That's right," Julie said. "Last week, Percy focused his sleazy reporting on Margaret. It seems she had worked as a stripper in a club in Louisiana for a few months when she was twenty-two."

"Margaret ... a stripper," T.J. mumbled. "It boggles the mind. Everyone in the club must have been blind."

"Late Night Edition" and its criticism of his determination to win was still on Rock's mind as he climbed into his bed that night. He mused that even Ben Sloan did not understand the depths of his determination to win. It was just as well.

> Had any of his old acquaintances on shore but half dreamed of what was lurking in him then, how soon would their aghast and righteous souls have wretched the ship from such a fiendish man! They were bent on profitable cruises, the profit to be counted down in dollars from the mint. He was intent on an audacious, immitagable, and supernatural revenge.
>
> Here, then, was this grey-headed, ungodly old man, chasing with curses a Job's whale round the world, at the head of a crew, too, chiefly made up of mongrel renegades, and castaways, and cannibals ...

6

AT THE TEAM MEETING Wednesday morning, Rock warned his players their constant bickering must stop.

"You need the killer instinct, but that doesn't mean killing each other. It's the other team you're after. Keep that in mind."

Sam had never enjoyed studying at libraries and liked it even less now. When he should have been memorizing the names of the czars of Russia and the inventor of the bicycle, he thought instead about the joys of savoring Chicago's pleasures with Julie Howard. He had a hunch that, under normal circumstances, Julie was a rational, sympathetic, even passionate young woman.

As the team studied at the Regenstein Library on Wednesday morning, Sam noticed Julie cracking the books at a nearby table.

"I know you said Julie is engaged," Sam told T.J., "but she isn't tied down yet. What would happen if I asked her out on a date?"

T.J. shook his head. "You've got a huge amount of work to do before Sunday. You'd better get your mind off her. ... Besides, Brian asked her out three weeks ago and she threatened to throw him into Lake Michigan."

Sam was not intimidated. "That shows she has high standards."

"Forget it, Sam."

WEDNESDAY AFTERNOON, THE TEAM viewed film of the Cleveland Middle Americans' most recent game as Rock evaluated strengths and weaknesses of the MAs' starting lineup.

"Hold the film while I go out for popcorn," Brian piped up, trying to ease the tension.

Rock was not amused. "Take your seat and watch the film, mister! Another remark like that and you'll be on the next plane back to Los Angeles."

"Promises, promises," muttered Brian.

The MAs grabbed an early lead against the Pittsburgh Bookers. Their history specialist, Ivan the Terrible Kolsky, a former Rhodes scholar, correctly identified Edwin Stanton as President Lincoln's secretary of war. The MAs' sports ace, Smokey Jorgenson, seemed to be a walking encyclopedia of trivia. Chase, haunted by a question he had fumbled against Dallas, asked Rock if he thought Smokey would know who had caught the biggest Dog Tooth Tuna.

"Smokey probably has the guy's address and phone number," Rock suggested.

"Crap," moaned Chase.

The popular arts expert, Maria Sebastian, sparked a second quarter surge, and by halftime the MAs led the Bookers 45-26. In the second half, R.W. Jessica Granger Brayton, who held a Ph.D. in nuclear science, answered a question about quantum physics correctly.

"Brayton is very smart when it comes to science," Freud noted, "but she's forgetful about other things. She was married three times, divorced once."

Carlton Fitzwalter, the MAs' quotations expert, knew that Jane Heap had said "no American with an IQ over ten was ever tried by a jury of his peers." This perplexed Edgar Woodford, who thought he had been the first to say it.

Lin Chan, the MAs' world specialist, dominated the Brain Busters faceoffs. She was a whiz at deciphering scrambled words. "Lin can make three sentences out of the letters in a bowl of alphabet soup," Rock noted.

"What possible practical application could that have?" asked Brian, who had suffered through a season of Rock's game film commentaries and couldn't take it any longer. "Why do you even mention it?"

Rock confronted the superstar. "What did you say, Mister?"

"Uh ... making three sentences out of the letters in a bowl of alphabet soup doesn't seem very ... uh ... relevant to what we're talking about, coach."

"*Relevant?* If it wasn't relevant, I wouldn't mention it. Have *you* ever made three sentences out of letters in a bowl of alphabet soup, Hot Shot?"

"No, coach."

"Damn right you haven't. It isn't easy, I can tell you. If she can do that, she can unscramble most of the word games. Now do you understand, Brian?"

"Yes, sir."

"Next time, think before you speak."

Brian whispered to Annie Jones, "I've got to get out of this asylum."

"Cleveland's coach is Abe Matthews," Rock said, returning to his commentary. "He's quiet, but strong on strategy. Some call him the John Wooden of Brains coaches." Wooden was the mild-mannered UCLA basketball coach who guided the Bruins to ten NCAA titles in twelve years.

"Trade me to Cleveland!" Margaret bellowed.

Rock grimaced. "I tried, but they only offered me three bucks and a third-round draft pick for you. It was tempting."

The MAs' easy 96-60 victory impressed and worried Sam. Rock and most of Chicago expected Sam to perform well against Cleveland after five days of preparation. That was like expecting a video game player to fly a Concorde across the Atlantic after five days of flight training.

Sam closed his eyes and prayed. "God, if You're listening, this might be a good time for a miracle."

"Amen!" said T.J.

SAM SURFED THE INTERNET in his hotel room Wednesday evening, accessing library web sites and other sites filled with resources touching on world and American history. He also read his e-mails and checked out the Brains League web site, where visitors were asked to vote for their favorite Brains player. Brian led the Phils voting with 248,236 votes. Sam, whose name had just been added to the list, had five votes. He cast a vote for himself, then shut down his computer.

By 11 P.M., his brain reeled from the intense studying. He poured himself a Coke and switched on the widescreen television in his room. A movie was just beginning ... *Champagne for Caesar.* Ronald Coleman played a genius trying to win the biggest game show prize ever, Vincent Price owned the company sponsoring the show, and Art Linkletter hosted the game show. Coleman advanced to higher and higher plateaus on his way to the big prize.

Finally, Sam couldn't take it any longer. He was nervous enough. He flicked off the television and went to bed.

7

As THE TEAM FILED INTO the Lockwood Restaurant for breakfast Thursday morning, the television and newspaper reporters who circled the hotel lobby like vultures cornered Rock.

"Do you really intend to start a raw recruit like Sam Winslow in the Phils' first playoff game?" demanded Harry Warton.

"That's what we hired him for," Rock said, as he pushed Warton out of the way. "Sam's got a job to do. He'll do it. He knows how important it is."

Sam turned pale. Newshounds blocked his path and stuck microphones in front of his face as cameras rolled. The other Phils looked on with amusement.

"How does it feel to suddenly find yourself under so much pressure?" asked a television reporter.

"Like a cow attending a barbecue. It's nice to be invited, but you wonder if you're going to survive the dinner."

"How do you like playing for Rock?"

"Technically, I haven't played for Rock yet. I've sweated for Rock, gotten migraine headaches for him and had a beer with him, but I haven't played for him."

Brian was stunned. "I've been on the team three years. I never had a beer with Rock."

"Think about what you're saying," Juanita said. "Do you really *want* to hang out with Rock? Don't you see enough of him during the day?"

Juanita was sometimes very good at putting things in perspective.

THURSDAY MORNING, SAM BURIED HIMSELF in stacks of books at the Regenstein Library and immersed himself in facts about the American Founding Fathers, the Declaration of Independence, the Constitution, the Bill of Rights and the economy of the young Republic. Then he fell asleep and didn't show up for lunch with the team. Rock slapped a $1,000 fine on him.

"It's the most expensive nap I ever had," Sam lamented.

"That's chicken feed," Chase said. "Rock fined me ten grand for missing the Phoenix game."

That afternoon, the Phils played a fast-paced version of Brains designed to sharpen their thinking. With even less time to ponder responses, Sam choked on six of nine questions.

"You need to get a lot smarter before Sunday," Rock growled. "Smart alecks like you join the team and think it's going to be a picnic. Well, it's not. It takes study and hard work—"

Rock's eyes glazed over.

"—and practice. We're going to run the old quarterback option again and again, until we get it right. The Packers are tough. They'll push you all over the field. You've got to be tougher. Put your head down and plow straight ahead. *Go for blood!*"

"He did it again," T.J. whispered to Sam. "He's back in

the Sixties. It may be a few minutes before he gets back to us. If you want to nap, now is the time."

THAT EVENING, THE IRRITATING RINGING of a telephone interrupted Sam as he boned up on the Ulysses S. Grant presidency. His father, Fred, was calling.

"The paper says you'll play for the Chicago Philosophers on Sunday, so I guess it's true. Are you really making a lot of money? You weren't kidding?"

"Am I talking to my father or my banker?"

"Don't get smart. You're talkin' to the father who bankrolled you most of your life."

"Sorry. I'm a little stressed out. It's all true. I'm making a bundle!"

T.J. stuck his head inside the door. Sam changed his tone. "It's really not that much, dad."

"You know, you could ship some of that dough home. We're still at the same address."

"I wouldn't forget you and mom, after all you did for me."

"You're a good kid. So how much are you sending?"

Sam's brother Joe took the phone away from their father. "Don't let dad bug you. I dropped by to convince him we should drive up to Chicago to see you play."

"No problem. Each player receives free tickets. Pick them up at the gate."

"That's great. ... Uh, there is one little thing I should mention. I called Martha Jean. We picked up where you left off. I was thinking about bringing her to the game with dad."

"That's just great, Joe. Just what I want to hear. I dump her because I want to start over and she's still hangin' around the family. How can I forget the past when you want to bring it up here to see me?"

"Okay. I get the point. Don't have a stroke. Dad and I will see you Sunday. ... Say, the Phils have a team shrink, don't they? Maybe you ought to talk to him. You've obviously got a few issues to work through."

"Right. Like the strong urge I have to kill my brother."

"Yes, that would be one of them."

Sam slammed the phone down.

8

By Friday morning, Sam felt like a lobster in boiling water. He had been in Chicago less than four days, but the pressure was suffocating. How had the other players survived an entire season? Why did they put up with all the stress?

After calisthenics, a curvaceous young brunette in a pink silk blouse and blue slacks waylaid Sam as he hurried into the dining room for breakfast.

"May I talk to you, Sam?"

"Well, I really don't have time."

The woman held out a hand for him to shake. "Diane Mercross, 'Late Night Edition'."

She grabbed Sam by his shirt and shoved him down into a chair. "Sam, I've got a proposition for you. We'll give you twenty-five thousand dollars!"

"Sounds fair. Give me the money. Now, if you'll excuse me, I've got fifteen minutes to grab some breakfast before the team bus leaves."

"All you have to do," she continued, "is talk to us. Tell us about Rock. Give us the inside scoop on his brutal coaching tactics … how he terrorizes the team, how he runs his players into the ground from dawn till the wee hours of the evening, how he squeezes every shred of human decency and dignity out of his crew."

Sam flinched. "Are you planning on doing a hatchet job on Rock, by any chance?"

"It's in your best interest to help us," Diane suggested. "We can be rough on you, if we need to."

Sam grimaced. "Are you threatening me?"

"Of course not, Sam! How did you get that idea?"

Sam pushed Diane away and managed to get to his feet. "Sorry, I can't help you, lady. Get your crummy paws off me!"

"You'll be sorry you didn't cooperate with us, Winslow!"

"So what happened?" Brian demanded when Sam joined the other players for breakfast.

"What do you mean?"

"What did Diane the Dragonlady want?" Julie asked.

"She offered me twenty-five grand if I exposed Rock's terrorist coaching tactics."

"Twenty five grand?" T.J. mused. "Prices have gone up. She offered me ten grand a week ago."

"What did you tell her?" Margaret asked Sam.

"I told her no, of course."

Brian shook his head. "You'll never make it in the big leagues, kid. You've got to think like a pro. First, get her in the sack, then get the money, then throw her out."

"Who are you kidding, Brian?" Julie snapped. "You never made it to first base with Diane Mercross."

"My standards are higher than Sam's. But this might be the best offer he gets all year."

"You are disgusting," Margaret snarled.

ROCK VARIED THE SCHEDULE on Friday by taking the team to the downtown Chicago Public Library to study, giving the players access to additional books and study aids.

Sam scanned historical writings. His favorite was *The Fifteen Minute War at a Glance.* As he flipped through a tome on Egyptian history late Friday afternoon, he noticed Julie speed-reading a book a few tables away. He still believed that under the Rock-damaged surface, Julie was a warm, gentle, loving person. She had never mentioned her fiancé. How could she really love him?

Sam gathered his books and moved to the seat beside her. Perhaps a plea for help would touch a sympathetic chord.

"I've got a lot of material to cover in a short time," he said. "Do you have any advice that would help me?"

Julie looked at him. The bags under her eyes suggested she was exhausted from a season of studying. "Can't help you much," she said in a low voice. "I find myself just staring at the books, numb. Nothing sinks in. Game preparation requires an effort, and I haven't got much effort left to give."

"The team is on the verge of a collective breakdown," Sam said. "Maybe—"

"We're making too much noise," Julie whispered. "Let's go back to the hotel. I'm done cramming for now."

She gathered her books and they left the library.

Not yet 5 P.M., it was already dark. Patches of ice and snow had slickened the sidewalks. People bundled in winter coats hurried along, ignoring Christmas decorations in the store windows.

After walking half a block, Julie asked, "How are you

holding up under Rock's outbursts? He's been rough on you."

"They're paying me a lot of money. And I'm beginning to think it's not enough."

She smiled. "You don't thrive on adversity?"

"Definitely not. Maybe I see some things more clearly than the rest of you, since I just joined the team. Like I was saying back at the library, the team is having a collective breakdown. We're all going bananas under the pressure. This isn't a team, it's a bunch of frustrated, overworked, overpaid, exploited individuals who are giving everything they've got so a few people can make a huge amount of money off of them."

"That attitude won't help you," Julie noted, as they waited at a stoplight on State Street. "Once you've signed on, you're committed. Cope the best you can."

They passed the huge Macy's department store that had once been Marshall Field's. Frigid winds sweeping into the city off Lake Michigan chilled Sam to the bones.

"What scares me," Julie said, "is that Rock is more stressed out and obsessed since we reached the playoffs. I don't know how much more pressure can build up inside him before he explodes. Every day, he's more unreasonable."

"That's exactly what I'm talking about!" Sam said. "Look, you need to get away from all this pressure. Let's go out for dinner tonight—get away for a while and relax. Then you'll be able to handle the pressure better when we get back."

She stopped walking and glared at her teammate. "So that's what this is about. I'm *not* going out with you, Sam. The first playoff game is two days away. It's your first game ever. There's no time to goof off. ... Good Lord, Sam. You've only been on Ahab's whaler four days and already you want to jump ship?"

"You bet! Why go through hell?"

"You'd better get your head on straight, Sam. You aren't helping me, you're adding to the pressure. *Now back off!*"

Sam slowed his pace and watched Julie hurry on.

She stopped a few feet away. "I didn't mean to be nasty. Just don't pester me. I can't handle it!"

Sam caught up and they passed silently through the busy streets as rush hour traffic hurried by. Obviously Julie was not interested in going out with him. He didn't need this humiliation. There were plenty of women out there begging to date him. He couldn't think of any offhand, but he was sure there must be, now that he was a Brains player. Besides, he could always ask Chase to share Brian's rejects with him. Yes, he was finished with Julie. She couldn't take his "pestering" and he couldn't handle her rejections. Fine. That would be the end of it.

But she looked so sexy when she showed up for morning workouts in shorts …

STILL SMARTING FROM JULIE'S REJECTION of his advances, Sam's mind wandered Friday evening as he attempted to concentrate on the Reconstruction period after the American Civil War. At 10:30, he heard Annie hollering down the hall.

"'*Late Night Edition' is nailing us again! You'd better see this, Sam!*"

The last few words hit Sam like a stake driven through his heart. Why did Annie think Sam in particular should watch it? Fearing the worst, he wandered over to Annie's room, where several of the Phils had gathered to view Percy Smathers on the boob tube.

"TONIGHT, A 'LATE NIGHT EDITION' EXCLUSIVE! THE CHICAGO PHILOSOPHERS MIGHT AS WELL GIVE UP—THEY BLEW THEIR PLAYOFF CHANCES WHEN THEY HASTILY RECRUITED SAM WINSLOW EARLIER THIS WEEK! 'LATE NIGHT EDITION' HAS LEARNED THE PHILS' RESEARCH CREW MISPLACED KEY DATA WHEN IT HUNTED FOR THE BEST CANDIDATE TO REPLACE TINA MEREDITH. SAM WINSLOW WAS NOT NUMBER ONE ON THE LIST. HE WAS ONLY NUMBER SIX!"

The Phils were stunned.

"I doubt if any of us were number one on the recruitment lists," Julie noted.

"Speak for yourself," said Brian.

"DIANE MERCROSS HAS THE STORY FROM CHICAGO."

"THANK YOU, PERCY. TONIGHT'S REPORT WILL COME AS A BOMBSHELL TO THE CITY OF CHICAGO. WHEN BEN SLOAN AND FREUD LAWTON HIGHTAILED IT TO FRANKLIN, INDIANA TO RECRUIT SAM WINSLOW, THEY DIDN'T KNOW THEY WERE SEALING THE PHILS' FATE AS LOSERS IN THE PLAYOFFS. INSTEAD OF RECRUITING THE BEST AND THE BRIGHTEST HISTORY PROSPECT IN THE COUNTRY, THEY SIGNED UP THE SIXTH BEST AND THE SIXTH BRIGHTEST. WITH SO MUCH AT STAKE, THIS SCREWUP BY THE PHILS HAS, FOR ALL INTENTS AND PURPOSES, DOOMED THE TEAM."

"Chicago's going to love me now," Sam moaned.

"WE ASKED RODERICK NORTON, A SCOUT FOR THE MEMPHIS MOONSHINERS, ABOUT THE PHILS' PROSPECTS WITH WINSLOW ON BOARD."

"IT'S A MAJOR BLUNDER," Norton declared. "WE SCOUTED WINSLOW WHEN HE WAS WORKING ON HIS DOCTORATE AT HARVARD. WE DIDN'T THINK HE WAS BIG

LEAGUE MATERIAL. HE WROTE HIS DOCTORAL DISSERTA-
TION ON 'HOW ECONOMIC DEPRESSIONS AFFECTED DOGS
IN THE MIDDLE AGES', OR SOME SUCH NONSENSE."

Sam grimaced. "It was 'Economic Depressions in the 14th Century'."

"Don't let it get you down," Juanita said. "They're only airing this piece of garbage because you didn't take the loot from Diane Mercross."

"Is it too late to take it?"

Juanita smiled wryly. "I believe it is."

"HOW DID SUCH A DISASTROUS ERROR OCCUR? WE
ASKED TRUDY LUND, A PROGRAMMER IN THE PHILS'
RESEARCH DEPARTMENT, THAT QUESTION."

"I CAN'T SAY ANYTHING ABOUT IT," Trudy insisted. She turned to go back inside the sleek new Phils office building on Wabash Avenue.

"IF YOU'RE SMART, YOU'LL TALK TO US," Mercross persisted.

"IF I WAS SMART, I'D BE PLAYING FOR THE TEAM, NOT
SLAVING AWAY ON A COMPUTER IN THE BACK ROOM FOR A
MEASLY NINE BUCKS AN HOUR."

"BUT HOW DID THIS DISASTER HAPPEN? WAS IT YOUR
FAULT?"

"NO! WHEN MANAGEMENT REQUESTED THE LATEST
SCOUTING REPORTS ON THE HISTORY PROSPECTS, ONE OF THE
DATABASES HAD NOT BEEN MERGED WITH THE OTHERS."

"SO SAM WINSLOW WAS NOT THE PHILS' NUMBER
ONE PROSPECT!" Mercross declared.

"THAT'S RIGHT," Trudy said, walking away from the cameras. "THERE WERE FIVE PEOPLE AHEAD OF HIM ON THE LIST."

"I know that girl!" Brian exclaimed. "I've dated Trudy."

"Like she said," T.J. noted. "She's not all that bright."

JUST HOW SMART *IS* SAM WINSLOW? CAN HE HELP THE PHILS WIN THE TITLE? WE ASKED ROBERTA MISCA, WHO TAUGHT HIM HISTORY AT THE UNDERGRADUATE LEVEL."

"WINSLOW? SMART? I NEVER THOUGHT OF THE TWO THINGS AS HAVING ANY CONNECTION. HE DAYDREAMED A LOT IN CLASS. KNEW VERY LITTLE ABOUT THE MIDDLE AGES AND EUROPEAN HISTORY. DON'T THINK HE EVER FINISHED HIS FINAL THESIS."

"That's sour grapes," Sam insisted. "She said she wanted to get in my pants and I said there wasn't room in there for both of us."

Brian gasped. "That is the *worst* line I have ever heard."

"I didn't want to screw around with her and that's the best I could do on short notice."

"SO THERE YOU HAVE IT, BRAINS FANS. YOU HEARD IT HERE FIRST. YOU MIGHT AS WELL WRITE OFF THE PHILS, BECAUSE THEY AREN'T GOING ANYWHERE IN THIS YEAR'S PLAYOFFS."

"Don't let it get you down, Sam," T.J. said, as he headed back to his room. "It doesn't matter how the scouts ranked you. Just help us win."

"That's right," Juanita added, patting Sam on the shoulder. "All that is water under the bridge. What matters now is how well you do in the game."

"*That* is what worries me," Sam muttered, as he returned to his room with a heavy heart.

ON SATURDAY, ROCK WAS EVEN MORE irritable and nervous.

"How nice of you to show up today," he told the players at a team meeting in the hotel. "Even Marvelous Maggie and Sam the Number Six Recruit are here. Sometimes I think trying to win the Brains Bowl with this crew is like trying to cross the Pacific Ocean in a leaky raft."

The short meeting was tense, but somehow Margaret, who insisted she had great difficulty sleeping, managed to fall into a coma. T.J., wearing a "Play Me or Trade Me" sweatshirt, tripped Ben Sloan as Sloan entered the meeting room. And, Annie popped a bubble with her bubble gum so loudly that Rock dropped to the floor, believing someone was shooting at him.

Margaret revived in time for lunch and mentioned that her doctor had called with results of procedures he had run on her. "He said my nerves are shot, I have arthritis in the hands and knees, diverticulosis in the colon, ulcers in the stomach and a murmur in my heart that sounds like John Denver singing 'Annie's Song'. He said if I take an aspirin a day, I'll probably live to be a hundred. I told the quack he'd better give me something stronger than aspirin because I don't want to hurt like hell for the next twenty-eight years. Sometimes I think they give out medical degrees in Cracker Jack boxes."

SATURDAY EVENING, SAM CRAMMED for the playoff game for three hours, then tried to relax by listening to music on the radio—a rock 'n roller warbling about "The Eve of Destruction."

Sam feared it was an omen.

9

THE DAY OF THE FIRST playoff game in the history of the Chicago Philosophers' franchise—and Sam Winslow's first Brains game—was a blustery one in Chicago. By 9 A.M., the temperature hovered around five degrees and snow clouds were moving in. It was the sort of day George Halas and the old Chicago Bears football team loved because they could use the weather to their advantage as they mauled visiting pansies from warmer climates. Since the game of Brains was played indoors, weather was a factor only to fans traveling to and from the game. Weather like this separated Fair Weather Fans from the True Believers.

Sam was so nervous he cut himself twice shaving with a straight razor. Perhaps television viewers would think gang members had slashed him with a knife as he heroically defended a young woman's honor. It wouldn't hurt to have a macho image.

AFTER LUNCH, THE PHILS BOARDED the team bus for the short journey to the huge new Windy City Dome.

A calm settled over the men's and women's locker rooms as team members slipped into their dark blue slacks and sky blue shirts. On the front of the shirts appeared the Philosophers' logo—a pipe resting in an ashtray in front of four books.

Then players gathered in the men's locker room for a few final words from Rock.

"We made it," the coach told his battle-weary brains. "We're in the playoffs. Nobody thought we would get this far, but we did. And do you know how? ..."

Brian whispered to T.J., "By pulverizing our brains."

"... By working hard and never giving up. Now we've got to prove that we belong here, that we're as good as any other team!"

He surveyed his nervous crew. "I'm not asking you to win this one for the Gipper. I'm not asking you to win it for me, although that wouldn't be a bad idea. I'm asking you to win it for *you*. ... This isn't one of those two-out-of-three deals, you know. We've got to win today. The Cleveland players are tough, but they have weaknesses. Exploit those weaknesses! Beat them up! Then open the wounds and pour salt on them! It's all right if a little blood is spilt today. That's part of the game!"

"Since when?" Sam wondered aloud. "This is supposed to be an intellectual game."

"Since Rock became a coach," Brian whispered. "He's got a point. I discovered my opponents can't concentrate on the game when their arms are broken and they're racked with pain."

"Did you say something, Mister?" Rock roared at Brian.

"No, sir. Ready for combat, sir!"

"That's more like it," Rock growled. "There is no tomorrow! Today, you must reach deep into your souls and find out what you are made of. Go out onto that playing floor with confidence and courage—and beat their brains out!"

As the Phils jogged toward the playing floor, the noise arising from the huge crowd grew louder and more nerve-shattering. Watching Rock lead the way, Sam thought again of Ahab.

> Small reason was there to doubt ... that ever since that almost fatal encounter, Ahab had cherished a wild vindictiveness against the whale, all the more felt, for that in his frantic morbidness he at last came to identify with him, not only all his bodily woes, but all his intellectual and spiritual exasperations.

THE FRANTIC HOMETOWN CROWD applauded and screamed as their heroes reached the playing floor. The huge scoreboard flashed "GO PHILS!" In the broadcasting booth, Moose Harrison described the scene for millions of viewers across the country.

> "THIS IS A HISTORIC DAY. FOR THE FIRST TIME THE PHILOSOPHERS ARE IN THE PLAYOFFS. THERE HASN'T BEEN THIS MUCH EXCITEMENT IN CHICAGO SINCE MICHAEL JORDAN CAME OUT OF RETIREMENT TO REJOIN THE BULLS.
>
> "AND NOW THE PHILS ARE TAKING THE FLOOR! LISTEN TO THE CROWD! ... OVER THERE IS THE NEWEST MEMBER OF THE TEAM, SAM WINSLOW. WINSLOW IS THE CENTER OF A CONTROVERSY OVER WHETHER THE TEAM COMMITTED SUICIDE BY SIGNING HIM. SAM MUST BE NERVOUS. IT LOOKS LIKE HE CHOPPED HIS FACE SHAVING ... AND HERE COME THE CLEVELAND MIDDLE AMERICANS! THE MAs, WHO HAVE BEEN TO THE PLAYOFFS THREE TIMES, HAVE ALREADY BEATEN THE PHILS ONCE THIS YEAR."

For the first time in his life, Sam literally could not think. The noise of the raucous crowd squeezed any thoughts he might have had out of his mind. He gazed dumbfoundedly at the mass of humanity—the tens of thousands of people who had come to see the Phils play. Six days earlier, Sam had been a nobody, a would-be writer playing basketball in a college gym. Now he had a chance to make a complete jackass of himself in front of seventy thousand people in the stadium and millions more watching on television.

After the playing of the National Anthem, Moose Harrison announced the starting lineups. In a restrained voice, he said, "AND NOW THE STARTING LINEUPS FOR THE CLEVELAND MIDDLE AMERICANS." Moose hurried through the MAs' roster without emotion.

Then the lights dimmed. Loud music with a torrid beat exploded over the public address system. A video tape running on the huge scoreboard showed a satellite photo of Earth taken from thousands of miles away. The camera zoomed down until the United States became visible, and then the city of Chicago, with lights shining bright. The camera zoomed in still further until the Windy City Dome could be seen, and then a new shot revealed the interior of the arena. In a voice suddenly loud and booming, Moose bellowed, "AND NOW THE LINEUP FOR THE CHICAGO PHILOSOPHERS! ... MARGARET KRAMER! ... EDGAR TOLIN WOODFORD ... BRIAN MARSHALL ... SAM WINSLOW ..." He introduced all the players, then Freud, and finally "THE AMAZING MENTOR WHO SHOULD BE THE LEAGUE'S COACH OF THE YEAR, ROCK NELSON!" The joyful fans went wild.

The six starting players on both sides seated themselves behind desks that would be transported to centercourt whenever it was their turn to compete—except on the team vs. team Shakespearean tipoff questions that began each half of a game. For those questions, the players faced each other from the sidelines.

At centercourt, the head referee read the Shakespearean tipoff as it appeared on the huge Brains Board:

"For four points: from which play is this quotation taken—'Was ever book containing such vile matter so fairly bound?' ..."

Julie slammed her buzzer first.

"Romeo and Juliet!" she declared.

The electronic scoreboard flashed "FANTASTIC!" as the crowd cheered wildly. No one could hear the referee proclaim that it was indeed the correct answer.

The sports specialists—Chase for the Phils and Smokey Jorgenson for the Middle Americans—moved to the Hot Zone. They looked like two fighters—Chase heavier and stronger, Smokey younger and more agile.

As the noise subsided, the head referee's voice again could be heard over speakers situated throughout the vast stadium. "For three points: in the 1950s three New York Yankees won the Most Valuable Player Award in the American League. Name them."

Smokey, a former baseball player, walloped his button for all it was worth.

"Mickey Mantle, Yogi Berra and ..."

He hesitated.

"Phil Rizzuto."

The "LUCKY GUESS" sign flashed only once—after all, it was the visiting team that scored—and the Phils led by a point, 4-3.

Two minutes later, the Phils held a 9 to 8 advantage when Sam was abruptly summoned to the Hot Zone to face the howling masses. Ivan the Terrible Kolsky, his Cleveland opponent, seemed relatively calm.

Moose Harrison remarked, "THIS IS THE MOMENT MANY CHICAGO FANS HAVE BEEN WAITING FOR—AND MANY HAVE BEEN DREADING. NEW RECRUIT SAM WINSLOW IS IN THE HOT ZONE. THE PRESSURE ON THIS YOUNG HOOSIER HAS BEEN BUILDING ALL WEEK. HE FINDS HIMSELF IN THE FIRE OF PLAYOFF COMPETITION WITHOUT EVER HAVING PLAYED A BRAINS GAME."

A hush settled over the crowd as the head referee read the question: "For three points: which of these United States presidents once served as secretary of war: a. John Quincy Adams, b. James Madison, c. James Monroe?"

The question and choices appeared on the Brains Board.

Rattled by the pressure but desperate to put points on the board, Sam punched his buzzer. A close-up shot on television revealed clearly the perspiration on his forehead and the razor cuts on his chin. The crowd waited tensely.

"James Madison," Sam guessed.

The "OOPS!" sign flashed. The crowd groaned.

"WELL, SAM CHOKED IN HIS FIRST TIME AT BAT," Moose told television viewers. "HE'S OFF TO A ROCKY START."

Ivan the Terrible took a crack at answering the question. "James Monroe!" he declared.

The "LUCKY GUESS!" sign flashed once. A collective moan surfaced from the crowd. On the sidelines, Rock shook a fist in anger.

From the bleacher seats on the left side, Sam's father and brother looked on glumly.

"Sam's not doing so good," Fred groused.

Joe shrugged. "It's early, Pop. It's his first game. He'll do better. There's a lot of time left."

Behind them, someone yelled, *"ship that loser back to Indiana!"*

Fred grimaced. "I'd like to see that blowhard try to ship me back to Indiana." He started to get up.

Joe restrained him. "He wasn't talkin' about you, Pop. He's talkin' about Sam. And you don't want to take on the heckler. He's about six-foot-five and built like a Hummer. Must weigh three hundred fifty pounds or more."

Fred settled back into his seat. "Well, it's a free country. I reckon he can say what he wants."

The MAs held the lead, but the Phils had a chance to tie it up when Renaissance Women Margaret Kramer and Jessica Granger Brayton faced off over a science question:

"For two points: he has been called our greatest genius in pure science. He laid the theoretical foundations for modern physical chemistry ..."

Before the referee finished reading the question, Margaret smacked her buzzer.

"Josiah Willard Gibbs!" she said.

The "HURRAY!" sign flashed as the crowd went wild. Then the scoreboard carried a new message: "WAY TO GO, MAGGIE!"

Margaret grimaced. "I told them not to call me Maggie."

A short time later, Sam, Julie and Brian were transported to the Hot Zone for the first Brain Buster of the game. Three MAs faced them.

"For four points," the head referee announced, "tell me the numbers in the next line of Pascal's Triangle, which represent values for 1 plus x to the seventh power."

On the Brains Board appeared the first seven lines of Pascal's Triangle:

$$1$$
$$1 \ 1$$
$$1 \ 2 \ 1$$
$$1 \ 3 \ 3 \ 1$$
$$1 \ 4 \ 6 \ 4 \ 1$$
$$1 \ 5 \ 10 \ 10 \ 5 \ 1$$
$$1 \ 6 \ 15 \ 20 \ 15 \ 6 \ 1$$

After a few moments, Lin Chan slammed her buzzer. "The next row is 1 7 21 35 35 21 7 1."

"That is correct," the head referee announced.

Rock grabbed his throat, letting his Phils know they had choked under the pressure. On his way back to the sidelines, Brian complained, "it's Rock's fault I didn't know that one. I prepared for the Brain Buster by making sentences out of vegetable soup."

Three minutes later, Sam and Ivan the Terrible prepared to rumble again.

"LET'S SEE IF SAM DOES BETTER ON HIS SECOND VISIT TO THE HOT ZONE," Moose said. "THERE ARE SEVENTY THOUSAND FANS IN THE STADIUM, BUT WINSLOW IS PROBABLY FEELING VERY LONELY RIGHT NOW. HERE COMES THE QUESTION."

"For four points: who fought in the Battle of Bannock-burn—and who won?"

Sam froze, terrified he might blow another answer. Ivan the Terrible swatted his buzzer.

"The Scots fought the English ... and the Scots won."

The "LUCKY GUESS!" sign flashed once. The crowd groaned in disappointment.

"OHHH, SAMMY," Moose moaned. "YOU'VE GOTTA FEEL SORRY FOR WINSLOW. HE'S IN A TOUGH SPOT, BUT IN A PLAYOFF GAME, JUST SHOWING UP ISN'T ENOUGH. YOU'VE GOT TO PRODUCE. AND SO FAR WINSLOW HASN'T."

At the end of the first quarter, the MAs led, 22 to 16.

IN THE SECOND QUARTER, Julie and Cleveland's Carlton Fitzwalter were hauled to centercourt.

The head referee called for quiet. "For three points. Who uttered these words on the occasion of his seventieth birthday?"

The quotation appeared on the Brains Board:

> "Of late years the public have been trying to tackle me in every way they possibly can, and failing to make anything of it they have turned to treating me as a great man. This is a dreadful fate to overtake anybody."

Julie slammed the buzzer. "George Bernard Shaw!" she declared.

"WOW!' flashed the Brains Board as the crowd applauded.

But Cleveland controlled the momentum and slowly built up its lead.

The world specialists, Edgar Woodford and the MAs' Lin Chan, met in the Hot Zone.

"For two points," declared the head referee, "which country does *not* share a border with Italy? a. France, b. Yugoslavia, c. Hungary, d. Austria."

Lin pressed her buzzer quickly. "C. Hungary," she said.

"NO BIG DEAL," flashed the Brains Board, as the head referee declared Lin's answer correct.

Brian and the MAs' Maria Sebastian rendezvoused at centercourt for a two-point popular arts faceoff.

"I'm curious," Brian said. "Why did you marry your

third husband before you divorced your second victim?"

"I merely forgot. Husband Number 2 was inconsequential. Like you."

"Believe me, honey. If you were married to me, you wouldn't forget me."

Laughter erupted.

"I would have forgotten you *before* I married you."

Brian was noticeably rattled as the head referee read the question. "For two points: who won the 1986 Best Director Academy Award for *Rain Men*? a) James Cameron (b) Bob Levinson (c) Oliver Stone."

Maria punched the buzzer. "b. Bob Levinson!"

The "LUCKY GUESS" message flashed on the Brains Board.

On the sidelines, Rock confronted Brian. "Rule Number Two, kid: Don't flirt with your opponent unless the coach tells you to!"

"What's rule Number One?" asked T.J.

"Don't put T.J. in the starting lineup," Rock growled.

Sam lost another encounter to Ivan the Terrible, and at half-time the Middle Americans led, 43 to 36.

"THINGS ARE LOOKING BLEAK FOR THE PHILS," Moose Harrison noted. "WITH SAM WINSLOW COMING UP EMPTY, CLEVELAND IS IN CONTROL. BUT A SEVEN-POINT LEAD CAN DISAPPEAR QUICKLY IN A GAME LIKE THIS. IT ALL DEPENDS ON WHETHER THE PHILS CAN GET THEIR ACT TOGETHER IN THE SECOND HALF. IS THIS HOW CHICAGO'S MIRACLE SEASON WILL END? WE'LL BE BACK AFTER THESE MESSAGES."

SAM HEADED FOR THE locker rooms, frustrated because he was having a terrible game and didn't have a clue about how to turn it around. The players with game experience all had more poise, more confidence, more correct answers than he did. He felt like a beachcomber in the path of hundred-mile-an-hour hurricane winds. There was no place to run, no place to hide.

In the locker room, a desperate Rock faced his weary crew.

"Why are you doing this to me?" he asked in anguish. "If you don't win today, there is no tomorrow! Everything we've done this season will be flushed down the toilet. You've got to pull yourselves together. *You've got to bite the bullet!* ... Seven points isn't a lot. You were down by eighteen against Buffalo and you came back. You can do it, but you've got to *focus on the game!* Use every bit of energy you can muster. Play better than you've ever played before!"

He directed his death-ray stare at Sam. "Winslow, if I wanted someone to sit in the Hot Zone like a dummy and blow every question I would have hired my mother. We can use one pass in each quarter, and I want you to use it. Ivan is killing us. We could try to terminate him, but you haven't got a question right yet and all that would do is send you to the bench. You've got to get it together, Winslow!

"All of you are playing in a daze. Brian, you were slow on the buzzer. Margaret, everyone knows you're seventy-two years old. Instead of whining about it, make it work for you. Wake up!"

Rock pulled a slip of paper from his hip pocket. "I wasn't going to read this letter to you, but I think you ought to hear it," he said somberly. "It's from the mother of Johnny, a little five-year-old boy. It says, 'Johnny is dying of an incurable disease. The doctor says he only has a few months to live. More than anything else in the world, Johnny wants you to win your playoff game. He'd like to be there to see you do it, but that isn't possible. Will you win the game for Johnny? It would mean so much to him.'"

Rock dabbed a handkerchief at his eyes to dry them. The locker room was quiet.

"So what is it going to be?" asked Rock. "Are you going to give up like craven cowards, or are you going to win this game for Johnny?"

"We'll win it for Johnny!" declared Julie, as she wiped away a tear.

"You bet we will!" said T.J.

"Damn right!" yelled Brian.

"Then, let's do it!" Rock bellowed.

He threw the letter in a wastebasket and led the charged-up team back to the playing floor.

Chase, who understood Rock better than the other players, fished the letter out of the wastebasket after the others had left. The letter wasn't from Johnny's mother—it was from a bill collector. Rock was three months late making a payment on his new lawn sprinkling system.

Chase shook his head and jogged toward the playing floor. The old son of a bitch was trying to con them. Wanted them to win the game for a bill collector. What would the team say if they knew?

Chase would tell the rest of the team … *after* the game. If the letter helped Rock get his victory, Chase reasoned, more power to him.

Yes, Chase understood Rock.

THE SECOND HALF OPENED with the inevitable four-point Shakespearean tipoff:

> "From what Shakespearean play comes the quotation:
> 'I do begin to perceive that I am made an ass'."

Margaret swatted her buzzer first.

"Is that any language to use on national television?" she asked. "You ought to be ashamed!"

The head referee was not amused. "One more outburst like that and I'll penalize you for unsportsmanlike conduct!"

On the sidelines a frustrated Rock Nelson pulled out a clump of his hair and looked at it forlornly. "At this rate I'll be bald by the end of the day," he told Freud.

"Do you wish to answer the question?" the referee asked Margaret.

"Of course I wish to answer the question. I hit the buzzer, didn't I? It was *The Merry Wives of Windsor.*"

The Brains Board flashed "YOU BETCHA!" as the crowd roared. The other Philosophers looked at each other and smiled. Margaret, in her own obnoxious way, had helped break the tension.

Chase and Smokey Jorgenson entered the playing area for a sports faceoff.

"For four points: in 1954, the Cleveland Browns and Detroit Lions met in the National Football League Championship playoff game. The Browns won, 56-10." A film clip from another game appeared on the screen. "In 1957, the same two teams met for the title again. Who won, and what was the score?"

Chase punched his buzzer. "Detroit, 59 to 14!"

The scoreboard exploded. Fans went crazy. "It was nothin'," Chase told Sam, when he returned to the sidelines. "I watched a tape of that game a dozen times."

The quotations specialists, Julie Howard and Carlton Fitzwalter, moved to the Hot Zone.

"For two points," the referee announced, his voice booming over the loudspeakers. "Name the author of these lines and the name of the poem from which they are taken." The referee read the lines as they appeared on the huge Brains Board behind him.

> Ten days and nights, with sleepless eye,
> I watched that wretched man,
> And since, I never dare to write
> As funny as I can.

Julie slammed her buzzer. "Oliver Wendell Holmes, 'The Height of the Ridiculous'!" she declared.

"RIGHT ON!" flashed the Brains Board.

The Phils and MAs were tied when Sam and Ivan the Terrible returned to the playing area. Boos and catcalls greeted Sam.

Moose Harrison commented, "I'M SURPRISED ROCK HASN'T PULLED SAM OUT OF THE GAME, BUT APPARENTLY HE WANTS SAM TO FIGHT HIS WAY OUT OF THE CORNER HE'S IN SO HE'LL DO BETTER IN THE PHILS' NEXT PLAYOFF GAME—IF THERE IS ONE. EVEN SO, I DON'T KNOW HOW MUCH LONGER ROCK WILL LEAVE SAM IN THE GAME. THIS IS TURNING UGLY."

The head referee called for quiet. "For two points: name the architect credited with designing the Washington Monument."

Sam hesitated a split second, then walloped the button so hard he thought he had broken it.

"Yes, Chicago," said the head referee.

Sam took a deep breath. "Robert Mills," he declared.

The stadium was quiet, then the Brains Board lit up: "SAM DID IT!"

Chicago fans shouted and hollered their approval.

"YES," said Moose Harrison. "SAM DID IT! HE FINALLY PUT

POINTS ON THE BOARD, AND THE PHILS HAVE SEIZED THE LEAD, 49-47. LISTEN TO THE CROWD! LOOK AT THE SMILE ON SAM'S FACE!"

When Sam returned to the sidelines, teammates congratulated him. Rock slapped him on the back. "That's more like it, Winslow!"

HEADING INTO THE FINAL QUARTER, the Phils led, 60 to 52.

Brian and Cleveland's popular arts expert, Maria Sebastian, met in the Hot Zone.

"For three points," the head referee declared, "which of these television shows was *not* a spinoff from another show: a. 'Maude', b. 'Benson', c. 'Diff'rent Strokes', d, 'Lou Grant'."

Maria walloped her buzzer. "'Benson'!" she said.

"TOO BAD!" flashed the Brains Board, and the crowd cheered.

Brian smacked his buzzer. *Oh, God, I love this game,* he thought, as attention was once more riveted on him. *This might be worth another $100,000 in advertising endorsements.* "'Benson' was a spinoff from 'Soap'," he declared. "The answer is 'Diff'rent Strokes'."

"HURRAY!" flashed the Brains Board.

Chase correctly named Roger Staubach of Navy as the college football player who won the 1963 Heisman Trophy, and Chicago fans were delirious. They couldn't believe their Phils, the underdogs, held a 65-52 lead in a playoff game.

Then the Middle Americans clawed their way back into the game. Margaret didn't know Krypton was denser than Chlorine, and Julie failed to identify the author of this passage: "From morn to noon he fell, from noon to dewey eve, a summer's day, and with the setting sun dropt from the zenith like a falling star ..." (Milton)

Two minutes remained in the game.

"THE PHILS ARE CLINGING TO AN EIGHT-POINT LEAD, 68 TO 60," Moose Harrison reported, "BUT THE GAME'S MOMENTUM HAS SHIFTED TO THE MIDDLE AMERICANS. CAN THE PHILS HANG ON?"

> In the stands, Fred Winslow got up. "Let's go."
>
> "But, dad, there's two minutes left in the game!"
>
> "There are seventy thousand people here," Fred grumbled, as he led the way to the exit. "I don't want to wait three hours to get out of the parking lot. We're leaving now!"
>
> "But, Sam might answer another question. Your own son is playing for the Phils!"
>
> "He hasn't exactly been shooting the bull's-eye out of the target. Let's go. We can hear the end of the game on the car radio."
>
> "But dad! ..."

With 1:48 remaining, Sam and Ivan were asked, for two points, to explain the highly unusual disappearance of a Soviet Union tank during Warsaw Pact maneuvers in Czechoslovakia in the mid-1980s.

Sam was stunned. "How would I know? I didn't take it."

Ivan said, "I didn't take it, either. But I knew the four soldiers who did. I was serving in the Soviet Army at the time. My four comrades traded the tank to a tavern owner for vodka, herring and pickles. Not a bad trade at all, but I told them, you just can't go around trading Soviet tanks."

Cleveland trailed the Phils by six points, 68 to 62, as Edgar Woodford and Lin Chan, the world specialists, were transported to centercourt. Lin immediately called out, "Double it!"

The head referee began reading the question, now worth four points, as it appeared on the Brains Board:

> Who served as United States ambassador to the United Nations under President John F. Kennedy?
>> a. Henry Cabot Lodge, Jr.
>> b. Adlai Stevenson
>> c. Robert F. Kennedy
>> d. Stuart Symington

Edgar knew the answer, but Lin Chan was faster at reading the question and pushing the buzzer. "B. Adlai Stevenson," Lin declared.

The "LUCKY GUESS!" sign flashed once as the crowd groaned.

"HANG ON TO YOUR SEATS," Moose Harrison said. "IT'S ALL COMING DOWN TO THE LAST QUESTION. CLEVELAND HAS CUT THE PHILS' LEAD TO TWO POINTS, 68 TO 66. THERE'S TIME FOR ONE MORE QUESTION, AND THE RENAISSANCE WOMEN—MARGARET AND JESSICA GRANGER BRAYTON—ARE UP NEXT."

Rock called a timeout. As the crowd shouted encouragement to their beloved Phils, the players gathered around Rock.

"You've got to nail it," he told Margaret. "You've got to be first and be right! *Everything* is riding on you. Civilization as we know it will crumble if you blow it!"

"And little Johnny will die," Chase noted.

Rock did a double-take. He had forgotten about Johnny. "That's right. You don't want *that* on your conscience, do you, Margaret?"

Freud pulled Rock aside. "Easy, coach. It's only a game. Only a game."

"Softball is a game. This is war!" He turned to Margaret. "Now go out there and annihilate the enemy!"

Margaret wiped sweat off her forehead with a towel. "So much pressure. I'll probably have a heart attack!"

"Have your heart attack *after* the game," Rock growled. "Rack up those points for us!"

Rock and Freud conferred.

T.J. smiled. "I've got just one question, Margaret."

"What's that?" she asked wearily.

He put a hand on Margaret's shoulder. "Are you ever going to turn seventy three? We're all pretty sick of hearing you're seventy two."

Margaret glared at T.J., but her grimace slowly gave way to a smile. "Why, you little pipsqueak. Just wait and see how irritating I can be when I'm seventy three."

"Go get 'em, Maggie."

"Right, T.J."

The players returned to their positions and Margaret and Jessica were whisked to centercourt. Jessica immediately pressed the Double It! button; Cleveland had no interest in tying the game, it wanted to win.

Margaret took a deep breath.

"For double the points," the head referee declared. "Four points." The question appeared on the Brains Board as he began reading it.

> In Greek mythology, the Trojan princess Cassandra was awarded to this king, who later was beheaded by his wife. Name the king.

Both players whacked their buzzers before he finished reading the question. Margaret hit hers first.

"Agamemnon!" she asserted.

The Brains Board flashed "YOU DID IT, MAGGIE! THE PHILS WIN!" The crowd roared its approval as fireworks exploded from the far corners of the arena. Fans mobbed the playing area. The other Phils surrounded Margaret and congratulated her as time ran out.

Moose Harrison described the scene for television viewers:

> "SEVENTY-TWO-YEAR-OLD MARGARET KRAMER HAS DONE IT! SHE'S THE HERO HERE IN CHICAGO AS THE PHILS BUILD UP A THIRTEEN-POINT LEAD AND THEN BARELY HANG ON TO DEFEAT THE CLEVELAND MIDDLE AMERICANS, 72 TO 66. IT'S BEDLAM IN THE WINDY CITY DOME AS FANS CELEBRATE THE FIRST PLAYOFF VICTORY IN FRANCHISE HISTORY. PLAYERS ARE HUGGING JUST ABOUT EVERYONE IN SIGHT.
>
> "THE WEARY PHILS WON'T HAVE LONG TO REST. NEXT WEEK, THEY HOST THE EASTERN DIVISION CHAMPIONS, THE BALTIMORE MENCKENS, WHO UPSET THE NEW YORK INTELLECTUALS TODAY, 78 TO 65. IN THE OTHER GAME, THE SOUTHERN DIVISION CHAMPION, THE HOUSTON SPACE CADETS, WILL TANGLE WITH THE DEFENDING BRAINS CHAMPIONS, THE SAN FRANCISCO HACKERS. WINNERS OF NEXT WEEK'S GAMES WILL COMPETE IN THE BRAINS BOWL."

Rock viewed the jubilation with growing uneasiness. His team had won another skirmish as time ran out.

In the locker room, Rock faced his crew. "All right, hold it down. ... You managed to win, but you almost blew the game in the fourth quarter. You've got to do better! We can't let up. Next week we face the Baltimore Menckens. It will be our toughest game yet. And Sam ..."

"Yes, coach."

"If you don't shape up, I'll ship you back to Fort Wayne!"

"Franklin," Sam muttered.

"What did you say?" Rock growled.

"Fort Wayne will be fine."

"You can't play like that in the big leagues and get away with it. *All of you* must work three times as hard this week. I'll see you at seven tomorrow in the workout room."

Ben Sloan congratulated Rock on the victory and posed with the coach as television cameramen and newspaper photographers closed in on them.

AS HIS TEAMMATES HURRIED OFF to change into street clothes, Sam remained on a locker room bench, lost in thought. He wasn't sure whether he should be relieved or disappointed Rock hadn't kicked him off the team. The game had been a rude awakening. Practices hadn't gone well, but Sam thought that somehow everything would work out during the game and he would be a hero. Instead, he almost blew the game for the Phils.

Suddenly, he felt a hand on his shoulder.

"I know it's a ridiculous idea, but I thought maybe you and I should get away from the pressure for a while," Julie said. "Let's have dinner somewhere tonight. I don't care where. Just so we can get away for a while."

As Julie headed toward the women's locker room, Sam watched in amazement. Maybe that was what it took. Julie was a sucker for men who were so overwrought they couldn't cope with life. All he had to do was be on the verge of a breakdown every time he asked her out.

That wouldn't be a problem as long as he was sailing on Rock's Whaler.

II

Thou Shouldst
Go Mad

MONDAY, DECEMBER 15 - SUNDAY, DECEMBER 21

10

AFTER THE GAME, THE TEAM RETURNED TO THE Palmer House Hilton. Sam showered and slipped on a blue knit shirt and jeans. He grabbed his black leather jacket and rendezvoused in the hallway with Julie, who was wearing a gold pullover sweater and jeans under a long tan wool blend coat.

Sam hailed a taxi and they headed for Coco Pazzo, an Italian restaurant nestled on West Hubbard Street.

The first thing Sam noticed when they arrived were the wooden beams that crossed the ceiling, stretching from one brick wall to another. Tables covered with white linen tablecloths were scattered across the hardwood floor. The open kitchen with a wood-burning stove added to the rustic ambience.

Despite the pleasant surroundings, Sam's mood was sour. "This was not a good idea. I'm not at my best after I humiliate myself in front of millions of people."

Julie smiled as she reached for her wine. "So you humiliated yourself. Big deal. We all do it. I humiliated myself when we played the Milwaukee Beer Heads. I'm surprised you don't remember. They threw me a curve, asking me to identify a line from Elvis Presley's 'Love Me Tender'. I said it was from a Charlotte Bronte novel."

"I think we have a problem with semantics," Sam suggested, as he picked at his tagliata alla fiorentina—a grilled rib-eye steak. "I'm not talking about annoying incidents that pass from memory within a day or two. I'm talking about real humiliation, on the order of, say, mooning the First Lady."

Julie reached across the table and caressed his right hand. "You may think everyone is staring at you thinking 'what an idiot', but no one holds it against you. We won the game! Everyone in Chicago is ecstatic!"

Sam's gaze trailed to other tables. The natives did not seem friendly.

> At a nearby table, a chubby young man wearing a Cubs shirt whispered to his blonde date, "Isn't that Julie Howard and that screwup—the new guy on the Phils?"
>
> "I dunno," she said. "It's hard to tell. They aren't in their uniforms."
>
> "Probably not them," he conceded. "I don't think the screwup would have the guts to walk the streets after today's game. ... Sure looks like him, though."

"So, let me get this straight," Sam told Julie. "This is a pity date. We're having dinner together because you took pity on me."

"Not exactly. I thought you needed someone to comfort you. A friend."

"That's a start. ... What kind of comfort do you have in mind?"

"Behave yourself!"

"Tell me about the competition."

Julie thawed out a little. "That's more like it. The Baltimore Menckens are tough and often obnoxious, but there are ways to beat them."

"That's not what I mean. Tell me about your fiancé. T.J. said you were engaged, but you haven't mentioned the unlucky victim."

"I don't have time to see him now. After I get away from Rock's Little Ship of Horrors, I plan to go back home to Philadelphia and marry David."

Sam sipped his wine. "What does he do for a living? Does he swindle people out of their payroll checks, or burglarize old ladies' homes?"

"He makes small missiles."

"For little wars?"

"No. He designs toys for a company."

Sam drummed his fingers on the table as he pondered this information. "Designing war toys for kids ... how does he sleep nights? How do *you* sleep nights, knowing you may marry a man who does such despicable things?"

"It's only a job. It's not like he peddles pornography to kids."

"Hard to know where to draw the line, isn't it? War toys for kids—O.K. Porno for kids—that's a no-no."

The Cub fan continued to scrutinize the couple at the nearby table.

"I know it's them! I'd like to tell that jerkball a thing or two. He almost ruined everything!"

The blonde grimaced. "For Pete's sake, Kirby. We won the game! Give it a rest!"

"But we *almost lost*. Next week, we could lose bigtime with him on the team. I gotta say somethin'!"

The Cub fan stomped over to Sam and Julie's table.

"You're Phils players, aren't you!" Kirby said, more as an accusation than a compliment.

Julie smiled. "Isn't that nice, Ralph. He thinks we look like Phils players."

"I'd like to get my hands on the money they make," Ralph—a.k.a. Sam—suggested.

"Look, I'm sorry. Guess I made a mistake," muttered the Cubs fan. He retreated to his table.

The blonde shook her head. "Are you happy now? You made a fool of yourself!"

Kirby stared at his plate of spaghetti. "It sure looked like them."

Sam sighed heavily. "So much for your theory Chicago fans have forgiven me. They're ready to lynch me. ... What were we talking about? Oh, yes. Your fiancé. Has David gotten to home plate with you?"

"What are you—the scorekeeper?" Julie asked, as she tasted the cappuccino ice cream.

"I'm a friend who's trying to keep you from ruining your life. David isn't right for you. I don't see any fireworks going off here. You talk about him like you would talk about your Aunt Mildred in Maine."

"I wasn't asking for your opinion, Sam! I suggested we have dinner together because I wanted to cheer you up, but we won't be doing this again."

"I should hope not," Sam mused, as he sampled his chocolate cake. "We should do something much more exciting next time."

"Why can't you take things seriously, Sam? We have another game next Sunday. We should be boning up for it right now. Rock will be a real bear this week because of the way we played."

As the waitress picked up the dirty dishes, a way out of the mess occurred to Sam.

"I don't know what I'm worried about. Rock will throw me off the team after the way I played today."

"No he won't! He doesn't have time to train anyone else. He knows you have potential."

"I ought to beat him to the punch and quit. I don't need all this aggravation."

Julie glared at her teammate. "How can you talk about quitting? You've been with the team less than a week. The rest of us have been in this pressure cooker all season!"

"That's your trouble. You've been on the team too long, Julie. You've forgotten there's a whole wide world out there, a world where Rock isn't king, a world where there's more to life than abusing your brain eighteen hours a day."

"There will be time for the rest of the world after the season. Right now, this is what I'm paid to do, and I'm going to do it!" Julie leaned forward. "Why did you join the team if you aren't willing to work hard? ... I'll tell you why. You thought how great it would be to be a Brains player. All the money, the glamour, the publicity ... you wanted the perks without working for them. Now you know how tough it is, and the first thing you do is look for the exit. When the going gets rough, you give up. Well, it's time you did some hard work! Being a Brains player isn't something you dabble in. You've got to be part of the madness." She noticed Sam's eyes had glazed over. "Are you listening to me?"

"You're beautiful when you're passionate. Your eyes sparkle and your body vibrates."

"And *you* are hopeless. ... We've got to leave, Sam. We have a half hour 'til the 10:30 curfew."

"All right." Sam noticed someone lurking in the shadows at the back of the restaurant. He whispered, "Julie! Do you see that man over there? Tall, brown hair. Wearing a blue suit."

"What about him?"

"He's been following us since we left the hotel. And he's got a gun."

"Are you sure?"

"Positive."

"Why would he want to harm us?"

"Who knows? Maybe he plans to kidnap us and hold us for ransom. Or, maybe Baltimore hired him to lock us up until after next week's game."

Julie smiled. "Maybe our fans hired him, to make sure *you* don't play in the next game."

"That was a low blow," Sam mumbled.

"Sorry. ... Let's call the police."

"No. If I'm wrong. I'd look like even more of a fool. We've got to lose him before we get back to the hotel."

Sam paid the bill and they put on their coats. Julie noticed the man in the blue suit was getting ready to leave, too.

"Hurry, Sam!"

SAM AND JULIE HUSTLED OUTSIDE and hopped inside a taxi. They were a half block away when the man in the blue suit jumped into another cab.

"He's following us!" Julie gasped.

The cabbie, a middle-aged black man, took a closer look in his side mirror. "What's going down here? Am I going to get my head blown off?"

"Hopefully not," Sam said. "Lose him!"

"Sounds good to me," the cabbie declared, as he swerved

onto a side street and pressed the accelerator to the floor. The second cab followed.

"This presents an interesting problem," Sam said. "Both of you cabbies drive for the same company. How do we know you won't radio our location to the other cabbie after you drop us off?"

"I can't do that," the cabbie insisted. "Your destination and anything you tell me are completely confidential. We have a code of conduct like the lawyers have. What do they call it?"

"Privileged communication," Julie noted. "But that doesn't apply to cabbies."

"It does to this cabbie, lady. You can trust me."

The taxi permit identified the driver as William Archerby.

Archerby turned onto Michigan Avenue and weaved in and out amongst the traffic.

"Why are we being followed?" Archerby asked.

"We aren't sure," Julie said. "But the man following us has a gun!"

"Oh, boy." Archerby squeezed the accelerator a little harder.

He took two quick rights, pulled into a parking lot and waited until the other cab whizzed by. Then Archerby immediately returned the way he came. He gassed it to the Palmer House Hilton, where Sam slipped him a twenty-dollar tip.

JULIE WAS STILL BREATHING HEAVILY when she rode the elevator to the eleventh floor with Sam. "That was a close call. We could have been killed!"

Sam shrugged. "I don't think Marty would have gone that far."

Julie was stunned. "Marty? Who's Marty?"

"He's a bodyguard Rock hired to keep an eye on the team. That's why he was following us in the other cab. I met him the other day. Nice fellow."

Julie pounded on Sam's shoulders with her fists. "Why did you let me think we were in danger?"

Sam put up his hands to block Julie's blows. "Because we needed to have a little fun on this date."

"Fun?" Julie exclaimed. "My nerves are frazzled and you tell me a man with a gun is following us and you think that's fun? You're crazy, Sam Winslow."

"And David isn't."

"That's why I like David. He's stable. Dependable."

"And boring," Sam noted.

As Sam and Julie headed down the corridor, they noticed T.J. approaching from the other direction. He was dressed in a gray sweatshirt and bluejeans.

"Where have you been?" Sam asked.

"Playing golf. There's a virtual golf course next to the swimming pool."

"I thought the swimming pool was off limits," Sam noted.

"It is. So is the virtual golf course."

"How did you do?" Julie asked.

"I flirted with par on the first hole. Then it was all downhill. Every time I looked at the ball, I saw Rock's face. I smacked the ball so hard I forgot I was trying to get it in the hole."

T.J. wandered off to his room. Sam mumbled to Julie, "Like I said, it's the pressure."

"I don't know. T.J. has always been three books short of a library."

When they reached the door to Julie's room, Sam said, "You're too young to roll over and die. Stick with me, kid, and you'll have adventures. We'll dangle off buildings, free-lance for the C.I.A., fight terrorists."

Julie unlocked her door. "Sounds dangerous," she said.

"So, when are we going to have a real date?"

Julie slipped inside the room. "You're actually somewhat likeable, Sam, but you need to grow up. Life isn't always fun and games. Rock has us in the middle of World War III and you're chasing rainbows."

"But it *isn't* World War III."

"To us it is. Goodnight, Sam."

"But, Julie …"

Suddenly, voices drifted out of the other rooms …

"Goodbye, Sam."

"Do it again, Sam!"

"I want to dangle off a building with you, Sam!"

"You struck out, didn't you, Sam!"

"Shouldn't you be studying, Sam?"

Sam returned to his room mumbling, "This team drives me nuts."

11

AFTER CALISTHENICS ON MONDAY, the team shared breakfast in the hotel's French Quarter restaurant. Sam leafed through a copy of the *Chicago Post* he had picked up in the lobby. On the sports pages, Harry Warton's column caught his eye.

> Thanks to dumb luck, the Philosophers won their first playoff game. If Sunday's match was any indication, the Phils might as well wave the white flag and surrender because they have about as much chance of beating the Baltimore Menckens as they do of winning $100 million in the lottery.
>
> It was a pathetic performance. This isn't a team. It's a street gang that puts on uniforms for games. They don't belong on the same court with the Menckens. But they somehow clawed their way into the game, so let's get this bloodbath behind us. The Phils can wrap up their season and spend the off-season crying about all the unfair questions and questionable referee calls they didn't agree with.

Sam skimmed down a few paragraphs …

Just who are the Menckens? Well, they have many of the traits of H.L. Mencken, their namesake. Mencken was born in Baltimore in 1880 and lived in the city nearly all his 75 years. During his career he held reporting and editing jobs on newspapers, wrote a memorable column called The Free Lance for the *Baltimore Evening Sun*, edited *The Smart Set* and *The American Mercury* with George Nathan and penned numerous books, including *The American Language*. Mencken was competent, organized, hard-working and driven to accomplish whatever task was at hand. So is the team named for him, and that is why the Menckens will overwhelm the Phils next Sunday.

Sam skipped down a few paragraphs …

As for Sam Winslow, the sheriffs in the Old West knew what to do with his kind. They would put him on the next stagecoach leaving town. The only chance the Phils have of winning Sunday's game is to send Winslow to Baltimore and hope someone there is dumb enough to put him on their team.

"Why does Harry Warton bash the Phils?" Sam asked Annie. "He works for a Chicago paper. You'd think he'd be on our side."

"Warton needs something to write about, and he figures if it isn't outlandish, people won't read his column," Annie said.

"Never give a guy with a low IQ and a peptic ulcer a sports column," Brian added. "It's a lethal combination."

"If you want to know what's really eating him," Margaret said, "I'll tell you. He asked me out a year ago. When I turned him down he went bonkers."

"Oh, come on, Maggie," T.J. said. "Harry Warton never asked you out. He's a lowlife, but he's not blind."

She rose from her chair and threw her fork on the table. "Why you little pipsqueak ..." She leaned over and placed her hands around T.J.'s neck and was about to choke him.

"Breakfast is over!" Freud barked, as he approached the table. "What's going on here?"

"Margaret is breaking off her affair with T.J.," Juanita said.

Freud seemed stunned. "Really? I had no idea. I'll try to be more observant. It's like Mark Twain said: Life is just one damn thing after another. Obviously, this is one of those damn things. ... Well, it's over so forget it."

Freud headed on out to the bus.

"You want me to tell you somethin' that'll make you feel stupid?," Chase asked his teammates.

"Lately *everything* makes me feel pretty stupid," Sam noted.

"We won Sunday's playoff game for a bill collector."

They all looked at Chase as though he had been doing hard drugs.

"What are you talking about?" Edgar asked.

"There was no letter from Johnny's mother. Rock conned you. The letter was from a bill collector. I saw the letter!"

"He lied about that?" Annie said.

"Why are you so surprised?" Brian mused. "You know he'll do anything to win."

T.J. shrugged. "We've been conning Rock all season. Guess it was his turn."

AFTER AN UNEVENTFUL BUS RIDE to the University of Chicago campus, Rock addressed his captive audience in the Regenstein Library.

"We were lucky to beat Cleveland," he grumbled, as he paced the seminar room. "We had a terrible, terrible game. All of you played like rookies who didn't have the faintest idea what was going on. Which brings me to you, Winslow."

"Oh, Lord."

"That was the worst performance I've ever seen in a play-off game. You need to improve a lot to be mediocre. Maybe you were trying to psych me out. Make me think you were the worst Brains player in history. Catch me off-guard, so this weekend, when we play Baltimore, we'll be amazed when you play a great game. Is that it, Winslow?"

"I did my best against Cleveland, coach."

"Don't tell me that, kid. That can't be your best. Your best is going to be this weekend, when you have a great game. Now, is that right, Winslow?"

"That would be terrific."

Rock glared at Sam. "Make it happen. And by the way, kid. Don't take the security guards on any more wild goose chases. I've given them orders to shoot to kill." Rock turned his attention to Brian. "And now you, Hot Shot. You blew two questions my seven-year-old niece could answer. What's the matter with you? What does it take to light a fire under you? This is our chance to make history!

"I won't tolerate any goofing off this week. I won't settle for anything less than perfection and your undying loyalty. You will work harder than you ever worked before. Any questions?"

Margaret screwed up her courage. "You're asking too much, Rock. I'm exhausted. I'm near my breaking point. And when I crack I'm going to grab a gun and take you with me!"

Rock gritted his teeth."That's traitorous talk! You're lucky I don't have you court-martialed. You don't pack up and go home in the middle of a war. Where would the country be if George Washington's troops had gone home before winning the Revolutionary War? Where would we be if Franklin Roosevelt had gotten tired of fighting Hitler? Now is the time to look deep into your souls and find out what you are made of!"

The Phils passed the day cramming at the Regenstein Library, then cracked the books in their rooms at the hotel until the wee hours of the morning.

12

Tuesday, a new calamity befell the team. Brian Marshall's new book, *PHILanderer: The Naked Truth about the Chicago Philosophers*, hit the bookstores. The publisher had rushed the book into print because the playoffs would boost sales. Crews at the printing company labored around the clock to get the autobiography out. Brian dropped off copies at the doors of all the Philosophers' rooms, and when the Phils gathered for breakfast, the book was the hot topic of discussion.

Margaret browsed through the tell-all account as she played with her scrambled eggs. "Incredible!" she declared. "To think you won all of our games by yourself! I'm not even mentioned until page forty-two."

"Take a look at page fifty-one," T.J. said.

> T.J., the bench warmer, is known on the team as the 'Strikeout Kid'. When it comes to women, he has all the sophistication and aplomb of a Skid Row wino. Women have been known to lock themselves into cells with death row inmates after T.J. asked them out on dates.

"What the hell is 'aplomb'?" Margaret asked.

Brian smiled. "It's poise. Something you wouldn't know anything about."

"You don't use words like that," Juanita said. "Who wrote the book for you?"

"No one! I wrote it myself!"

Annie flipped ahead a few pages. "What an imagination! It sounds like every woman in Chicago tried to get you into bed!"

"Every word of this book is true, more or less," Brian insisted. "I may have taken a little literary license with a few nonessential facts ..."

Julie screamed. *"How dare you! We never had an affair! Listen to this."* She read from page 73.

> Julie couldn't keep her eyes off me in the Dallas game. By the time we reached Portland the next week, she had lured me into her bed. When we returned to Chicago, she pestered me so much I had to tell her to back off.

"You are slime, Brian! There's not a word of truth in that!"

Freud joined the team at the table. "I see you're all reading *PHILanderer*. I skimmed my copy. How do you expect us to have team spirit if you write trash like this, Brian?"

"He nailed you too?" asked Juanita.

"Page 112," said Freud. Everyone except Brian turned to page 112.

> Freud is the team's resident flake. He holds a degree in psychiatry from some cow college in North Carolina. He's into Buddhism, meditation, Transcendentalism and chicken plucking. In short, he's a spare tire left over from the Love Child Syndrome of the 1960s.

Chase finally found a reference to him in the book. He glared at the superstar. "You're a little careless throwing around the word 'murderer', aren't you, Bone Head?"

Beads of sweat formed on Brian's forehead. "The editors changed the meaning entirely. You're absolutely right. That reference will be dropped in the next edition!"

Edgar, who had been browsing through the book as he picked at sausage and eggs with a fork, said, "For your information, I did *not* ask the President to invade Cuba because I was running out of cigars!"

TUESDAY AFTERNOON, ROCK SHOWED the team film clips of the Baltimore Menckens' playoff victory over the New York Intellectuals.

"T.J., douse the lights," Rock ordered. Film of the game began rolling. "In case you meatballs haven't figured it out, I'll spell it out: the only way we can get to the Brains Bowl is by defeating Baltimore. The Menckens are riding an eight-game winning streak, and I think they're looking past us to the bowl. That's their mistake, because we're going to beat them, come hell or high water!"

"We've already been through hell," Edgar Woodford grumbled in the darkened room. "Bring on the high water."

"I heard that!" Rock roared.

"Thank God our coach isn't deaf *and* dumb," Brian said.

"As most of you know," Rock continued, "the Menckens are known for their dirty tricks. You've got to be alert. You never know when they're going to screw you. When Houston played in Baltimore, the Menckens told the cops the Space Cadets were heavy cocaine users with big stashes of drugs. The cops raided the Space Cadets, but all they found

were Prozac, Valium and amphetamines. When the Menckens visited Denver, they hacked into the Brains Board computer. They had the crowd cheering for the Menckens and
booing the home team. They're slicker than a greased pig.
If they pull any dirty tricks on us, we'll be ready. I want
Chase the con artist and Annie the hacker to come up with
something that will put the Menckens in their place. Understood?"

"No problem," said Chase.

"Jawohl, herr Nelson," said Annie.

"All right. Start the film, Freud."

As the game film rolled, Freud offered commentary.
"Now, this is Betty Lou Carruthers, the Menckens' popular
arts specialist. She was a film critic before she joined the
team. She writes romance novels in her spare time. She
seems easy going, but if you get in a fight with her she'll nail
your hide to the wall. She's tough."

Brian sighed. "I suppose I must sacrifice myself by dating
the poor little wench. That will get her mind off the game."

"It will also turn her against men for the rest of her life,"
Juanita suggested.

"I wouldn't advise asking her out on a date," Freud said.
"Her husband is a three-hundred pound wrestler. ... Now,
this is Rusty Dobson, their world specialist. He may not look
like a genius, but he was the league's third leading scorer
this year."

Rock said, "You've got to stop him, Edgar. Any ideas?"

"I know some people who could put him on a rendition
flight to Albania. He wouldn't be heard from for years."

"Terrific!" Rock said.

"Let's try something a little less extreme," Freud suggested.

"All right," Rock conceded reluctantly. "But we'll keep our options open."

Freud continued: "This is Crazy Legs Stearn, their sports ace. He's a sports nut. Wrote a doctoral dissertation at Ohio State on sports as the most powerful force in the history of nations. He drives a car shaped like a football and there's a basketball court in his living room."

"Why is he playing Brains?" Juanita wondered. "He should be locked up in an institution."

"If he wasn't such a winner, he would be," Rock said.

The team watched as Scooter Daniels, the young prodigy who was Baltimore's Renaissance Boy, quickly identified the queen sacrifice that enabled Gary Kasparov to defeat Anatoly Karpov in a world championship chess match in 1985.

"Did you know that move, Margaret?" Rock demanded.

"Do I look like I give a crap about chess?"

T.J. had an idea. "If Scooter gets too many points, maybe we could drain the battery on his electric wheelchair," he suggested facetiously.

"Now you're talkin'!" Rock said. "That's the spirit!"

Freud cleared his throat. "Or, perhaps we could rely on less mischievous methods. ... The Menckens recruited their quotations whiz, Rory Thunderheart, from Harvard, where he was a distinguished professor in the literature department. Offhand, Julie, I'd say your best bet is to psych him out."

"That's right!" Rock roared. "Get Rory thinking about sex. Confuse the hell out of him."

"That's her specialty," Sam suggested.

Freud resumed his narration. "Now, Sam, this is their

history hotshot, Dr. Emily Putnam. She holds a Ph.D. from Princeton. She's the world's leading authority on the War of 1812. She's sixty-seven, so she's lived through more history than you have. You'd better have your head on straight!"

T.J. switched the lights back on.

"You have your work cut out for you," Rock grumbled. "I wasn't kidding when I said this would be the toughest game yet—the toughest game you've ever played. Why aren't you cracking the books right now?"

13

WEDNESDAY WAS FILLED WITH hours of intense cramming inter-mingled with arguments about religion, the meaning of life and Chicago hot dogs.

That evening, the Phils decided it was time for another visit to The Dumping Ground.

Sam shared a table with T.J., Brian, Julie, Juanita and Edgar, while Margaret, Chase and Annie occupied the next table over. Annie was served only Cokes and 7-Up. Rock and Freud huddled on the far side the bar.

"You look worried," Juanita told T.J. "Uncle Sam looking into your taxes?"

"My girlfriend Mary back in Detroit is pressing for an answer. Wants to know if I'm going to marry her or if she's wasting her time with me."

"Obviously, you should wed the poor misguided lass," Brian said. "You won't find anyone else dumb enough to marry you."

"If you aren't sure what you want to do, drop her," Edgar Woodford suggested. "There are plenty of other fish in the barrel."

"Fish in the barrel?" Julie repeated. "Is that how you think of women?"

"It's just an expression," Woodford countered. "Like 'dogs in the kennel'."

"*What?*" Margaret bellowed. "You call women 'dogs'?"

"You're reading things into what I said, just like the reporters in Washington did. I didn't mean anything by it."

"The bottom line," Brian told T.J., "is that you'd better grab this girl if she's even remotely interested in marrying you. On the other hand, *I* won't rush into marriage because, as I pointed out in *PHILanderer,* over the past two years I received more than three hundred proposals from women of all colors and creeds. It's a buyer's market, and I can afford to be choosy."

The others groaned.

"I hear you talk about these women," T.J. said, "but I never see any of them. I don't think you receive any proposals."

Brian grabbed a handful of letters from a coat pocket.

"This is just today's batch. They come from all over the country. These women are hungry for love, hungry for me!"

"And woefully ignorant and naive," Annie suggested.

"Go ahead and laugh," Brian snarled. "I don't see the rest of you getting mail like this."

T.J. retrieved one of the letters and speed-read it. "You're right. I don't get mail like this. The bank says your check bounced and if you don't send them a cashier's check in five days, they're going to repossess your Porsche."

Brian grimaced. "That one got into the wrong pile." He handed T.J. another letter. "Read this one."

T.J. scanned it. "This is from Cynthia. She wants you to know she's out of prison, she's read in the newspapers you're fooling around with other women, and she's coming after you."

"She's threatening you!" Juanita exclaimed. "You'd better tell Security."

"Nonsense. I get letters like that all the time."

"You're right, Brian," Julie said. "Your mail *is* more interesting than ours."

"You're all jealous," Brian insisted.

"I'd like to know what kind of women send you proposals," Sam said. "Suppose you call one of them and arrange a date."

"That's not a good idea," Brian said. "I don't want to lead them on. They could be stalkers or murderers."

Julie shook her head. "You have an incredible imagination."

"Come on, Brian," T.J. goaded. "I challenge you to make a date with one of these affection-starved females so we can see if it's on the level or if you're just blowing smoke."

"Back home we call it 'farting into the wind', not blowing smoke," Chase pointed out.

"All right. I'll do it—on one condition. *You*'ve got to make a date with one of them, T.J. I want to prove once and for all that when it comes to women, I'm the master and you are a klutz."

T.J. shook his head. "These women didn't write me. They are *your* groupies."

"Scared, T.J.? What would it hurt?"

"He's right," Margaret said. "It's time you both put up or shut up."

"All right," T.J. declared. "I'll do it to shut you and Brian up once and for all."

"You'd be doing a public service," Annie suggested.

"Am I the only one here," Edgar interjected, "who realizes Rock will kill you two if he finds out you're partying before a playoff game?"

"Relax," said Brian. "He won't find out. He's so worried about the playoffs he's lost all contact with reality."

Julie placed Brian's letters face down on the table. "Both of you pick one."

Brian and T.J. each selected a letter and opened it.

"You're also behind on mortgage payments on your Gold Coast condo," T.J. noted.

Brian grimaced as T.J. selected another letter. It was agreed they would call their dates Thursday and double-date Friday evening.

"Twenty bucks says Brian's date walks out on him first," Annie declared.

"I'll take you up on that," Chase snapped.

"The smart money says they both strike out," Juanita suggested.

Freud stopped by the table. "Hold the noise down! Rock will kill you if he finds out what you're doing." He added quietly, "Twenty bucks on T.J."

Freud headed back to Rock's table with drink in hand.

"Oh-oh," Julie moaned.

"What's the matter?" Margaret asked.

"Over there." Julie nodded toward the television set. "Late Night Edition" was starting. The lead story: Brian's book.

"Your luck just ran out," Annie told Brian.

"Quick! Turn off the television!" Brian pleaded.

"Too late," Chase said, as Rock and Freud glanced over at the television set.

"UP FRONT TONIGHT: THE CONTROVERSY SWIRLING AROUND THE PUBLICATION OF BRIAN MARSHALL'S NEW TELL-ALL BOOK, *PHILANDERER: THE NAKED TRUTH ABOUT THE CHICAGO PHILOSOPHERS*. BRIAN PROVIDES A REVEALING

LOOK AT LIFE INSIDE THE CHICAGO PHILOSOPHERS' CAMP. AMONG OTHER THINGS, THE PHILS' ROMEO REVEALS:

"• HIS SIZZLING AFFAIR WITH TEAMMATE JULIE HOWARD."

Julie slunk lower in her seat. "I'm going to kill you," she growled.

"• HIS CLOSE CALL WHEN A CRAZED FAN STALKED HIM AND TRIED TO STAB HIM IN PORTLAND LAST YEAR."

"What an imagination!" Margaret exclaimed.

"That wasn't a crazed fan," T.J. said. "That was *me*."

"• AND, HIS ROCKY RELATIONSHIP WITH COACH ROCK NELSON, WHO BRIAN REFERS TO AS THE 'ROCK OF RAGES'. BRIAN SAYS ROCK'S WHALER IS ACTUALLY A SLAVE BOAT. AND HE REPRINTS ROCK'S COLLEGE GRADE TRAN-SCRIPTS, WHICH DOCUMENT WHAT 'LATE NIGHT EDITION' REPORTED LAST WEEK—ROCK IS THE ONLY BRAINS COACH WHO FLUNKED OUT OF COLLEGE!"

"Oh, crap," moaned Brian.

"Nice touch," Juanita said. "That will earn you points with the coach."

The Phils scrutinized Rock to determine his reaction to the revelations. They couldn't tell if Rock had been paying attention or if he was lost in reverie.

Rock put down his bourbon and water and leaned over toward Freud. "Did he say Brian published my college tran-scripts?"

Freud cleared his throat. "Well, uh … it did sound like that, Rock."

Rock coddled his drink. "Why does everyone make such

a big deal about me flunking out of college? Hell, hundreds of thousands of kids flunk out of college every year. Why pick on me?"

"I suppose it's because you're a Brains coach, and people expect … uh …"

"They expect Brains coaches to be geniuses. Is that it?"

"More or less."

"Hmph."

Freud took a swallow of Kahlua as "Late Night Edition" turned to more pressing things, such as which actresses had been seen dancing naked at a Hollywood party. "You seem more withdrawn than ever this week," Freud told the coach. "I'm worried about you."

"After we win the trophy, I can relax. Not before."

"Rock, open your eyes. You're at the breaking point and the team is at the breaking point. You've got to back off."

"You've had your say, Freud. I don't want to hear it again."

Freud sipped his Kahlua. "All right. But if we win this week, I want you to take the team to a quiet secret retreat, where they can prepare for the Brains Bowl without all the pressure. I'm telling you, Rock, the players need it, you need it and God knows I need it."

"Hmph. Might be a good idea. … Get away from all the reporters and the bedlam. The team could focus on the game."

"That's right, Rock!"

"Okay. Set it up. … Maybe you should find *two* hide-aways. One where we'll train next week, if we beat Baltimore on Sunday. And one for you to use if we lose Sunday's game, because I'll hold *you* responsible!"

Freud gulped. "Good idea," he mumbled.

14

Shall we keep chasing this murderous fish till he swamps the last man? Shall we be dragged by him to the bottom of the sea?

BECAUSE HIS TEAM WAS BESET by problems and practices were marred by mistakes, Rock became more obsessed than ever with whipping his crew into shape. The Phils did not have the talent—the raw brain power—to be a super power in the Brains League. Like the old Chicago Bears under George Halas, they scrambled for every point they got. Harry Warton called the Phils the "Rescue Mission team of the Brains League—any bum off the street has a shot at becoming a starter".

As the week wore on, Rock became increasingly moody, and spent hours alone in his room pondering strategy.

AT THE UNIVERSITY OF CHICAGO'S Regenstein Library on Thursday, the Phils endeavored to focus on the task at hand. Brian occupied a strategic location in the main reading room, where attractive co-eds could recognize him and ask for his autograph—or hotel room number. Chase snatched volumes he needed out of the hands of undergraduates. T.J. found a corner back in the stacks where he could use his laptop to access resources on the Internet. Edgar penned a rough draft of a letter to the President asking if he could have his old job as secretary of state back. Juanita skimmed through *Shocking Scandals From Around the World*. Every so often Margaret could be heard screaming, "This is the last straw! Rock has gone too far!"

As Julie speed-read her way through Homer's *Iliad*, Sam pulled up a chair at the same table.

"Would Chaucer's *Canterbury Tales* fall under history or literature?" he wondered.

"It's literature," Julie said. "but they might ask you historical questions about it, such as when Chaucer wrote the *Tales*."

"Of course."

"Do you know when he wrote it?"

"Of course ... give or take a few hundred years."

"That's not precise enough. Late fourteenth century."

"Oh, right. That's what I thought ... more or less."

"Sounds like you have a little more cramming to do."

"You are a master of understatement."

Sam headed off toward the shelves that held books on the Middle Ages.

THURSDAY EVENING, BRIAN AND T.J. called two of the women who had sent marriage proposals to Brian, asking them to go out on dates the next night. Being celebrities gave the teammates some leverage.

"Is this Kathy Lamaster?"

"Yes."

"I'm Brian Marshall of the Phils. You wrote me."

"I did? What did I say?"

"You said you wanted my body."

"Oh-oh. I think there's a misunderstanding. I didn't write you. My girlfriends wanted to fix me up with you."

"Well, it worked. Let's have dinner Friday evening so we can get acquainted. No pressure. We'll double-date with my teammate T.J. and his date."

"Well, all right. It might be fun. Why on earth did you call me? You must get dozens of letters."

"Hundreds, babe. But I've got to start somewhere. I'll pick you up at seven tomorrow evening."

"All right. I hope you won't be disappointed."

Brian hung up. "Me, too."

"May I speak to Denise Ubanga?"

"Who's calling?"

"T.J. Collins. I play for the Phils."

"I'm Denise."

"You wrote Brian Marshall, and he suggested I call you. He read your letter, and he thought that since you sounded like a very nice girl and he's a total jerk, *I* should ask you out."

"Sounds groovy. What did you have in mind?"

"Dinner. We'll double-date with Brian and his date. Nothing extravagant."

"All right. ... Do you have a whip and a chain?"

"What?" T.J. was sure he hadn't heard her right.

"I'm a sucker for men with a whip and a chain. When shall we get together?"

"Uh, Friday night. I'll pick you up at seven. ... Are you *sure* this is Denise Ubanga?"

"See you then, T.J."

As T.J. hung up, he had the nagging feeling Denise was more than he had bargained for.

15

ON FRIDAY, MARGARET reached the breaking point.

The team meeting was half over and Rock had just made his ninth threat involving bodily harm when Margaret suddenly turned paler than usual and blurted out, "No, Rock. There's a limit. I don't have any more to give." Then she slumped to the floor. Archie Bolton, the team physician, rushed over and felt her pulse. He tried to revive her.

"Call the hospital," he said.

Freud ran out of the room to find a telephone since no cell phones were allowed in team meetings.

Margaret regained consciousness while the team waited for the ambulance attendants. "Did I shoot Rock when I lost it?" she asked Archie.

"No. He's fine," Archie assured her.

"Damn. It would have been the perfect time to do it. No jury would convict me."

"It's not too late," Annie suggested. "Maybe we can find a gun!"

As ambulance attendants loaded Margaret onto a stretcher, other team members watched in stunned silence. Then they retreated to various locations in the Regenstein Library, though they were not in the mood to study.

Julie tracked down Sam in the history section. He had fallen asleep with his legs propped on a table and a book in hand.

"*Winslow!*" she barked.

Sam fell out of the chair as Julie laughed.

"Good grief. It's you. ... What do you want?"

"Do you still want to go out with me?"

Sam picked himself up off the floor.

"Well, sure."

"All right. We'll tag along with Brian and T.J. tonight. I've got to get away from the pressure for a while."

Sam stared at Julie as she headed to an exit.

"That is one screwed-up broad," he mumbled.

Sam informed T.J. that he and Julie would be triple-dating with T.J. and Brian and their dates.

"Great," T.J. said. "I've got a feeling I'm going to need some help with Denise. ... By the way, do you have a whip and a chain? I called the discount stores, but I don't think they have what I need."

AFTER RETURNING TO THE HOTEL late Friday afternoon, Brian, T.J., Sam and Julie dressed for their dates.

Brian stopped by Sam's room. "Can I borrow a tie, Winslow?"

"Sure. What happened to yours?"

"They all have lipstick on them. I hear you and Julie will be slumming with us tonight."

"That's right."

"I'm curious. How did you get her to go out with you?"

"I didn't. She asked me."

Brian did a double take. "Really?" He turned to leave. "That is one screwed-up broad."

"Hey! Don't talk about my date that way!"

When Sam stopped by Julie's room at 6:30, he discovered there was a small problem.

"I've decided I don't want to go, Sam. If we go out again, you might think I'm interested in you. It wouldn't be fair to you—or David."

"What? This was *your* idea. You asked *me* out!"

"A woman has a right to change her mind. Haven't you learned that by now?"

"But this was a commitment. An oral contract. You can't toy with my feelings like that!"

"I'm sorry, Sam. I just think it wouldn't be a good idea."

Sam took fetched his cell phone from a coat pocket. "Just one minute. I know how we can settle this."

He dialed Carl Jeffries, the lawyer who shot baskets with him in Franklin.

"Carl? Sam. … Thanks. Who knew I'd be playing in the Brains Bowl? Look, I've got a little problem you could help me with. A breach of promise thing. Julie Howard, one of the players, asked me to go out on a date with her this evening. I'm ready to go—took a shower, put on a sport coat, the works. Now she's trying to back out of the agreement."

Sam handed her the phone. "My attorney wants to talk to you."

She grabbed the phone. "Let me be perfectly clear: I thought I might hang out with Sam tonight but I changed my mind. It's no big deal. I never promised him anything!"

"Why would he lie?" Jeffries asked.

"Why would he lie? Do you even *know* Sam Winslow?"

"He doesn't have the promise in writing?"

"Of course not. I didn't put anything in writing, and I doubt that he can read or write!"

"Hmm. Well, he obviously is interested in you. Maybe you can work this out."

She relaxed a little. "Perhaps. ... Are you really a lawyer, or one of Sam's pals?"

"I am an attorney. I have a law degree, passed the bar exam, been accused of malpractice, been thrown in jail for contempt of court ... I've done it all, baby!"

"Hmm. How much would it cost me to get a restraining order against Sam?"

Sam took the phone from her and hung up. "The conversation was obviously deteriorating. ... So, will you quit wasting time? We've got to leave!"

"You are the most persistent man ... This isn't a date! We'll just hang out for a while. Agreed?"

"All right."

She slipped on her coat as they headed for the elevator. "Next time I'll call my own lawyer."

16

THE BOILER ROOM, A NIGHTSPOT on the south side of Chicago, was off the beaten path. To Philosophers who had been mauled and slandered by "Late Night Edition" it seemed the perfect destination for a night out on the town.

As a waitress led Sam and Julie to the table reserved for the group, Sam noticed the unconcealed pipes and concrete walls. The Boiler Room indeed seemed to be a boiler room. As a concession to the Christmas season, colored lights and green wreaths trimmed with red bows draped the otherwise barren walls.

"I don't approve of this," Julie said, as Sam held her chair for her. "Brian and T.J. are doing this as a macho thing. They aren't really interested in their dates."

"It's too early to say. Wait and see what happens."

As Sam and Julie sipped cocktails, a waitress escorted Brian and Kathy to the table. Kathy, slender and not particularly well-endowed, had glasses on. She wore black slacks and a red cotton blouse that was buttoned to the neck. Brian, decked out in a brown cashmere sport coat, seemed ill at ease.

"Kathy insisted we take the 'el'," Brian said. "She wanted a lot of people around in case I attacked her."

Kathy smiled. "A girl can't be too careful."

"I'm impressed you understand Brian so well after only one phone call from him," Julie said.

"Excuse us a minute," Brian said. "Sam and I need to use the powder room."

The women laughed as Brian nearly dragged Sam toward the men's room. As they watched their table from afar, Brian pleaded, "I'm dying here, Sam. What should I do?"

Sam looked at Kathy closely. She seemed to be the quiet librarian type, bookish and prim. Brian was more the caveman who thought libraries were best used for picking up lonely women. "It's very funny, really. If you could step back and see yourself ..."

"Don't mess with me, Sam. I've had a rough week. This might push me over the edge. Kathy is not the kind of woman I usually date. I mean, she's so timid she thinks a man and a woman shouldn't shake hands until the third date."

"She seems like a nice girl. Give it time. You got yourself into this. Just don't do anything to hurt her feelings."

Brian straightened his sportcoat. "My reputation will be worthless after this."

"Sorry, Brian."

Brian and Sam returned to the table just as T.J. and Denise arrived. When Brian noticed Denise, his jaw fell in amazement. She wore a leather jacket and leather miniskirt. She had the colorful makeup, wiggling walk and smooth moves of a successful hooker.

"Hi, everyone," T.J. said. "This is Denise—"

"Ubanga," she purred.

"I would've guessed that. I'm Brian Marshall. I believe you wrote me proposing marriage."

"Heavens, no! I did propose a few other things, though."

"We had an interesting taxi ride over here," T.J. said. "It seems Denise works evenings—"

"I would have guessed that, too," Brian said.

"— as a cocktail waitress."

"That wasn't my first guess."

Denise leaned over toward T.J. "Did you bring them?"

"The whip and the chain?" he whispered. "No, they're back at my place."

"We'll need them later," she purred.

"Yes, ma'am." T.J. cleared his throat. He was sweating.

"Take it easy," Sam whispered to T.J., as Julie gossiped with Denise and Kathy. "So Denise has been around the block a few more times than you. You can hold your own."

"I think we've been around different blocks," T.J. said. "In some cities they call her block the Red Light District. Sam, I usually date women who are a little less eager to discuss sexual accessories and certain parts of the anatomy."

"Hang on for the ride. She could teach you a lot."

"I don't doubt that for a minute."

After they ordered dinner, Brian asked Denise if she had lived in Chicago long.

"Including the two months in jail? About two years."

T.J. choked on his water. "Jail? Uh ... what were you in for?"

"I offered to do a man a favor."

"Why would that land you in jail?" Kathy asked.

"Because I charged him for the favor, honey."

Kathy's face reddened as she realized what Denise was saying. She took a swig of the gin and tonic Brian had ordered for her.

"That's a beautiful blouse," Julie told Kathy.

"Thanks. I made it myself."

"Yeah, nice threads," Brian said. "So tell me, Denise—why did you decide to pick up a pen and write me?"

"Because you're one handsome hunk," she purred.

"Did you see that?" Sam asked. "Someone over there behind that post seemed to have something pointed at us. A camera, I think."

The others surveyed the far corners of the restaurant, but did not see anyone.

"Maybe it was Marty," Julie suggested.

"I could have been mistaken."

After dinner, Denise whispered suggestive little nothings to T.J.

"Where did you learn to do *that*?" T.J. said.

Embarrassed, Julie and Kathy took swigs of their drinks.

Denise whispered something else.

"Aren't there laws against that?" T.J. asked.

Julie and Kathy took another swig.

"Slow down, Julie," Sam cautioned. "I didn't know you liked the sauce so much."

"I don't," she mumbled. "Order me another one."

"Me, too," Kathy said.

An hour later, the evening was winding down and Denise was hot to trot. Brian, Sam and T.J. watched Denise's every move as Kathy and Julie indulged in Kahlua and cremes. Finally, Julie decided she could not sit through any more foreplay. "Well, this has been fun, but we've only got an hour till curfew. Sam and I must get back to the hotel."

"Curfew?" Denise laughed. "You're kidding."

"I'm not kidding," Julie said. "We must wrap this up. Isn't that right, Sam?"

Sam had been watching Denise fondle T.J.'s left leg with her bare foot under the table.

"What? … Uh, what did you say?"

"We've got to get back before curfew, don't we, Sam."

"Oh, right. It's the law on Ahab's ship."

Julie and Sam slipped on their coats. "We'll see you back at the hotel," Julie said.

"You can count on it," Denise purred.

"I was talking to T.J. and Brian," Julie snapped.

SAM AND JULIE STOPPED OFF FOR a quick dessert at The Cheese-cake Factory on North Michigan Avenue before heading back to the whaler. The Cheesecake Factory's decor had been described as looking like the inside of a cheesecake. Hold-ing a dish with a double chocolate upside-down Jack Dan-iels cheesecake in his hands, Sam had a surreal feeling, but he shook it off because his whole day had been surreal.

"I had to get out of the Boiler Room," Julie said. "I was afraid that any minute Denise would be making out on the floor. I just wasn't sure who would be down there with her. Brian, T.J. or you."

"I'm shocked, Julie. You know I only have eyes for you."

"Yeah. Right." She toyed with her chocolate mousse cheesecake. "Maybe I shouldn't be eating this after having a couple drinks. I'm a little woozy." She smiled at him coyly. "You know something, Sam Winslow? You're kind of cute when you're drunk."

"I'm not drunk. You are."

"Oh." She moved closer and snuggled up to him. "I'm really not as straight-laced as you think I am."

She planted a long, lingering kiss on Sam's mouth. Sam thought he saw a light in the distance.

"Must be what they mean when people talk about fireworks going off."

"What?" she asked.

"Nothing."

He kissed her more passionately.

"Would you mind taking it outside?" the waiter said. "People come here to eat. Not to watch people make out."

Julie quickly backed off. She primped her hair. "Oh, my. I don't know what I was doing. It must have been the drinks."

"C'mon, Julie. We're just getting warmed up."

He tried to kiss her again.

"Back off, Sam! Behave yourself. Let's not get carried away."

Sam glared at the waiter. "If you think I'm leaving a tip, you're crazy."

By the time they returned to the eleventh floor of the Palmer House Hilton, Julie had sobered up a little.

"We must do this again," Sam said, as he brought his lips near hers.

"Oh, no! This was a mistake. A friendly little dinner and we got carried away. What kind of woman do you think I am, anyway?"

"*My* woman," Sam said.

"Wrong. I'm engaged to David. Remember?"

"You weren't thinking much about him over dessert."

"That was a dreadful mistake. It won't happen again."

Sam grimaced.

She took his right hand and caressed it. "I don't want

to hurt your feelings, Sam, but when I go out with you, it's nothing personal. I needed to unwind. We could never have a long-term relationship because you're flighty and impetuous. I mean, let's face it. You haven't decided what you want to do when you grow up—and you are grown up! Two weeks ago you were unemployed in Franklin, now you're a Brains player. Who knows what you'll be doing next month. I need someone like David, who knows where he's been and where he's going."

"He's been in Philadelphia all his life, and he's going nowhere."

Julie thought about that. "Well, you must admit, it shows stability."

"I didn't realize I was such a mess."

"Now, you understand! *That's* what I've been trying to tell you. So you can understand why I won't go out with you anymore ... *you are a mess!*"

"But, Julie! ..."

She slammed the door.

As Sam returned to his room, he heard a loud voice coming from one of the rooms.

"Oh, T.J.! Don't stop, T.J.!"

17

ROCK DECIDED TO CONVENE a team meeting Friday evening, but he couldn't find half the team. Saturday morning, he mentioned this to the players in his usual subtle way.

"Where the hell were you? Our next playoff game is one day away, and you're off doing who knows what to who knows who."

"Whom," Edgar said.

"What?" Rock snapped.

"Doing who knows what to who knows *whom.*"

"Good grief, man. We're fighting for our lives. Everything is at stake. And you're worried about grammar? *I want to know where half the team was last night!"*

No one said anything. Finally, T.J. offered an explanation. "We were in church, praying."

"For three hours?"

"We had a lot to pray about."

"You'd better pray I can't find you if you lose Sunday's game," Rock warned.

"That was very high on the list," Julie noted.

Rock grimaced. "By the way, Margaret is still in the hospital. If we lose a few more people, we'll be playing Baltimore from the emergency room. Edgar will replace Margaret as the R.M. Juanita will sub for Edgar as the world special-ist."

"All right!" exclaimed Juanita.

Sam could tell by T.J.'s face that he was crushed not to be selected for the starting lineup.

THE MOOD WAS SUBDUED and apprehensive Saturday evening as players crammed in their rooms, taking occasional breaks to listen to music or television. At 10:30, T.J. flicked on the week-end edition of "Late Night Edition". The lead-in announced they were about to air another special report on the Philoso-phers. The subject: "Wild Nights in Chicago."

"Oh, no," groaned T.J. *"You'd better see this!"* he hollered down the hallway. *"'Late Night Edition' is nailing us again!"*

Several Phils wandered over to T.J.'s room. Julie wore a cream-colored bathrobe. Her hair was wrapped in a towel. Sam, bleary-eyed from reading, scuffled into the room decked out in an old sweatshirt and jeans.

"What's all the commotion?" Brian snarled, as he stepped inside the room.

"This ain't goin' to be purty," T.J. said.

> "WHILE OTHER PLAYOFF TEAMS BUCKLE DOWN AND PREPARE FOR THIS WEEKEND'S GAMES, THE CHICAGO PHI-LOSOPHERS SEEM TO HAVE TIME FOR PARTYING. FRIDAY EVENING, A 'LATE NIGHT EDITION' CAMERAMAN SPOTTED BRIAN MARSHALL, SAM WINSLOW, JULIE HOWARD AND T.J. COLLINS CAVORTING IN CHICAGO NIGHTSPOTS."

"Oh, no!" Julie muttered. "They've got us on camera!"

> "T.J. HAD A WILD TIME WITH HIS DATE, DENISE UBANGA, A COCKTAIL HOSTESS AND HOOKER WHO HAS AN

ARREST SHEET LONGER THAN CHASE'S. WAITRESSES OVER-
HEARD DENISE MAKING SUGGESTIVE PROPOSALS TO T.J.,
WHO PRETENDED TO BE SHOCKED. THE TRUTH CAME OUT
LATER, HOWEVER, WHEN T.J. HUSTLED DENISE BACK TO
HIS HOTEL ROOM, WHERE THE TWOSOME MADE PASSIONATE
LOVE."

"Rock is going to kill you," Julie told T.J.

"If Rock doesn't kill me, mom and dad will!"

"MEANWHILE, BRIAN'S FANS WILL BE STUNNED TO
DISCOVER THEIR YOUNG IDOL PAIRED OFF WITH MOUSY-
LOOKING KATHY LAMASTER, A LIBRARIAN. BRIAN DIDN'T
MAKE IT TO FIRST BASE WITH MISS LAMASTER."

"Well, my reputation is shot to hell," Brian moaned.

"ROUNDING OUT THE DATING GAME WERE JULIE
HOWARD AND SAM WINSLOW. THEY STARTED SLOW, BUT
BY THE END OF THE EVENING JULIE WAS CRAWLING ALL
OVER SAM. WE HAVEN'T SEEN KISSES LIKE THIS SINCE LIZ
TAYLOR AND RICHARD BURTON LIT EACH OTHER'S FIRES IN
CLEOPATRA. THE PHILS CERTAINLY HAVE STRANGE IDEAS
ABOUT HOW TO PREPARE FOR CRUCIAL PLAYOFF GAMES!"

"Oh, no!" Julie moaned. "They got it wrong. I didn't do
that. Or, if I did, it was temporary insanity."

"The whole country knows I dated Kathy," Brian complained. "I'll get letters from every dog-faced girl from here
to Timbuckto."

"Welcome to the real world," Chase said.

"They sure screwed up the facts," T.J. said.

"What do you mean?" Sam asked.

"Nothing. Just that they always screw up the facts."

"That isn't what you meant," Brian said. "How did they
screw up the facts?"

"If you must know," T.J. said, "it wasn't Denise who was in my room last night. Now will you forget it?"

Everyone looked at T.J. in shock.

"Who was it?" Edgar Woodford asked. "Who was making that awful racket? It sounded like chains."

"It was somebody else. Can we forget it?"

"Was it Annie or Julie?" Brian guessed.

"I resent that!" snapped Annie.

"I think I'm going to be sick," Julie grumbled.

"Just forget it," T.J. said. Then, after a few moments of silence: "All right. If you must know ... it was Kathy."

"*My date?*" exclaimed Brian. "Your date was so hot to trot she couldn't see straight, but you dumped her for the Librarian From Hell?"

T.J. smiled slyly. "Kathy was wild. You don't know a good thing when you see it."

"What happened to Denise?" Brian asked.

"Denise hooked up with another guy after you passed out at the table. I think 'hooked up' is the apt phrase. He recognized her, invited himself over to the table, and two minutes later she was all over him like syrup over waffles. They left, and you were still passed out, so Kathy and I got to talking, and I guess Denise's foreplay had started Kathy's motor running, and one thing led to another. When Kathy and I left the Boiler Room, we told them to put you in a cab and send you back to the hotel."

"Well, I guess that settles once and for all who the Romeo is on this squad," suggested Annie.

"It certainly does," Edgar Woodford agreed. "It's obviously me. The other men are such klutzes!"

"You're all losing sight of the big picture," Julie pointed out. "If Rock hears about this, he'll go off the deep end."

Juanita shrugged. "So what's new?"

Sam escorted Julie back to her room.

"I hope David wasn't watching," Julie said. "He'll kill me."

Her phone rang.

"Hello ... Oh, David. What a surprise. ... You did? Look, David, they got it all wrong. ... Yes, that was me kissing Sam, but it wasn't like that. Sam and I are just friends, and I had too much to drink, and for a few brief moments I got carried away. It meant nothing! ... Well, I know what it looked like, but I'm telling you it wasn't like that!"

"Actually, it *was* like that," Sam said.

Julie grimaced. "Yes, that was Sam. He's just trying to be funny. If you knew him, you would understand I couldn't possibly be interested in him. He's very unstable and flighty and unpredictable."

Sam took the phone from Julie.

"I'm afraid she's right, old man. I'm not Julie's type. When she asked me out on dates twice, I couldn't believe it because I know I'm not her type, and as for the kisses, well you know how she is when she drinks. ... You don't?"

Julie grabbed the phone back.

"Thanks a lot, Sam ... Look, David, you must trust me. Things were taken out of context. We've been under a lot of pressure here. It didn't mean anything, and when I see you, I'll make it up to you. ... Yes, I'll kick him out of my room right now. Goodbye, sweetheart."

"You hung up too soon. I wanted to ask him how many lethal weapons he designed for children today."

"Goodnight, Sam."

Julie pushed him out the door.

"You're a wonderful kisser, Julie."

"Will you shut up!" she said, as she slammed the door.

THE MESSAGE LIGHT ON THE TELEPHONE in Sam's room was flashing. Sam called the front desk and was informed that his brother Joe had called.

Sam dialed Joe's number. After two rings an answering machine message kicked in. "You have reached Joe Winslow Enterprises. For newspaper delivery, press one. To submit applications for venture capital, have your twenty-five dollar application fee ready and press two. To order a copy of Joe's autobiography …"

Sam grimaced. Joe had a newspaper delivery route, but he didn't have any venture capital and no one could possibly be interested in his autobiography. "Answer the phone, Joe!"

"Sam! You sly old dog. I thought you were working yourself to death in the Windy City, but all you're doing is makin' out with Julie Howard."

"It's not like that, Joe."

"I saw it all on 'Late Night Edition'. Saw it with my own eyes. I just have one question. Does she have a sister?"

"Knock it off, Joe. Julie had a couple drinks and got carried away. That's all. Is that why you called?"

"No. I wanted to tell you Dad and Mom won't be at the game tomorrow. The first playoff was too much for Dad— the pressure of finding a parking space, seeing you screw up, and all. And Mom doesn't want to go to Chicago because she thinks a soda pop can will freeze to her lips. I haven't figured that one out. But I'll be there to see you play!"

"Fine. I'll leave a ticket for you."

"Leave two."

"Why? Who's coming with you?" Sam frowned as a thought occurred to him. "Oh, man. Not Martha Jean!"

"It's a long trip, Sam. I need company."

"Buy a dog."

"It's not the same. Why didn't you get a dog instead of smooching with Julie? … Why do you care, anyway? You dumped her."

"I know. I thought I was getting rid of her. Now she's still hanging around my family."

"You won't even know she's there."

Sam gritted his teeth. "All right. Two tickets. By the way, if she says anything about me falling asleep while we were having sex, it isn't true. I closed my eyes for a minute."

"She said you were snoring."

"See what I mean? No good can come of this."

18

AT THREE IN THE MORNING on game day, the Chicago players heard someone rapping loudly on their doors.

Brian was the first to open his door. He hadn't been to bed.

"Room service!" said the hotel employee, who pushed a cart loaded with chicken, steak and vegetables into Brian's room.

"What the ... I didn't order this!"

The young man checked the bill. "No, sir! It was all charged to Rock Nelson's room."

Brian let the cart stay and nibbled on the food. The other Phils, who had been trying to get some sleep before the big game, were irate.

"*Get outta here!*" T.J. told the room service man at his door.

"*Are you crazy? Waking me up at three in the morning?*" Juanita told another.

"*I don't want any food. Get out!*" Sam snarled.

Edgar glared at the security guard. "Why didn't you stop them? That's what you're getting paid for!"

"They told me Rock ordered the food!" the guard said.

The Phils conferred in the hallway. "Rock and Freud

wouldn't wake us up at three in the morning on game day," Juanita said. "The Menckens or their fans are behind this."

"They don't want us to get a good night's sleep," Julie concluded.

"Those jerks," snapped Annie. "Wait till I get my hands on them."

"Go back to bed," Edgar suggested. "Victory is the best revenge."

"He's been hanging around Rock too long," T.J. mumbled.

THE DAY OF THE BALTIMORE GAME dawned with Rock pacing restlessly in his hotel room, Sam lying awake in his bed, Annie surfing X-rated web sites on the Internet, and Brian sneaking into T.J.'s room in a futile attempt to steal Denise Ubanga's telephone number.

As a crowd of more than seventy thousand people rocked the rafters in the Windy City Dome, Rock faced his weary troops in the locker room below. His hair disheveled, bags the size of cantaloupes hanging under his eyes, he looked as though he had been to hell and back.

"The time has come," Rock said. "Battles like these separate the men from the boys, the heroes from the cowards. We are on the brink of war. Are my troops prepared for this war?" He surveyed his crew. "No. They were playing around and partying when they should have been preparing for battle."

"Oh, crap," whispered Brian. "He heard about Friday night!"

Rock glared at his crew. "I notice 'Late Night Edition' filmed you going to church the other night. ... I can't believe you were partying. What's the matter with you? Don't you realize what's at stake? Don't you know *everything* depends on us winning today's game, and then the Brains Bowl?

"That's the trouble. You're too soft. Too relaxed. I don't understand it. How can you be calm at a time like this? We're about to play in the most important game you've ever played in and you look like you're getting ready for a picnic.

"You've never learned to make sacrifices. Sometimes, you've got to sacrifice everything—food, health, body and soul—to reach a goal. If you don't throw everything into the effort, you're cheating yourselves, you're cheating the team, and you're cheating me!

"Before we go out to that playing floor, you'd better get your heads on straight and focus on the job you've got to do.

"There's nothing else I can do. It's out of my hands now. I can only look to God and hope He deals mercifully with my troops, for they are sinners. Forgive them God—*but only if they beat Baltimore!*"

The players, subdued and pensive, filed out of the locker room.

> Thy shrunk voice sounds too calmly, sanely woeful to me. In no Paradise myself, I am impatient of all misery in others that is not mad. Thou shouldst go mad, blacksmith; say, why dost thou not go mad? How canst thou endure without being mad?

AS THE TEAM REACHED the playing floor, a roar erupted from the Chicago fans.

"LISTEN TO THAT CROWD," Moose Harrison told the millions of people around the world watching the game on television. "IT'S BEEN A ROUGH WEEK FOR THE PHILS—MARGARET

KRAMER LANDED IN THE HOSPITAL, BRIAN MARSHALL'S TELL-ALL BOOK STIRRED UP A WHIRLWIND OF CONTROVERSY, AND FOUR PLAYERS WERE CAUGHT CAROUSING AT CHICAGO NIGHTSPOTS. THOSE PROBLEMS AND THE LACKLUSTER PLAY OF NEWCOMER SAM WINSLOW HAVE LED ODDS-MAKERS TO RATE THE BALTIMORE MENCKENS NINE-POINT FAVORITES TODAY."

It was time for the introduction of the starting lineups. Lights in the dome dimmed and loud music blared from loudspeakers as spotlights shone on the Menckens. The Phils and their fans immediately realized something was wrong. All the hoopla was supposed to occur *after* Baltimore's players had been given a quiet, low-key introduction. This was the Phils' home territory; this was *their* city, *their* stadium.

The Menckens jogged out to the playing floor with big smiles on their faces as Moose Harrison introduced them—what else could he do?—and then the music stopped, the lights came on and the Phils took the floor without any fanfare.

"IT LOOKS LIKE THE MENCKENS PULLED OFF ONE OF THEIR TRADEMARK DIRTY TRICKS BEFORE THE GAME EVEN STARTED. THEY APPARENTLY HACKED INTO THE STADIUM COMPUTER AND RIGGED IT SO THE MENCKENS—NOT THE HOME-TEAM PHILS—WOULD RECEIVE THE BIG INTRODUCTION."

"They're dead meat," said Brian.

Rock protested to head referee Crawler Destry and wanted an unsportsmanlike conduct call assessed against the Menckens, but Destry would not listen. "In the first place, Rock, the game has not even started. I *can't* penalize them. In the second place, you can't *prove* the Menckens did it. You've got other enemies. Maybe Percy Smathers and 'Late Night Edition' did it."

"Percy isn't smart enough to think of something like that," Rock insisted.

Destry called for quiet and read the four-point Shake-spearean tipoff:

"Name the play from which this quotation comes."

The words appeared on the Brains Board:

> "When we are born, we cry that we are come to this
> great stage of fools."

Edgar Woodford slammed his buzzer.

"An apt description of Brains games," he said. "The passage is from *King Lear*!"

The crowd cheered as Rock shouted at Edgar: "Don't do that! The half-wit referee will nail you for unsportsmanlike conduct!"

The half-wit referee nailed Rock for unsportsmanlike conduct—a penalty that wiped out the four points Edgar had just racked up.

Brian and the Menckens' popular arts specialist, Betty Lou Carruthers, moved to the Hot Zone.

"In 1963, William Faulkner won the Pulitzer Prize for fiction. What was the title of the prize-winning novel?"

Brian slammed the buzzer.

"*A Fable*!" he said.

"Wrong!" declared the referee. "Baltimore?"

"I thought everyone knew it was *The Reivers*," said Betty Lou. "Faulkner won a Pulitzer for *A Fable* in the 1950s."

Humbled, Brian returned to the sidelines.

Sam and the Menckens' history expert, Dr. Emily Putnam, were transported to centercourt for a three-pointer.

"Which American President apparently was a Canadian citizen and therefore held the presidency illegally?"

Sam racked his brain, but couldn't think. Dr. Putnam punched the buzzer.

"Chester A. Arthur!"

"LUCKY GUESS" chided the Brains Board. Chicago fans groaned. Early in the first quarter, Baltimore led the Phils, 8-3.

Moose Harrison commented, "THE PHILS ARE BATTLING THE MENCKENS, THE MENCKENS' DIRTY TRICKS AND THEMSELVES TODAY, AND SO FAR THEY'RE LOSING ALL THREE BATTLES."

In the 93rd row, Martha Jean peered at the stage through binoculars. "Anyone can sit there looking like a jerk and give the wrong answer. Why are they paying Sam so much money?"

Joe shrugged. "I don't know. It's like one of those *koan* questions the Zen Buddhists ponder. There's no obvious answer. You've gotta think about it a long time."

"I could use some popcorn," Martha Jean said.

"Wait until halftime. I don't want to miss any of the game."

Martha Jean grimaced. "Why? It's not like Sam is going to put any points on the board."

IN THE SECOND QUARTER, Edgar Woodford and the Menckens' Renaissance Boy, Scooter Daniels, moved out to the Hot Zone. Scooter, handicapped since he was seven years old, rode in his electric cart.

Head Referee Destry asked, "Which of these gases and vapors is most dense?"

On the Brains board appeared the choices: "hydrogen sulfide, krypton, chlorine?"

Edgar hit the buzzer.

"Chlorine."

The "OOPS!" sign flashed on and off.

"Baltimore?" said the referee.

"Krypton." Scooter glared at the former secretary of state. "Shouldn't you be out starting a war or something? You're no Renaissance Man!"

"Keep it up," Edgar grumbled. "You'll find out what my friends in high places can do to a little squirt like you."

First-time starter Juanita Lorez and the Menckens' world expert, Rusty Dobson, took over the playing area.

"For three points," announced Crawler. "What was the name of the area where most of Britain's codebreakers worked during World War II? (a) Benchley Park (b) Bletchley Park (c) Nottingham Park (d) Manchester Park."

Rusty slammed the buzzer first.

"B—Bletchley Park!" he declared.

"LUCKY GUESS" noted the Brains Board.

At Northwestern Memorial Hospital, Margaret Kramer shared a room with Tina Meredith, whose collapse in the Phils' final regular season game resulted in Sam's recruitment. Tina's condition remained precarious. Margaret's nerves were shattered, but her strong, pioneer-woman constitution kept her from becoming a complete basket case.

Doctors left orders that the two nerve-frazzled Phils must not watch the playoff game, but Margaret's eyes were glued to the set anyway. She kept Tina posted on what was happening. After Edgar and Juanita blew their questions, Margaret growled to a nurse, "get my clothes! I gotta get out of here. They need me!"

"No way, Margaret. Doctor Murphy said you must stay here a few more days."

"What does that quack know? I'm ready to check out of this joint. I'm good as new!"

Margaret tried to rise out of bed but couldn't make it. She was weak and groggy.

"On the other hand," Margaret said, "maybe I'll watch the game from here. Get me a daiquiri, will you, dear?"

The nurse hesitated. "Margaret, I can't."

"Do it!"

The nurse scrambled toward the door. "Yes, ma'am!"

"Make it two," the weak voice from the other bed said.

Back at the Windy City Dome, emotions ran high in the second quarter. A Brain Buster sent three players from each side to the Hot Zone—Brian, Edgar and Juanita for the Phils and Emily Putnam, Scooter Daniels and Rory Thunderheart for the Menckens.

"For six points: Sixteen people board a passenger train in New York City. At Baltimore, three people get off the train and five get on. At Richmond, Virginia, two people get on the train and five get off. At Savannah, Georgia, no one gets on and three people get off. When the train arrives in Miami, Florida, how many people are on the train?"

Edgar slammed the buzzer. "The answer is none," he said. "If a train carries so few passengers, the railroad would have discontinued that run long ago because it isn't cost efficient."

"GOOD GRIEF!" exclaimed the Brains Board.

"Wrong!" proclaimed the referee.

On the sidelines, Freud tried to restrain Rock.

"I'm going to kill that pompous bureaucrat!" the coach roared.

"Would you care to answer?" the referee asked Baltimore.

Scooter hit the buzzer. "I certainly would. The answer is twelve. Twelve people."

"That is correct!" the referee declared.

BY THE END OF THE FIRST HALF, the Menckens rolled up a solid 45-31 lead over the Phils.

Before Rock addressed his dejected troops in the dressing room, Freud took Rock aside to confer.

"The team is trying, Rock! They're doing their best. You've pushed them to the breaking point. Try to be reasonable and calm."

"Losers are reasonable and calm," Rock griped. "Winners are unreasonable and emotional."

He faced his players. "All right. Listen up, you meatballs!"

The players moaned. Bottles of Excedrin and Prozac were passed around the room.

"You trail by fourteen points. Giving the Menckens a lead that big in a playoff game is like giving God the top seed in a tennis tournament. You're falling apart out there. Pull yourselves together! Use your passes and psych out your opponents. Exploit their weaknesses! Rattle their concentration!"

Rock surveyed his motley crew. "You won a lot of games this season. You can't go belly up now. Quit looking for the easy way out. Throw yourself into the game. If you don't, you'll always regret it. Play your best for twenty-four minutes and we'll go to the Brains Bowl. *Twenty-four minutes.* Is that asking so much? *You can do that, can't you! You can win this game!!"*

Chase leaped off the bench. "Yes, we can!"

Brian jumped up. "We can win!"

The others joined in. "We can do it!"

The team jogged back to the playing floor with more energy and team spirit than they had shown all season. Rock and Freud watched in amazement.

"What happened?" Rock asked. "What got them fired up? I've got to know so I can use it again."

Freud sighed. "Sorry, Rock. I wasn't listening. I was trying to figure out the fastest way to the airport in case we lost the game."

Even Sam was caught up in the frenzy. He couldn't help himself. It was just like *Moby Dick*:

> How was it that they so aboundingly responded to the old man's ire—by what evil magic their souls were possessed, that at times his hate seemed almost theirs, the White Whale as much their insufferable foe as his ...

As THE SECOND HALF OPENED, Julie nailed the Shakespearean tipoff. A few moments later, Chase and Crazy Legs Stearn moved to centercourt.

"For three points: Name the team that won the 1994 world series."

Chase confidently punched the buzzer. "There was no world series that year. A dispute between players and owners forced cancellation of the series!"

The board flashed "YOU BETCHA!" The crowd roared.

Rock called a timeout and signaled for T.J. to come over to confer.

"I'm putting you in for Edgar at R.M. We've got to neutralize Scooter Daniels. Our dirty tricks response crew, Annie and Chase, came up with a plan to get rid of him. All you've got to do is call a terminator and *get the answer right!*"

"We're doing dirty tricks now?"

"No. When *they* do it, it's dirty tricks. We're getting even. You got a problem with that?"

"No."

T.J. returned to his seat.

"I trained the kid well," Rock told Freud.

After the timeout, Edgar took a seat on the sidelines and T.J. was transported to centercourt to face Scooter, who smiled confidently. "Terminator!" T.J. told the head ref. Then he turned his attention to Scooter. "You're taking it well."

"What are you talking about?"

"If fire destroyed my parents' house it would shake me up."

"Our house didn't burn down!" Scooter replied.

Suddenly, video of a house—Scooter's parents' house—engulfed in flames appeared on the Brains Board. Scooter was stunned.

Head referee Crawler Destry's voice boomed over the loudspeaker: "For three points: Who discovered the mathematical laws that apply to the orbiting of the planets?"

T.J. popped his buzzer. "Kepler!"

"GOODBYE, SCOOTER" flashed the Brains Board.

Scooter returned to the sidelines muttering, "My parents' house burned down?"

Menckens' Coach Lou McGiver berated Scooter. "What's the matter with you? You let them snooker you. They took a video of your house and used special effects to make it look like it was burning!"

"But, coach, my home ..."

"You dumb jerk. Your house is safe! They conned you!"

Sam and Dr. Putnam met in the Hot Zone to tackle another history question.

"Sorry to hear your house burned down," Sam declared.

"You're full of if," she said.

"It was worth a try."

"Name the year these events occurred," the referee said. "A bomb explosion on Wall Street killed thirty people; about 2,700 Communists and radicals were arrested throughout the U.S. in a five-month period; *Main Street* and *This Side of Paradise* were published ..."

Sam stabbed at his buzzer. "It was 1920."

The Brains Board flashed "SUPER, SAM!". The Phils excitedly cheered for their teammate.

When Sam returned to the sidelines, Rock roared, *"That's more like it!"* Then he slammed Sam on the back so hard the rookie flew into the first row of seats.

In the 93rd row, Joe stood up and cheered for the Phils as Martha Jean used a compact to freshen up her makeup.

"Wow! Sam did it!" Joe shouted.

"Honey, would you get me a hot dog?"

"Not now, Martha Jean. I can't leave the game!"

"I can be awfully nice when I'm not hungry. Very, very nice."

Joe swallowed hard. "Be right back, honey."

On the playing floor, Julie Howard and Rory Thunderheart were asked to identify the author of these lines:

> For though from out our bourne of Time and
>   place
> The flood may bear me far,
> I hope to see my Pilot face to face
> When I have crost the bar.

Julie slammed her buzzer. "Alfred Lord Tennyson!" she exclaimed.

"YES! YES! YES!" declared the game board.

Annie Jones, substituting for T.J. at the Renaissance Person position, didn't know Thomas Jefferson was the father of American cryptography, so Rock sent Edgar back into the game as R.M. By the end of the third quarter the Menckens' lead was cut to two points, 61-59.

IN THE FOURTH QUARTER, Julie and the Menckens' quotations ace, Rory Thunderheart, headed back to the Hot Zone.

"It's unfortunate we are rivals," Rory said. "Under different circumstances, you and I might have shared a torrid passion."

"That might be true," Julie conceded, "if I didn't find your slimy Conquistador approach to love revolting."

Rory was stunned. "Revolting? Who do you think you are talking to?"

"That's telling him!" Sam shouted from the sidelines.

Crawler Destry declared, "Identify the author of this passage."

On the Brains Board appeared the quotation:

> From morn to noon he fell, from moon to dewy
> eve, a summer's day, and with the setting sun
> dropt from the zenith like a falling star.

Julie punched the buzzer.

"Milton!"

The "WE'RE NO. 1!" sign flashed as the crowd roared its approval.

Rory returned to the sidelines in a daze. "Revolting? She finds my slimy Conquistador approach to love revolting? Who does she think she is?"

Coach McGiver glared at Rory. "She's the player who just psyched you out, you dumb moron."

At Northwestern Memorial Hospital, a nurse holding a syringe barged into the room and cheerily announced to Margaret, "It's time for your shot, dear!"

"Get out," Margaret commanded. "I'm watching the game."

"Well, aren't we naughty. The doctor strictly ordered that you not watch—"

Margaret interrupted her. "Before you give me that thing, let me look at it." Margaret took the syringe. "There must be enough medicine here to knock out a horse."

"Now, dear ..."

Before the nurse had time to react, Margaret stabbed the syringe into the nurse's arm. A stunned look washed over the nurse's face as she collapsed onto the floor.

"Now, we can watch the game in peace," Margaret declared.

Tina, who was due to get the next injection from the nurse, muttered, "I owe you one, Maggie."

Back at the Windy City Dome, Sam and Emily Putnam were whisked back to the Hot Zone.

"For four points, identify the muckraker who wrote *The History of Standard Oil* in 1904."

Sam punched the buzzer first.

"Ida Tarbell!"

"YOU BETCHA, SAM!" flashed the Brains Board. The crowd roared its approval.

"You did good, kid!" Chase said.

Brian and Betty Lou Carruthers were asked to identify who wrote the lyrics and music for "Love Me Tonight".

"Rogers and Hart!" Betty Lou shouted.

"LUCKY GUESS," flashed the big board.

Neither team would fold in the closing minutes. The lead changed hands five times. With nineteen seconds remaining in the game and the score knotted at 79. Rock called a timeout.

Moose Harrison described the scene:

"THIS ONE IS COMING DOWN TO THE WIRE. EVERYTHING IS RIDING ON THE LAST THREE-POINT CHALLENGE. THE RENAISSANCERS, EDGAR WOODFORD FOR THE PHILS AND BAINBRIDGE KRAWLER FOR THE MENCKENS, WILL BE UP NEXT. "

Edgar and Bainbridge moved to the Hot Zone. Edgar took a deep breath, exhaled slowly and waited for the question.

The referee asked: "How much more damage will an earthquake registering 6.3 on the Richter Scale do than one registering 4.3?"

Bainbridge hit his buzzer first. The crowd groaned.

"THIS COULD BE THE END OF THE GAME AND THE END OF THE SEASON FOR THE PHILS," Moose Harrison reported.

"One hundred times," Bainbridge asserted confidently.

The board flashed, "YOU BLEW IT, BAINBRIDGE!"

"Chicago?" said the referee

"It's a trick question," Edgar said. "You didn't ask how much more damage a 6.3 'quake was *capable* of causing, you asked how much more damage it *would* cause. And that depends on where the 'quake strikes."

Crawler Destry was confused. He looked to the board of judges, who hastily conferred.

The lead judge took the microphone. "The Chicago player is correct!"

"Thank God," Edgar mumbled.

The "WAY TO GO EDDIE!" sign flashed, fireworks exploded and the crowd cheered wildly.

The other players mobbed Edgar. Sam and Brian lifted the former secretary of state to their shoulders.

"It wouldn't kill him to lose some weight," grumbled Brian.

"Thirty pounds of it is ego," suggested Sam.

Moose Harrison was ecstatic:

THE PHILS HAVE DONE IT! THE PHILS HAVE DONE IT! THE HEART ATTACK KIDS ARE IN THE BRAINS BOWL! FOR MOST OF THE GAME, THE PHILS TEETERED ON THE VERGE OF SELF-DESTRUCTION, BUT ROCK GUIDED HIS WEARY CREW TO VICTORY. NOW THE PHILS HAVE TWO WEEKS TO PREPARE BEFORE THEY FACE THE POWERFUL SAN FRANCISCO HACKERS IN SEATTLE. CAN THE PHILS PUT THEIR PROBLEMS BEHIND THEM AND WIN THE BRAINS BOWL? THAT'S THE BIG QUESTION.

IN THE LOCKER ROOM, THE TEAM celebrated, but their exhilaration was tempered by the enormity of the task ahead.

Rock signaled for quiet.

"Now, it all comes down to one game," he said, his voice hoarse from yelling. "Monday morning, a bus will take us to a secret training location. You won't know our destination until we are on the bus. I don't want prying reporters—especially those weasels from 'Late Night Edition'—knowing where we are going. I will tell you this ... bring along your heavy clothing."

"That figures," Brian moaned. "Why couldn't we train in a warm climate?"

"Because I don't want any distractions, Hot Shot. And remember—if you are captured, give only your name, rank and serial number!"

AT THE PALMER HOUSE HILTON, Sam escorted Julie to her door, where a Federal Express package had been left for her.

"It's from David!" she noted, as she ripped it open. Inside was a light brown stuffed bear, about a foot high. Printed on the bear's tee shirt were the words "Good luck, Julie! Love, David."

"Look, Sam! Isn't it adorable!"

"Cute," said Sam. "So, what now, Julie? Christmas isn't a good time to be lonely."

"I'm not lonely. You'd better go on, Sam. I had a good time, but we're just friends. I'm going to relax now and call David."

"I live down the hall. It's not like I'm going to miss the last train to the suburbs if I stay a while."

"Goodbye, Sam!"

She shut the door.

Shaking his head, Sam tramped down the hall to his room. Suddenly, he heard voices from the other rooms.

"Goodnight, Sam."

"Go home, Sam."

"You're really screwed up, Sam!"

Sam grumbled, "you people need to get straightened

out. You could start by getting decent jobs!"

"Amen!" said Edgar Woodford.

"You've got that right," agreed Juanita.

"Isn't that the truth!" Annie chimed in.

19

As the Phils tried to unwind after their playoff victory, a taxi whisked Percy Smathers through snow-slickened Chicago streets to the "Late Night Edition" regional studio on State Street. Percy was in a foul mood. The Phils and their despicable coach, RockNelson, had somehow managed to win two playoff games and would now compete in the Brains Bowl. This was an abomination. It proved to Percy there was no God, at least not in his world, for no righteous and just God would ever allow the Phils to advance that far in the playoffs. Furthermore, the whole situation was a personal affront to Percy. Rock was flaunting the Phils' success in Percy's face. The senile old coach had even left a message on Percy's answering machine: "We will win the Brains Bowl to show you up for the sleazebag you are, Smathers!"

Something had to be done. Rock and the Phils must be stopped. Half-measures would not do. They must be totally humiliated, and crippled so badly they would not be capable of winning the Brains Bowl.

At the "Late Night Edition" offices, Diane Mercross told Percy about Rock's plan to take the Phils to a secret location to prepare for the big game. "He told reporters he didn't want 'Late Night Edition' and other 'frauds who pretend to be legitimate journalists' distracting his team." *That* sent Percy's blood pressure up another thirty points.

Percy convened an emergency staff meeting. "Rock doesn't know who he's screwing with," Percy told his crew. "How the hell does he think he can hide an entire sports team in this age of GPS tracking, instant communications and surveillance cameras? He's got to be insane.

"Diane, hire twenty more people. Everyone here and all the new hires will be responsible for keeping the Phils under surveillance. If the Phils try to escape to a hideaway, I want our people right there with them. There will be no place they can hide. We'll find Rock and the Phils and humiliate them—and then we'll exploit it for all it's worth! We'll get into their heads so deep they'll all be basket cases by the time the Brains Bowl begins!

"Okay. You've got your orders. *Go get 'em!*"

Diane squirmed in her chair. This wasn't what she had in mind when she signed up for a career in journalism. No journalist intends to spend her career doing hatchet jobs on sports teams or chasing celebrities who can't keep their private parts in their pants. She had imagined she would be doing important work, piling up Pulitzer Prizes.

Well, welcome to the real world, she thought. This is tabloid TV journalism Percy Smathers style, and she was up to her eyeballs in it. She had worked for the old charlatan for two years, and it was a little late in the game to develop a conscience.

Percy's grating voice interrupted her reverie. "What are you waiting for, Diane? Haul ass!"

III

Philosophers in Hiding

MONDAY, DECEMBER 22 - THURSDAY, JANUARY 1

20

MONDAY morning Sam waited with other players in one of the Palmer House Hilton's meeting rooms as Rock and Freud made last-minute preparations for the journey to a secret location. Sam was surprised to see Margaret had rejoined the team.

"So what's the story?" Brian inquired. "Are you back at full strength or running on one cylinder?"

"That's one more than you're running on," she snapped.

"Now, Margaret. I was hoping we could be friends, since Rock assigned you and me to bunk together the next two weeks."

"*What?*" she screamed. *"Not in a million years!"*

Julie pulled Brian away. "Relax, Margaret. Brian is playing with your mind. Freud says we all will have our own rooms."

"Thank God."

Julie turned to Brian. "Shame on you! She just got out of the hospital!"

Rock and Freud arrived with their arms full of scarves, hats and sunglasses.

"These are your disguises," Rock said. "Put them on!"

"Disguises?" Juanita muttered. "What kind of place are you taking us to?"

"The disguises should fool any reporters who try to follow us."

Everyone on the team—including Rock and Freud—slipped on scarves, hats and sunglasses. Everyone but Archie Bolton, who would join the team in Seattle.

Rock no longer looked like the quintessential football coach. Dressed in a shabby coat and weather-beaten hat, he could have been mistaken for a short dirty old man peddling porn on the street.

"Just what is it you do in the off-season?" Brian asked.

"Get outta here, wiseguy," Rock growled.

Rock took Freud aside, out of hearing range of the players.

"With Margaret out, we had a rough night at the Renaissance slot, and moving Edgar out of the world chair was a disaster. The subs struggled all game.

"Keep an eye on Margaret. Make sure she doesn't go completely nuts. We can't afford to lose her for the Brains Bowl!"

"I'll do my best," Freud said, "but we've got a lot of players on the verge of losing it."

"Your job is to make sure they don't!"

FOUR BUSES PULLED INTO the hotel parking garage. Rock and the team boarded the bus nearest to them. Then the team watched in amazement as a motley assortment of people who bore some resemblance to the real Philosophers boarded the other three buses. They were the decoys, and they also wore disguises. Rock had thought of everything.

"That bum could never be mistaken for me!" Edgar complained. "He's too dorky, too ugly!"

"He looks exactly like you, Eddie!" Annie exclaimed.

Edgar slumped in his seat. "Don't call me Eddie. Why is it my fate in life to be surrounded by lunatics and idiots?"

"I was wondering the same thing," Margaret said.

"Me, too," T.J. mumbled.

"Isn't it the truth," Chase moaned.

"Peasants," grumbled Edgar.

Sam intended to sit next to Julie, but she placed an overnight case and the stuffed bear from David in the seat next to her. Sam made himself comfortable across the aisle. Brian settled into the row of seats in front of Julie.

"This is not a good idea," Brian insisted. "There are at least ten women out there who will go bananas because they can't contact me. Who knows what they'll do! What if they commit suicide?"

"Aren't you exaggerating?" asked Julie.

"Not at all. I tell you, it's a dangerous situation."

"They'll probably get along fine," Sam suggested. "Maybe it's *you* that can't cope without companionship from the opposite sex."

Brian shrugged. "I don't know. I never tried it before. At least, not since I was fifteen."

Julie laughed. "Do you know what you need, Brian?"

"A cold shower?" he guessed.

"I was going to suggest a really long session with Freud."

The buses began rolling.

As the buses pulled out of the parking garage, crews from "Late Night Edition" and other TV news and entertainment shows were waiting, but they didn't know which bus to follow.

"Don't lose them!" Percy Smathers shouted to his people. "I want two vehicles following each bus! Don't let them get away!"

Percy's people scrambled for their cars and vans as one bus headed north, one south, another west and another east. Rock hoped reporters would follow the decoy buses. And he had some tricks up his sleeve in case they didn't.

The bus carrying Rock and the team headed south on Interstate 55. Percy Smathers and Diane Mercross were in a Ferrari following the bus traveling west. Diane was at the wheel. Percy held a two-way radio.

"Anybody have a positive ID?" Percy asked.

"Impossible to tell who they are," a northbound driver said.

"I'll second that," said a southbound driver.

"I'm already in Indiana," said an eastbound driver.

His other drivers also were clueless.

"Stay with them!" Percy barked.

Diane pulled the Ferrari alongside the westbound bus. The lighting inside the bus was dim and the passengers all wore disguises.

"No way to tell if they're the Phils," she said.

"Fall back. We'll keep following them," Percy said. "They'll have to stop sometime."

"Let me know if you see anyone trailing us," Rock told the team. "We've got a surprise for them a few miles ahead."

Sam and T.J. spotted a blue Chevy and a gray van behind the bus. Other vehicles passed the bus, but the Chevy and the van showed no intention of passing. "Coach, I think we're being followed. Two vehicles."

Rock hiked to the back of the bus and gazed out the window. "All right. We're prepared for this!"

Henry Clover, the driver, grabbed the CB and radioed ahead: "Code Twelve. Blue Chevy and gray van behind us. Lose them!"

A voice crackled over the receiver: "Roger, Tin Man."

The bus rolled on. The trailing vehicles stayed close. Two miles up the highway, Henry barked, "hold on to your seats!"

He pressed the accelerator. The bus roared to ninety miles an hour. Before the Chevy and the van could adjust, a semi trailer pulled across the southbound lanes of the interstate, cutting the vehicles off from the bus and sending them rolling through a field, where they cruised for thirty or forty yards before smashing into trees.

"This isn't an ordinary bus," Henry said. "It's got a jet engine."

"He's joking, isn't he?" Margaret muttered.

"What's the matter?" Henry asked. "No guts?"

"The southbound bus ditched us!" a voice crackled over the two-way radio.

"Is someone still following them?" Smathers asked.

"Negative. We're both stuck in a farm field."

"Oh, my Lord," Percy moaned. "How could you lose a damn bus? You're fired!"

Diane glanced at her boss. "Should we keep following the westbound bus?"

"No. We'll let the Ford keep following them, in case the other situation was a diversion."

Mercross turned the Ferrari around as Smathers pulled out a map. Soon the Ferrari was headed back east toward I-55. Perhaps they could still locate the southbound bus.

As the bus carrying the team barreled south on Interstate 55, Rock rose from his seat next to the driver and addressed his crew.

"All right, you meatballs. Listen up! Freud thought we should train for the bowl in a secret location so you wouldn't be at the mercy of distractions and temptations. I agreed. Freud picked a hideaway a few miles outside a sleepy burg where no one will pay much attention to us. What's the name of that town?"

"Moberly, Missouri," grumbled Henry.

"Oh, yes. Moberly. No one will bother us there. If we go into town for anything, we'll wear disguises. Don't tell *anyone* where we will be. We are going to Moberly for one thing, and only one thing!"

"Sex?" guessed Brian.

"No! To prepare for the bowl! Any questions? ... Good! Now, we've got about seven hours before we arrive. I suggest you crack the books!"

T.J. turned to Edgar. "Did you bring any books?"

Edgar shrugged. "Nobody said anything about books."

Annie sighed. "I assumed the team would bring everything we needed."

Rock was aghast. "You didn't bring any books? What the hell did you think you were going to study for the next two weeks? Your belly buttons? Freud, did you bring the books?"

"I tried to arrange all the details. I forgot the books."

Rock hurried to the front of the bus and checked a map. "Henry, when we get to Bloomington, Illinois, find a bookstore."

"You mean a restaurant, don't you?" Henry asked.

"No, a bookstore!"

Henry shrugged. "Strangest group I ever hauled."

TWO HOURS LATER, HENRY found a bookstore in a mall in Bloomington, Illinois. As Rock and the Philosophers scrounged for books, Freud ordered carry out food from Jethro's Family Restaurant. Twenty minutes later the team was headed south on Interstate 55 again.

"Wait 'til Sloan gets the bill for twelve hundred dollars," Rock moaned.

"Might have been cheaper to buy the bookstore," suggested Freud.

"Just make sure all the books the team needs are shipped to us from Chicago—fast!"

An hour later, Brian noticed T.J. typing on his laptop computer.

"Forget it, T.J.," said Brian. "Nobody reads books by second-stringers."

"I'm not writing a book, you twit. I'm devising a code. Rock wants secrecy, so I thought I'd come up with a code the newspapers and the Hackers could never break. If our notes or important papers get into the wrong hands, they'll appear to be complete gibberish."

"Like Margaret's love letters," noted Juanita.

"I'm serious," T.J. asserted. "This code is a combination of the Great Cipher of Louis XIV and the Navajo Code Talkers from World War II, with a little of Britain's Playfair Cipher from World War I thrown in."

"You're wasting your time," Brian said. "By the time you encode and decode a message, the Brains Bowl will be over. Besides, I don't think you could handle anything more complicated than pig Latin."

"Go bug someone else," T.J. snapped. "I'm busy."

Percy Smathers and Diane Mercross sped south on Interstate 35 and joined Interstate 55 near Bloomington-Normal, Illinois. Percy had no idea if the team bus was still on I-55, or if it ever had been.

"This is hopeless unless someone reports seeing the bus," he complained. "Just stay on 55 and pick up speed. Maybe we'll spot them."

As the Phils' bus rolled through southern Illinois thirty miles south of Smathers and Mercross, Brian noticed Annie playing chess on her laptop computer. The computer was winning.

Brian slumped into a seat on the other side of the aisle. "The computer is strong on logic. Your best chance of winning is to use creativity and fake it out."

"Do you mind?" Annie grumbled. "This is a private game."

She moved her queen to E3. Brian couldn't believe it. "Why are you giving up your queen? You don't sacrifice your queen unless it helps you win. You don't give it up just because you can't think of a better move."

"Brian, I don't try to straighten out your love life. Don't mess with my chess!"

Brian got up. "All right, Annie. I'm just trying to stop you from embarrassing yourself."

"Admittedly, that's a subject you know a lot about, but I can manage. Thank you anyway, Brian."

T.J. shouted, "That's telling him, Annie!"

Juanita snapped, "Don't bother the working people, Brian!"

Rock had fallen asleep, but the noise roused him from his slumber.

"What's goin' on?" he asked Henry.

"I'm a bus driver," Henry said. "You want information, buy a newspaper."

Rock turned around.

"What's goin' on back there?" he demanded.

"We're excited because Brian finally got a four-point question right," T.J. said.

"About time," Rock grumbled. He slumped back in his seat and resumed his nap.

"How long have you been a bus driver?" Juanita asked Henry.

"About a year."

"What else have you done?"

"Over the last thirty years, I held a lot of jobs. I was a bartender. Then I played in a band that had gigs across the Midwest. When that didn't pay the bills, I became an auto mechanic. Then I drove a truck for a few years. I was a private detective. Then I took up computer programming and worked my way up to vice president of a corporation. When it looked like they were going to name me president, I got out of there fast. I wanted to travel again, so I decided to give bus driving a whirl."

"When are you going to settle down?" Annie asked.

"When I'm dead."

Brian's voice came wafting up from the fifth row. "The way you drive, that could be tonight."

"What's the matter with him?" Henry asked.

"There are many theories about that," Annie said. "I believe his problem is geographical."

"Geographical? What do you mean?"

"Brian's ego is bigger than Alaska and his brain is smaller than Rhode Island."

"Figured it was something like that," Henry said.

NEAR ST. LOUIS, THE BUS left Interstate 55 and merged onto Interstate 70, heading west into Missouri.

"This is the first time I've been here since I graduated from St. Louis University," T.J. noted.

"The Billikens!" Brian declared, recalling the nickname used by the school's athletic teams.

"Didn't Ogden Nash write a limerick about the Billiken?" Juanita asked.

"Nash wrote about the Pelican, not the Billiken, you ninny," Margaret snapped.

"You're only half right," Julie noted. "The limerick was about the Pelican, but Ogden Nash didn't write it. Dixon Lanier Merritt did."

"Obviously, we've got work to do before the Brains Bowl," Edgar suggested.

The towering arch, the most distinctive landmark in the St. Louis area, loomed ahead.

"First time I've seen the arch," Juanita commented. "Why was it built?"

"To celebrate America's addiction to fast food," Edgar suggested.

As the Phils headed west into Missouri, Percy Smathers and Diane Mercross continued south on I-55 in southern Illinois. Percy consulted a map.

"This interstate cuts through Missouri, Arkansas and Mississippi before winding up in Louisiana. The Phils could have gotten off 55 just about anywhere. This is hopeless.

Let's pack it in. We'll head for the St. Louis airport, fly back to our Chicago studio and regroup. We'll rely on tips from the public to track them down."

ABOUT A HUNDRED MILES west of St. Louis, Henry exited Interstate 70 and highballed it north on 65. Forty minutes later, the bus rolled into the small Missouri city of Moberly. It was a quiet burg, with a small downtown area, a few fast food restaurants sprinkled along the roads and hundreds of small wood and brick houses, many of them adorned with Christmas lights. As the bus passed the police station, Freud told the crew what he had learned about Moberly when he was hunting for a hideaway: "The population here is about thirteen thousand. It lost residents in the 1990s, but in the last few years it's been growing again. On the Fourth of July in 1995, a tornado ripped through the town."

Annie, who had lived only in big cities, was uncomfortable. "It's awfully small."

"Is this some kind of joke?" Edgar demanded.

"This is Small Town America," Sam said. "It's different in small towns."

The bus passed through the business district, where stores squatted along the streets. Christmas decorations were draped over intersections, making it difficult to pick out the traffic lights from the red and green Christmas decorations. Wreaths and multi-colored lights adorned storefronts.

"I think we've gone back in time about sixty years," Margaret said.

A FEW MINUTES LATER, light snow tumbled to the ground as Henry parked the bus outside a large, rambling wood frame house three miles outside Moberly. The building appeared to be in good shape—no broken windows, no doors missing—but it did not look like the type of five-star establishment some of the Philosophers expected.

"All right. Everybody out," Rock ordered. "This is it."

Edgar surveyed the building carefully. "You can't be serious."

"It's just what the doctor ordered," Rock grumbled. "Get out!"

"It's nothing but a big old house!" Margaret said. "I thought we were going to stay at a resort."

"We've got this hacienda all to ourselves," Rock said, "and it's off the beaten track. This is where you will spend the next ten days."

"Including Christmas and New Year's," Julie noted sadly.

"Exactly," Rock said. "Let's get the luggage inside."

Rock and Freud led the wary team up steps leading to the front porch. Freud rapped on the door.

21

A SHAPELY BRUNETTE IN A BLUE sweatshirt and gray workout pants opened the door. She seemed to be about fifty. She surveyed the motley assemblage of visitors.

"The team is here, in case you haven't figured it out already," Freud announced.

"Come in and warm up. I'm Irene Harper. ... Sorry I'm not more presentable. I was doing some last-minute cleaning."

Freud shook hands with her.

"Amos Lawton, better known by this outfit as Freud. We spoke on the phone when I rented the house. This is Rock Nelson, the coach."

Rock grunted. Freud introduced the rest of the team and Henry, who would be staying so he could drive the bus.

As the Phils stepped inside the rather ordinary looking house, they discovered a larger and more elaborately decorated interior than they had expected. The spacious living room was furnished with thick brown carpeting, comfortable leather and vinyl recliners and armchairs and a large, plush brown sofa. A bookcase stocked with hundreds of volumes stretched along one of the sand-colored walls, flanked by two large Christmas wreaths. Along another wall could be seen a large brick fireplace and two paintings depicting scenes along a river bank in autumn and spring. A stairway led to the second floor.

Sam's eyes were drawn to the dining room, which housed an oak table large enough to accommodate all the Phils. Snowman decorations added an elegant touch to the room. Plates and silverware had been placed in front of each chair.

"I'll give you time to settle into your rooms, then we'll have dinner," Irene said. "You've got a choice—spare ribs and scalloped potatoes or chicken and dumplings. ... Four of you will have rooms on the first floor. The rest will be upstairs. You will find the living room and den comfortable for reading and lounging, and the living room or dining room will be useful for team meetings."

"Where do I bunk?" Chase asked.

"I'll be on the first floor," Rock said. "And so will Freud, Margaret and Henry. The rest of you crazies will be upstairs."

Irene showed the downstairs occupants to their rooms. Then the others—T.J., Chase, Annie, Brian, Juanita, Edgar, Sam and Julie—followed her up the wide, carpeted wooden staircase to the second floor.

"Do you live here alone?" Julie asked Irene.

"Yes, at the moment. My daughter is a junior at Stanford. My son lives in New York City. He works for a book publisher. I make the house available for small corporate retreats and that pays the bills. Lizzie lives down the road and she helps me with the cooking and housekeeping."

They could see a middle-aged woman in the kitchen. Her black hair was wrapped up into a bun and she wore an apron.

THE PHILS DUMPED THEIR LUGGAGE in their rooms, washed up a bit and then returned to the living room, ready for dinner.

"This is a wonderful old house," Julie remarked.

"I'm not sure about that," Brian grumbled. "The house and Irene are too good to be true. This could be Rock's idea of a joke. Suck us into a phony, homey atmosphere and then we discover it's not the Old Homestead, it's the Amityville Horrors, and good old Irene turns out to be Lizzie Borden. I think I'll sleep with my door locked tonight."

"You're crazy," Annie said. "You've been playing for Rock too long. You forget there are people who live fairly normal lives."

"I'm with Brian on this one," T.J. said. "Rock's gotta have an angle. He always does."

During dinner, something coming around the corner on its way into the living room caught Edgar's eye.

"Good heavens! I didn't know there were cats in the house!"

"Just one," Irene said. "Her name is Glory."

"Cats and I don't get along," Edgar noted.

"It dates back to one of his visits to Africa," Brian suggested. "Something about superstition, twilight, evil spirits and negotiations for machine guns worth twenty million dollars."

"Nothing of the sort," Edgar scowled. "I just don't like cats. And they don't like me."

"I'll try to keep Glory away from you," Irene assured him.

After dinner, some of the Philosophers retired to their rooms to crack the books while others lounged around the living room with study materials in hand. Before long, they all noticed the same thing.

"It's so damn quiet!" Brian said. "How can we concentrate?"

"Turn on the television," Chase said.

"In case you haven't noticed, there isn't any," Julie pointed out.

"There's got to be!" T.J. insisted. "It must be in one of the other rooms."

A search of the house turned up no televisions and no radios.

"We're in a time warp," Juanita complained.

"We've died and gone to Farmer Hell," Brian declared.

When Freud emerged from the dining room, he ran into a barrage of complaints about the lack of televisions.

"Just calm down," he pleaded. "Rock has laid down a few ground rules. No television. All televisions have been removed from the house and put into storage. No radios. You can use your computers, but there will be no Internet connections. The telephone service has been disconnected, and cell phones and house phones have been confiscated. And no one is allowed to go into town. Rock doesn't want anyone to know where we are."

"No television? No Internet? No telephone calls?" Brian muttered. "That's barbaric! It's a violation of our constitutional rights."

"Rock is going too far," Annie declared.

Edgar emerged from his room smoking a pipe. He didn't notice Irene coming in from the kitchen carrying a tray of soft drinks, tea and coffee.

"The residence is not without its charms," Edgar noted, "but it's a little primitive for my tastes. This is one step up from having an outhouse in the backyard."

"Why, Mr. Woodford," Irene said, as she offered beverages to Margaret. "There *is* an outhouse in back, but since we installed indoor plumbing last year, we don't have much use for it. Now, we let former secretaries of state go out there to meditate."

Edgar's face reddened as the others laughed. "Point taken," he said.

After Julie retreated to her room, Sam knocked at her door. He carried a duffle bag. "Rock changed the sleeping arrangements. We're bunking together!"

"Nice try, but it won't work," Julie said. "Rock is crazy, but he's not *that* crazy. Get lost, Sam!"

22

Tuesday morning, the Philosophers awoke to the aroma of hot sausage and biscuits. Because bathrooms were on a first-come, first-served basis, some of the Phils studied in their rooms or in the living room while awaiting their turns.

"This place could use about six more johns," suggested Brian.

"Must you always complain?" Annie said. "Try to look on the bright side of things."

"Easy for you to say. You got to the bathroom first and barricaded yourself inside. What do you do in there for forty minutes?"

"I make myself beautiful."

"It didn't work. Try again."

"All right, knock it off," Rock grumbled, as he hustled into the dining room wearing a workout suit. "Where is everybody?"

"There's a bottleneck at the johns," Brian said. "The others should be here in two or three hours."

"There will be no more of that!" Rock declared. "From now on, no one takes more than five minutes for a crap or twelve minutes for a shower and shave."

"Could you clean that up a little?" Annie said. "There's a lady present, you know."

Rock looked around. "Oh. Sorry, Irene."

"That's all right, Rock," she said.

Annie cringed. "I meant *me.*"

"You're just a kid," Rock said.

"I'm a lady, although no one on this team seems to have noticed."

The others scrutinized Annie.

"Nope, you're a kid," Brian said.

"Yep. Maybe next year you'll be a lady."

"Sorry, Annie."

Annie grimaced. "I will be *so* glad when this season is over and I'm surrounded by normal people again."

"Make yourselves comfortable," Irene said. "Breakfast is ready!"

"I didn't sleep well last night," Edgar lamented, as he commandeered a seat at the long oak table in the dining room. "That obnoxious cat tried to break into my room all night."

THE PHILS PILED BISCUITS, gravy, scrambled eggs, sausage and pancakes on their plates.

"You will be happy to know there will be no calisthenics while we are here," Rock announced.

"That's great!" T.J. said.

"Praise the Lord!" Edgar declared.

"What a relief!" Henry muttered.

"I was talking to the team!" Rock scowled.

"What's the catch?" T.J. asked warily.

"Starting today, you will be chopping wood and jogging along the countryside."

Annie gritted her teeth. "You've gotta be kidding. It's twenty degrees out there."

"Really?" Rock said, as he reached for his cup of steaming coffee. "Must have warmed up. I thought it was ten."

"I can't do it, Rock!" Margaret declared. "I just got out of the hospital!"

"Oh, all right. See if you can do some exercises in the house. Everyone else—outdoors in ten minutes!"

"I told you this was Amityville," Brian whispered to Annie.

Edgar Woodford managed to pull almost even with Rock as they jogged along a country road.

"(Huff) Did it occur to you Rock (huff huff) that it's a little cold (huff) to be running out here? (huff huff) That maybe (huff) we'll all get pneumonia? (sneeze)"

"No," Rock growled, and he pulled ahead of Edgar.

"Just (huff) checking," Edgar wheezed.

When the Phils returned to the house, Rock faced his weary crew in the living room. Logs burned in the fireplace, lending a feeling of coziness and warmth to the room. Because several Phils wore sweaters, the group could have been mistaken for skiers at a lodge in Aspen.

"Out here in the sticks, far removed from the craziness surrounding the Brains Bowl, we can focus on preparing for the game," Rock declared. "There is no excuse for you not to study!"

SKIMMING THROUGH BOOKS filled most of the day, just as it had in Chicago. Julie browsed the titles in the living room bookcase and discovered they included many of the greatest books western civilization had produced ... Plato's *Repub-*

lic; Homer's *Odyssey* and *Iliad*; Augustine's *City of God*; Flaubert's *Madame Bovary*; Pascal's *Pensees*; and many more.

"If you find any Batwoman comic books, let me know," Annie said.

After an early and solitary supper, Rock retired to his bedroom to pace, plot strategy and mutter to himself.

Freud joined the players for dinner in the dining room an hour later.

"How does it feel to be the shrink for a team of basket cases?" Brian asked, as he helped himself to swiss steak and potatoes.

Freud sighed. "Sometimes, I feel like I'm working in a psychiatric hospital, but there are moments of pleasure and exhilaration, too."

"Let's face it," T.J. said. "As long as things are like this, we don't have much chance of beating the Hackers. We're disorganized, and our nerves are shattered. And having Ahab for a coach doesn't help. He's getting worse. Can't you do *something* to help Rock see what's happening to him and the team?"

Freud reached for the bowl of green beans. "It's not that easy. He doesn't know how he can do things any differently. He's living in a very small world right now, and he doesn't have any perspective on how things are in the real world."

"What about shock therapy?" asked Juanita.

"Of course!" T.J. said, waving a steak knife in the air. "We could fry Rock in the electric chair. Is that a form of shock therapy?"

"Rock isn't the only one having difficulty coping," Freud observed.

"The ironic thing," Edgar said, "is that Rock is so obsessed with winning he can't see that his obsession makes it harder for us to play well."

"You see him as an obstacle," Freud said. "I've developed a theory about this. Look at it this way: You're on a road that leads to a big city where there's all sorts of good things—ice cream, theaters, Chinese food, sex. And Rock is a huge ferocious bulldog squatting in the middle of the road. You think the bulldog is an obstacle preventing you from reaching your goal. But look at it differently—it's *your* bulldog. He's big and fearsome. If you come up against any enemies or obstacles, your bulldog will tear them to shreds. He's on *your* side. It's all in the way you look at it. Work *with* the bulldog, not against him."

The players pondered what Freud had said.

"That's the biggest load of crap I ever heard," Margaret muttered.

"Is that what they taught you in shrink training?" asked Julie.

"It's known as the 'bulldog in the road' theory," Sam suggested. "Late in life, the real Freud was going to throw out everything he said about sex and use the bulldog theory instead."

"The real Freud? I thought *this* was the real Freud," Brian said. "You mean our team shrink is an imposter?"

"Behave yourself, Brian," Annie said. "When it comes to you, everything *can* be explained in terms of sex."

"Or lack thereof," suggested T.J.

"There was no lack thereof until I hit this place," Brian mumbled.

The Philosophers ate in silence for a minute for two. Then Edgar piped up.

"I want to say something that's been bottled up inside me a long time. If I don't talk about it, I'll explode!"

"Oh, my Lord. You're going to have a sex change operation!" Juanita guessed.

"Where on earth did you come up with that idea?" Edgar said. "It's nothing like that."

"Talk about it, Edgar," Freud said. "This is good. Let it all hang out!"

"I wish I could feel like part of this team, but I don't," Edgar lamented. "I feel like I don't belong. I'm not like the rest of you ... thank God. But I try to fit in. Why can't I?"

"Because you're a pompous, conceited ass," Margaret said.

"Yes, but that never stopped me from being a part of things before. Whatever happened to the good old days, when the President and I sat around chewing the fat and discussing little things like which country we would invade next so he would look more macho? There's nobody on this team I can have an intelligent discussion with."

"I think we all feel like outsiders," Juanita said. "That's why there's no team spirit, no teamwork. We don't feel like we're part of a team. We're headstrong individuals who happen to play for the Phils."

"I think you're on to something," Freud noted. "Being part of a team means working together toward a common goal. Giving up something of yourself for the good of the team. *Caring* about other players. I haven't seen much of that on this team. Perhaps you're too quick to blame all your troubles on Rock."

> Queequeg, who had just plunged into a wintry sea to save the life of a fool, said to himself, "We cannibals must help these Christians."

23

When Percy Smathers and Diane Mercross returned to the "Late Night Edition" offices in Chicago, they set up a command center. He deployed to major cities across the country the people he had recently hired to trail the Phils and ordered them to be ready for action.

Tuesday evening, Percy told his television audience that Rock Nelson and his "band of misfits" were holed up somewhere and he asked that any sightings of the coach, the team, or the bus be phoned in to the show's free 800 telephone number.

Percy set up a huge map of the United States in the "Late Night Edition" studios. Every time a sighting of the Phils was reported, he would order his operatives to check it out and would place a tack on the board to indicate the location.

After Tuesday evening's broadcast sightings poured in, but none could be confirmed.

"Why is it we can not find an entire Brains team?" he lamented to Diane. "One or two players, sure, but a whole damn team?"

"Percy, you're obsessed with this. There are other people,

other teams you can pick on. Forget about the Phils. They'll show up soon enough."

"Oh, no. Rock isn't going to get away with it. This isn't just another story. We are on a mission. I intend to destroy the Phils, and Rock can't stop me by hiding the team!"

The phone rang, irritating Percy's already shattered nerves.

"Someone has found them!" Percy said. "I can feel it in my bones. Grab the phone!"

Diane dived for the phone.

"Yes? ... Really. ... You saw them ..."

"I knew it!" Percy exclaimed.

"... in West Virginia, going into a coal mine? Uh-huh. How do you know it was them? ... I see. ... Well thank you very much."

She hung up. "The lady said they were wearing Chicago Phils tee shirts and singing 'Off to work we go'."

"Don't bother putting that one on the board," Percy grumbled.

He pondered the map. "If I were Rock, where would I take the team? If I were a crazy man in my fifties, where would I go?"

24

THE NEXT DAY—WEDNESDAY—was Christmas Eve. A private shipping company delivered a load of books from the team's headquarters in Chicago. Irene and Freud arranged the volumes on shelves in the study.

Irene had placed a few wreaths, boughs of holly and snowman decorations around the house, but there wasn't much holiday spirit because of the intense preparation for the Brains Bowl. After a strenuous day of jogging, cramming and practice games, Rock again retired early.

In the living room, Juanita noticed Margaret seemed sad and her eyes were moist. "What's wrong, Margaret?"

"Nothing. Nothing is wrong."

"You've been crying."

"I was just thinking of the Christmases my husband and I spent together. All the holiday meals and presents and relatives. ... We lived in the Seattle area, you know. Bernard is buried there. I moved to Arizona after he died."

From her recliner, Julie looked up from the book she was speed reading. "No wonder Margaret's sad. It's Christmas Eve." She gestured toward the walls. "Where's the Christmas tree? Where are the presents?"

The others glanced around the room.

"Nothing wrong with that," Edgar said. "I've always dreaded Christmas. The sooner it's over, the better."

"Julie's right!" declared Juanita. "I've never had a Christmas without a lot of celebrating, decorating and going to church."

"Not much we can do about that," suggested Brian.

"Oh, yes there is!" Julie insisted. "We're surrounded by trees. Get your coats on!"

"It's cold out there!" Brian complained.

Chase rose from the sofa. "You heard the lady. Get your coats on!"

They all retrieved their coats from the large closet at the entryway.

"Thank you, Chase," Julie said.

He blushed.

OUTSIDE THE HOMESTEAD, an inch of snow covered the ground. A cool breeze rattled the trees. Daylight was quickly giving way to darkness.

Julie told Brian and Sam to search Irene's garage for axes. They found one. Then the team headed to a nearby field.

"Chop down one of the pine trees for us!" Julie ordered.

"We don't even know if this is Irene's property," Brian pointed out.

"Let's do what the lady says," Sam suggested. "She's not going to let technicalities stop her."

They inspected the pine trees more closely. Some were scrawny. Others were obviously too tall for the living room.

"Which one do you want us to chop down?" Brian asked. "What do you think, Margaret? Would that one make a good Christmas tree?"

"Or this one?" T.J. asked.

Margaret seemed surprised Brian and T.J. were looking to her for advice.

"I reckon that one will do," she said, pointing at an eight-foot pine tree about ten yards away.

Brian and Sam chopped down the tree and the men hauled it back to the house.

Irene fetched an old tree stand out of the basement.

MINUTES LATER, A CHRISTMAS TREE stood tall in the living room.

"This won't do," Juanita lamented. "We don't have anything to put on the tree."

"Or under it," Annie noted. "We need decorations and presents."

"Well, it's obvious we must pick up a few things in town," Sam declared. "Can we take your pickup?" he asked Irene.

"How many of you are going?"

"Are you up for this?" Sam asked Brian.

"Sure. Anything to get away from studying for a while."

"You bet," T.J. said.

"Chase?" asked Sam

Chase nodded. The others did, too.

"Well, you don't want to take the pickup," Irene said. "Half of you would freeze to death. Besides, my pickup is in sad shape. You need to take the bus."

"Good idea!" Edgar declared. "It's about time we put Henry to work!"

Edgar pounded on Henry's door. Three minutes later he returned with Henry in tow.

"Rock won't like this," Henry muttered.

"Go back to bed," Chase growled. "I'll drive the bus!"

"Just hold on. I'll go! You don't think I'd let you drive that temperamental bus, do you?"

Brian led the way to the front door. "All right. Let's hit the road!"

"Wait a minute," Annie said. "We're forgetting something."

"We can't take Rock," Sam said. "Let him sleep."

"I didn't mean Rock. We should wear our disguises!"

"The lady has a point," Brian noted.

Annie and T.J. retrieved the sunglasses, hats and coats from a closet. As the players slipped them on, Freud wandered into the living room. He glanced at the tree, then at the players and their disguises.

"Whatever you're doing, I don't want to know about it," he said. "I'm already on Rock's shit list for forgetting the books." Then he retreated to his quarters.

After making sure Rock had barricaded himself in his room, the players ventured out into the brisk winter air once more.

Henry revved up the bus engine as the Phils settled into seats. "Next stop, Moberly," he announced.

As the bus barreled over the country road, the players were unusually quiet. T.J. broke the silence.

"You know, we're overpaid," he said.

"You're crazy," Brian snapped. "We're playing for Rock. We couldn't possibly be paid enough."

"What I mean is, we all have more than enough money. Let's all chip in and buy Irene a Christmas gift."

The Phils coughed up cash and T.J. collected the loot.

As the bus rolled along, T.J. broke out in song—his own version of "The Twelve Days of Christmas":

"On the first day of Christmas, my Brains coach sent to me—a car bomb in an LTD.

"On the second day of Christmas my Brains coach sent to me—two hand grenades and a car bomb in an LTD."

By the time T.J. reached the fifth day, his teammates couldn't take it any longer. "Everyone in favor of leaving T.J. by the side of the road say 'aye'," Juanita said.

A chorus of aye's filled the bus.

"All right. I get it," T.J. said. "You don't appreciate good music."

"That's the problem," Annie said. "We *do* appreciate good music."

In Moberly, the bus rolled past the offices of the daily newspaper, the *Monitor-Index*. Henry parked behind a five-and-dime. Most of the Phils ventured inside the store in search of decorations and gifts. Chase hightailed it to the other end of the main street with the money T.J. had collected for Irene's gift. He was on a special mission.

Inside the five-and-dime, Julie and Sam checked out the stock of men's clothing.

"Pick out something for Brian," Julie said.

"That's not easy. What do you give an egomaniac who has everything?"

"A sweater. You can't go wrong with a sweater."

Sam shuffled through a pile of sweaters and pulled one out.

"What do you think?"

She shuttered. "Find one that doesn't have Santa and reindeer on it."

Sam dug further into the pile and pulled out another one. "What about this?"

"Mickey Mouse and Goofy? C'mon, Sam. We haven't got all night."

"I like it. Maybe you're overestimating Brian's taste in clothes."

"And yours."

"This isn't Neiman Marcus. The selection is limited."

"Forget it. We'll get him a bathrobe."

"The second greatest cliché in men's gifts."

"What would *you* get him?"

"A one-way ticket to Tahiti," Sam said. "He'd be happy, and so would the rest of the team."

Julie and Sam settled on a baby blue dress shirt for Brian, then hunted for presents for their other housemates.

Sam wandered into the toy aisle. One shelf held boxes containing the Brains Board Game. Apparently it was a popular item.

He picked up a Chicago Philosophers version of the hand-held Brains arcade game. Within minutes, he was losing and an annoying digitized voice that sounded hauntingly like Rock's lambasted him: "You blew it, meatball! Go to the bench!"

Annie came up behind Sam. "Scary, isn't it. Why would anyone want to hear Rock's bellyaching?"

"Beats me," Sam said, placing the game back on the display.

Sam and Annie browsed around the stuffed animals. A few minutes later, Julie showed up.

"Over here, Sam," she called out.

She pointed to boxes of toy rockets. "David designed these!"

Sam lifted one of the rockets out of a box and examined it. Then he picked up a bigger box containing a more sophisticated rocket and removed the rocket from its box.

"Watch this," Sam said. "Now, this is David's rocket, whizzing through space. And this ..." he lifted up the bigger rocket "is part of a missile defense system that tracks down David's rocket and shoots it out of the sky!"

He threw David's rocket up, then threw the bigger one at it, altering the smaller rocket's course. Both came crashing to the floor, breaking into pieces.

"What do you think you're doing?" demanded a gray-haired woman whose name tag—which identified her as Zelda— suggested she was a store clerk.

"Demonstrating that the smaller rocket is defective," Sam explained.

"It is now. You must pay for both rockets!"

"Gladly," Sam said, as he peeled off four twenty-dollar bills. "It was worth it."

"That was a childish thing to do," Julie chided, as they hurried away from the toy aisle. "David spent months designing that rocket!"

"Months? He's crazier than we are, and he's not even working for Rock."

Chase traveled two blocks on foot before he found the business establishment he was looking for. A half hour later, he used the cash T.J. had collected to pay for Irene's present.

After an hour-long assault on the unsuspecting city of Moberly, the Phils returned to the bus for the trip back to The Homestead. All except Chase, who was doing fine on his own.

BACK AT THE HIDEOUT, Annie and T.J. wrapped presents for teammates as the others—with the help of Freud—decorated the tree in thirty-five minutes.

"A record!" Freud declared.

Suddenly, the bolt on Rock's door snapped.

"He's coming!" Brian whispered.

All the Phils grabbed books so they would look busy. They watched as Rock, deep in thought, shuffled out of his room and advanced towards the kitchen. Suddenly he stopped, surveyed the room, then resumed his journey.

"He must have seen the tree, but it didn't sink in," Julie suggested. "He's got other things on his mind."

Brian slumped in his chair. "Like how to make our lives even more miserable."

"Quiet!" cautioned Margaret. "Here he comes!"

Returning from the kitchen, Rock again stopped for a moment, surveyed the room, then returned to his quarters and bolted the door.

LATER THAT CHRISTMAS EVE, MOST of the players retired to their rooms. Edgar was skimming *The History of Marbles* in the living room when Irene, obviously weary from a long day of dealing with Philosophers, settled into a nearby armchair.

"It's very comfortable here," Edgar noted. "Reminds me of the house my family lived in when I was a teenager."

Irene eyed him closely. "What was all that bluster last night about an outhouse?"

"I suppose I'm a snob. I don't think of rural Missouri as having much in the way of culture. And of course being on Rock's team has warped my judgment and sensibilities. I can only throw myself on the mercy of the court."

Irene smiled. "The court finds you innocent because of temporary insanity. ... Where did you live when you were a teenager?"

"Gloucester, Massachusetts."

"And fine country that is," Irene said.

"You've been there?"

"Oh, yes. I have a sister who lives in Weymouth, Massachusetts. Such a beautiful area, with fine old homes. A person feels connected to history there."

Edgar nodded. "I haven't thought about it lately. It seems so long ago, so far away."

"Over the weekend I'm going to fix clam chowder and lobster for all of you," Irene said.

"Telling a New Englander that is like saying you're pregnant with his child. I should do the right thing and marry you."

"Why, Mr. Woodford. Are you flirting with me?"

"I suppose I am. I'm a little rusty. Could you tell? ... Of course you could, or you wouldn't have asked."

"What would your wife say?"

"Not much. She died seven years ago. ... And what would Mr. Harper say about my flirting?"

"Even less. I divorced him eighteen years ago."

"Let's retire to the den so we can talk in private. We must try to get past the grieving."

"But, Mr. Woodford, I'm not grieving."

"Tsk tsk. Don't talk so much. Come along ... and call me Edgar."

"But Edgar, why are you flirting with me? Juanita said you intend to have a sex change operation."

"You misunderstood her. Juanita is having a sex change operation. I tried to talk her out of it. Now, come along."

They headed to the den as Glory tagged along, a few feet behind.

25

ROCK SLEPT LATE ON Christmas Day, but Margaret didn't give the rest of the team the same opportunity. She rounded up the players, Freud and Henry and told them to forget about disguises and put on their best clothes because after breakfast, they were going to church. She figured no one would recognize them in dresses, suits and sport coats since they were seldom seen wearing them.

"Not me," Chase growled.

Margaret screwed up her courage. "Chase, you are going to church and that's final! This is Christmas!"

Chase meekly nodded.

Henry borrowed a suit Irene's husband had left behind when he moved out eighteen years earlier and at 9 A.M., the Phils boarded the bus.

The bus rocked and rolled down the country road. It was not long before they came across a Baptist church on the outskirts of town.

"This will do," Margaret said. "It's large enough that we won't be conspicuous. We'll go in quietly, scatter throughout the back pews and leave quietly when it's over. There are three things you need to remember: First, we're here to worship. Show respect! Second, don't tip the ushers. And, third, if Brian, T.J. and Chase attempt to sing, muzzle them. They can't carry a tune."

Chase grimaced. "Does the church still frown on bodily harm?"

"Oh, heavens, yes," Margaret replied.

The Phils filed into the worship hall.

The preacher, Hawthorne Blaine, moved to the podium. He was a tall, stern looking man, clothed in a dark blue suit.

"Before we begin, I have a few announcements," he said. "The potluck supper will be Tuesday evening at George and Mollie Relford's home. Last time, six people showed up with potato salad and no one brought any meat. Perhaps the Good Lord will help us to be more creative in our choice of food. On Thursday, a Bible study will be held ..."

After the first hymn, "Silent Night", the pastor led the congregation in a prayer, followed by the passing of the collection plate. The Philosophers dropped twenty, fifty, or hundred-dollar bills in the coffer.

After the singing of two more hymns, one of the deacons whispered a few words to the pastor, who appeared stunned.

"You fine people nearly gave me a heart attack!" the pastor declared. "Our usual collection is about two hundred dollars. This week, it is eight hundred and thirty-eight dollars. Bless all of you for your generosity, and let's try to do better next week!"

T.J. whispered, "He'll have a heart attack next week when we aren't here and the offering drops back to two hundred bucks."

"Shhhhhh!" Margaret said.

The pastor continued: "For my Christmas sermon, I have selected the topic 'The Sinners Amongst Us'."

As Pastor Blaine spoke, Freud shifted uneasily in his seat. He attempted to listen to the pastor's preaching, but his mind wandered. Had Rock noticed his crew had jumped ship? Had he called the police or the F.B.I. to hunt them down?

26

Now, in his heart, Ahab had some glimpse of this, namely, all
my means are sane, my motive and my object mad ...

BACK AT THE HOMESTEAD, Rock slipped into a deep slumber,
but the demons that haunted him gave him no rest. He
dreamed he was captain of a small dingy with no crew in a
pool of water inhabited by a killer whale. It was Rock against
the terrifying beast from the deep. Although fear gripped
him to the depths of his soul, Rock persevered, determined
to slay the whale at any cost. The huge whale circled the
boat, relentlessly moving closer and closer. Rock had little
chance of getting out alive, but he fought on. Suddenly, the
whale surfaced at the edge of the dingy, showed off its huge
teeth and attacked the boat. Water poured in ...

Rock awoke, soaked in sweat and shaken by the realism
of the dream. He slipped on a bathrobe and slippers and
unbolted the door to his room. Then he wandered through
the house looking for his team.

No one else was there. Was he still dreaming?

He started toward the kitchen, but stopped when he
heard a strange, guttural noise. *The whale,* he thought. *It
was coming after him.* He tensed up. He hurried over to a
window, but he could see no whale ... only the bus loaded

with his team coming down the road toward the house. He was relieved.

Then it hit him. *The bus? Why was the team on the bus?* Henry had driven the players somewhere—in direct violation of Rock's orders about leaving The Homestead! Heads would roll for this! Insubordination would not be tolerated when so much was at stake!

Rock wandered outside, still wearing only pajamas and a bathrobe. The cold wind quickly penetrated his consciousness.

Annie was the first player to see Rock. "We're in trouble now!"

"Keep your cool," Freud advised.

The players stepped down from the bus.

"What are you doing, Rock?" Julie called out. *"You'll catch pneumonia out here!"*

Freud slipped his coat over Rock, and Freud and Julie led the distraught coach back toward the house.

"Where were you?" Rock asked, still confused.

"We went to church," Julie said.

"Oh, no. I fell for that once before. Where did you really go?"

Freud opened the door to the house. "We really did go to church, Rock. All of us. It's Christmas."

"It's Christmas?"

"That's right."

"Christmas," Rock muttered, as Freud led him into the living room. "Uh … You didn't happen to run into any whales out there, did you?"

"Whales?" repeated Freud. "No, Rock. We didn't see any whales."

"Good. I didn't, either."

Freud helped Rock into a comfortable recliner. Through a window, Julie could see Irene pulling up in front of the house in her pickup. Freud and Julie went back outside and joined the others. Irene climbed out of her pickup.

"What's going on?" she asked. "You're all dressed up. Have you been somewhere?"

"Church," Julie said.

"That's wonderful," said Irene. "I dropped by a neighbor's house. She just had surgery. ... Well, I'd better get dinner cooking. Today we're having turkey and all the trimmings."

"Wait a minute, Irene," Brian said, as Chase headed around to the back of the house.

"Yes? What is it, Brian?"

"Well, since it's Christmas," T.J. said, "we all chipped and bought a present for you."

"For me?"

Irene was overcome, but she didn't see any present. Suddenly, a new red Chevy pickup truck came barreling around the side of the house with Chase in the driver's seat.

"Merry Christmas, Irene!" Edgar said.

"We noticed your pickup was on its last legs," Annie explained. "So we chipped in and bought you one. Wouldn't seem like Christmas unless we gave someone a special present."

Irene wiped away a tear. "You shouldn't have done it." She inspected the pickup. "Why, it's wonderful. Just wonderful. You spent all that money on me?"

"You should feel honored," Margaret said. "Buying you this truck was one of the few things this team has agreed on all season!"

"Amen!" said T.J.

"I'm overwhelmed," Irene said. "I can't wait to drive it,

but right now I'd better get back to the kitchen. I've got a hungry team to feed."

THE PHILS CHANGED INTO casual clothes and passed around plates of sandwiches and chips for a light lunch. Then they lounged around the living room, books in hand, most of the afternoon as Irene prepared Christmas dinner. As the time drew near, the aroma of the turkey and dressing was almost too much to endure.

Shortly after 4 P.M., the hungry crew gathered around the dining room table. Irene and Lizzie filled the table with turkey, mashed potatoes, stuffing, green beans and cranberries.

"I may not stop eating till New Year's," Chase declared.

"Any woman who can cook like that ..." Edgar said. "I think I'm in love."

"Me, too," Annie said. "Do you think she's into that sort of thing?"

"You're disgusting," grumbled Edgar.

After dinner, Rock and Freud conferred in the den in the north end of the house as the players returned to the living room. The floor seemed to sink under the added weight the players had put on. Glory jumped up on the armrest of Edgar's chair and brushed against his arm. The cat obviously wanted to be petted.

Edgar considered shooing Glory off the armrest, but it was obvious that, for some unfathomable reason, Glory had adopted Edgar.

"Oh, what the hell," he said, and he rubbed Glory near her whiskers.

27

Rock was among the missing when the Phils gathered for breakfast on Friday, the day after Christmas.

"He barricaded himself in his room," Freud told the team. "Probably got very little sleep. He's still tormented by worries about the big game."

Brian's face brightened. "Does that mean we won't be jogging this morning?"

"That's right," Freud said. The players cheered. "But Irene tells me we need wood for the fireplace. We'll be chopping wood for a while this morning."

"It snowed last night," T.J. pointed out. "Isn't it too cold, or too white, to chop wood?"

"Spoken like a true city boy," Margaret noted.

Fifteen minutes later, the Phils gathered near the woodshed behind the house. Brian and Sam had managed to chop down the pine tree, but now the other team members were ready to try their luck swinging an axe.

Edgar picked it up. "This doesn't look so difficult." He raised the axe over his head, brought it down—and completely missed the tree trunk.

"Nice going," Annie suggested.

Edgar handed her the axe. She raised it ... and completely missed the tree trunk.

"You guys are pathetic," T.J. muttered. "Give me the axe."

He raised the axe and brought it down—and splintered the tree trunk badly.

"Well, that clears everything up," Julie noted cheerfully.

Henry, who had ventured outside to see what everyone was doing, wandered over and took the axe out of T.J.'s hands. "At this rate, you'll be here all day. Let me show you how it's done."

Henry took the axe, examined the edge of the blade to see how sharp it was, then lifted it and brought it down swiftly. It made a clean cut in the tree trunk.

"I forgot to mention I've had some experience chopping wood, too," Henry said.

Each of the Phils took a turn at chopping and a half hour later Irene had enough logs to last a month.

WHEN THE PLAYERS RETURNED to the house, they found Rock, unshaven and weary, pacing the living room.

"Sit down," he commanded. "We're going to look at films."

Brian plopped into a recliner. "Terrific! How about a disaster flick?"

"Or a Bruce Willis movie," suggested T.J.

"I vote for *Shakespeare in Love*," Julie chimed in.

"Knock it off," Rock grumbled.

The players and Glory made themselves comfortable as Freud slipped film of the San Francisco Hackers' playoff victory over the Houston Space Cadets into a projector.

"All this holiday celebrating has messed up your brains. You've had your fun. Now it's back to work. You're playing the team everyone considers the best. The Hackers are the Green Bay Packers, Dallas Cowboys and San Francisco Forty-niners all wrapped into one. They are awesome. They're going after their third straight Brains Bowl title. But they lost one game this year and they aren't unbeatable. You can whip them if you play the best game of your lives!"

The game film began to roll as Freud provided the narration.

"First up is Wolfgang Heller, the Hackers' world specialist. Heller graduated from the Free University of Berlin, then bounced around Europe studying in London, Paris and Heidelberg."

Wolfgang's long hair endeared him to women, but Rock was not impressed. "If he played for me, I'd make him get a haircut. Who knows—maybe he's like Salmon. Cut his hair and he loses all his powers."

"Samson," Margaret said. "Not Salmon."

"Too bad you aren't that quick with the answers on game days," Rock noted.

Freud continued: "As you know, Wolfgang is the leading scorer in the game, hair or no hair … Up next is Jake Clayton, their sports ace. He's a former pilot and he's nuts. He gets under your skin and while you're trying to figure out what he's doing, he beats you to the buzzer and answers the question. Watch him, Chase. He'll confuse the hell out of you."

"Like Margaret?"

"Be careful, Chase," Margaret warned. "I can put evil spells on people who upset me."

Rock grimaced. "Yeah. Like Margaret."

"Up next is Maxwell Tweed, their quotations guru," Freud said. "We all know about Tweed's adventures—how he climbed Mount Everest, raced on the NASCAR circuit for four years, then joined the F.B.I. Now, he's a fearless and reckless player who loves to intimidate people. Julie, he'll probably feel you out, then go for the kill. Don't let him scare you.

"This is Jaycee Yancey, their popular arts specialist. She was a colonel before she retired from the Army. Don't flirt with her, Brian, unless you want to lose a couple teeth. She has no interest in romance."

"She just hasn't met a man who can handle her," Brian suggested.

"My money's on Jaycee," T.J. said.

"Next up," Freud said, "is Cynthia Medlow, their history starter." Cynthia was an attractive brunette, about twenty-two or twenty-three years old.

"How come Sam gets to tangle with a bombshell like Cynthia and I have to butt heads with a military tightass?" Brian complained.

"Luck of the draw, kid," Rock snarled. "Deal with it."

"Medlow may look like a swinger, but don't be fooled," Freud said. "She's a history fanatic, a real history junkie. She's written books like *The Last Time I Saw Babylon* and *The Louisiana Purchase Exposed*. You'll need all your wits to beat her, Sam!"

"And you'd better do it, kid," mumbled Rock.

"Yes, sir."

"Any idea how you're going to do it?"

"None at all."

"That's what I thought." Rock turned to Freud. "Where did you say you found him?"

Freud resumed his narrative: "This is Leroy Hollinger, their Renaissance Man. He was a preacher before his church kicked him out. He's well versed in religion, science and astronomy. Weak in some other areas. Hit him where it hurts, Margaret."

Margaret was shocked. "I beg your pardon?"

"I meant, exploit his weaknesses."

"Oh. I can do that."

"And this is Hackers' coach Bronco Griffin," Freud noted.

"An insufferable snob and a bore," Rock commented.

"Not to mention, two-time winner of the Brains Bowl," Brian noted.

Rock scowled, "Yeah, well, he was lucky. We'll put him in his place."

After dinner, Rock and Freud conferred on strategy in the den while the rest of the team gathered to study in the living room. T.J. had trouble concentrating. "I can't stop thinking about Kathy and our night together. Brian, give me her phone number so I can call her when we get back to civilization."

Brian shrugged. "I don't have her number. It was obvious I wouldn't need it, so I threw it away."

"*What?* You jerk! How am I going to find her?"

"Isn't she in the phone book?" Julie asked.

"No. I looked before we left Chicago."

"Did you check the Internet?" asked Juanita.

"Couldn't find a phone number or e-mail address."

"Maybe she'll contact you," Annie suggested.

"I doubt it. She probably wants to forget me. She was a nice girl. She'd never done anything like that before."

"Well, cheer up," Edgar said. "There are plenty of other—"

"If you say 'dogs in the kennel', I'll lock you out of the house," Margaret growled.

Edgar, ever the diplomat, paused. "Let's say there are plenty of other women out there."

"Not bad, Edgar," Margaret noted. "You're doing better."

Juanita picked up her guitar and strummed it. "After listening to Sam complain about all the trouble he was having with Julie, I wrote a country song about it. It's called 'Goodnight, Sam'. Would you like to hear it?"

"No!" Sam and Julie snapped.

"Sure, why not," T.J. said.

"It beats working," Margaret suggested.

"All right. Here goes ...

"When we're together, it's not a date;
When we stay out, we don't stay late;
and when I get home, you've got to leave—
my love is in Philadelphia.

"Don't ask me out, but if I ask you
We'll have some fun and then we'll kiss;
but when I get home, you've got to leave—
my love is in Philadelphia.

"Goodnight, Sam; Goodnight, Sam;
close the door as you leave;
sure, you're fun, but you've got to go
my love's in Philadelphia."

The other Phils applauded as Sam and Julie slipped lower in their seats.

IN THE DEN IN THE BACK of the house, Rock and Freud heard the applause.

"They're goofing off again," Rock grumbled. "They just

don't get it. What does it take to make them realize Armageddon is waiting for us in Seattle?"

Freud leaned back in his chair. "If they don't let off steam once in a while they'll explode. You'll have a team of zombies playing for you."

"They're *always* letting off steam. In Chicago, they caroused around the nightspots. When we got here, they went gallivanting off to town behind my back, and I still haven't figured out where the tree in the living room came from. I don't think Irene chopped it down, carried it in on her back and decorated it. It's time those meatballs stopped letting off steam and focused on the game!"

Freud nodded. "You're right. But at the same time, you need to take a page out of their book and unwind a little. You're becoming more withdrawn and morose every day."

Rock thought that over. "I had a dream Christmas morning. Scared me bad." He told Freud about the pool and his ferocious battle with the whale. "What do you think it means?"

"Maybe you've been eating too much tuna."

Rock glared. "I'm serious, you two-bit shrink. It was more than a dream—it was an experience ... almost as real as this is. What does it mean?"

Freud thought about the dream as he sipped a cup of coffee. "All right," he said, at last. "You dreamed of a large, terrifying whale. You're aware that a lot of people—sportswriters, team members, fans—have compared your quest for the Brains title to Ahab's quest for the great White Whale, Moby Dick, aren't you?"

"What's your point?"

"You've been overwrought with all this bowl pressure, Rock. The dream was a symbolic depiction of your obsession. Take it as a warning that you've got to change. Your system can't take it anymore."

Rock grimaced. "So what am I supposed to do?"

"See what's happening to you. That's the way to conquer the demons that are driving you to madness!"

"How?"

"By rising above it! Take charge of your life. Win the bowl on your own terms—don't let obsessions destroy your life. Your team finds ways to let off steam. You must do it, too. Put things in perspective. There's more to life than the playoffs."

"But this is *the Brains Bowl*. If I don't give it everything I've got, and we lose, I don't know what I'd do."

"But we have a *better* chance of winning if you aren't so intimidating and obsessed—if you and the team aren't basket cases. The team will think clearer and play better."

Rock glared at him. "What if you're wrong? What if they lose because they didn't try hard enough? You going to say, 'Sorry, Rock. Guess I miscalculated. Tough luck.'"

"I'm *not* wrong, Rock. It's my business to know these things."

Rock sighed. "I'll think about it." He rose from the recliner and started back to his room. "But when the lion's at the door, it's a little late to change the lock." He hesitated as he reached the den door. "And tell Irene to cut back on the tuna salad sandwiches!"

As time passed that evening, the Phils wandered off to their rooms. Sam noticed Julie was nowhere to be seen. Perhaps she had retreated to her room for quiet time alone.

He ascended the stairs, careful not to attract attention, and approached her door. The wood floor creaked under his weight. He paused. She undoubtedly would reject his advances again and throw him out of her room. Did he really want that kind of aggravation? Wasn't he under enough stress? He started back toward the stairway.

Suddenly, Julie's door opened. Dressed in a pink nightie, she grabbed Sam by the arm, led him into her room and gave him a long, passionate kiss.

After a few moments, she let go of him. He sprawled on the bed.

"I've got to face the truth," she said.

"You love me?"

"No. I'm lousy at handling pressure. ... You've got to get out of here."

"But, Julie. You're obviously attracted to me!"

"I suppose so, but I'm engaged to David. Let's be honest. The only reason you're in my room and he isn't is that he's hundreds of miles away and you're here."

"Sounds good to me."

"But it's not right, Sam. I'm engaged. I can't let the passion of the moment screw up a long-term relationship. You understand, don't you?"

"Not in the least."

"Good. Get out!"

She pushed him toward the door and forced him into the hallway. As she closed the door, Sam stared at it. *"Stop toying with me, Julie! ... I know! I'll change my name to David. Then when we're together, you'll be with David and you won't have a guilty conscience. What do you say? How's that for thinking outside the box? ... Julie? ... Did you hear me, Julie?"*

As THE TEAM RETIRED FOR THE NIGHT, Rock barricaded himself in his room to study charts which listed questions the Hackers' had answered incorrectly over the course of the season. It was reminiscent of Ahab's "yellowish sea charts."

> At intervals, he would refer to piles of old log-books beside him, wherein were set down the ... places in which, on various former voyages of various ships, sperm whales had been captured or seen.

28

PERCY SMATHERS GAZED DOWN on State Street from the temporary "Late Night Edition" command center in Chicago as snow flakes fluttered to the pavement Friday afternoon. The Phils, alas, were nowhere in sight.

"We've wasted enough time," he told Diane Mercross. "Now we pull out all the stops. Tonight we'll offer three hundred thousand dollars to the first person to tell us where the Phils are hiding out. People will turn the country inside out trying to find them. There won't be any place safe for them to hide."

He plopped into his leather office chair and propped his feet on his desk. "Hell, I'd offer twice that if they were found dead, but I can't. The network is a little squeamish about things like that."

He stared at the ceiling. "You know, Diane, I kept asking myself ... if I were as dumb and obsessed and depraved as Rock, where would I hide the team? ... You know what I came up with? I'd hide the team in the basement of the Windy City Dome. I'd have people looking for me all over the country, and I'd be down there preparing for the game. What do you think?"

She smiled. "Interesting idea, but I think someone would have seen them by now."

"Wouldn't you feel like a damn fool if that's where they're hiding out?"

"Yes, I would."

"Then I suggest you take a half dozen people over there and search the stadium thoroughly, from top to bottom."

"Yes, sir."

She hadn't budged from her chair.

"Now!"

"Yes, sir!"

Three hours later Diane returned to the office. "We searched the stadium thoroughly. I can state unequivocably they are not there!"

"All right," Percy said. "Let me think a little more about this. If I were Rock Nelson—God forbid—where would I take the team? Where would I hide the players? ... Hell, I don't know. If I were Rock Nelson, I'd shoot myself to put me out of my misery."

29

ON SATURDAY, AFTER THE JOGGING and wood cutting were finished, the Phils engaged in a game-length scrimmage, with the six starters going up against the other three Phils and Henry, who said he was considering giving up bus driving to become a Brains player.

Henry stunned the Phils by slamming the buzzer first and answering questions about which of the fifty states had the largest Asian population (California) and the author who wrote *The Bridge Over the River Kwai* and *Planet of the Apes* (Pierre Boulle).

"That settles it," Rock declared. "Henry is on the team and Sam can drive the bus."

Freud hurriedly pointed out that it was too late for Henry to sign on as a player in the Brains Bowl. He also whispered to Rock that he had better do something to build up Sam's self-esteem, since he had just torn it down another notch.

"I was joking," Rock told the team. "I didn't really think Sam could drive the bus. "

AFTER DINNER SATURDAY, when Rock was safely barricaded in his room, Sam, T.J., Brian and Chase entered the kitchen dressed in disguises.

"Halloween already?" asked Irene.

"We need to ask a favor," Brian said.

"Ohhh, no! I'm not going to let you take the pickup into town. Rock was very angry when you took off in the bus. He used language I haven't heard before."

"Irene, darling," said T.J., "let's not forget that you wouldn't have the pickup if it wasn't for us."

"You play dirty, T.J. Do you play dirty in the games, too?"

"Whenever I can. C'mon, Irene. This is important!"

"Rock will kill me if he finds out."

She pulled the keys out of her apron and dropped them on the counter. She started off toward the living room. "Of course, if you stole the keys, I suppose there wouldn't be much I could do about it."

"You're a dear!" Sam said.

"And don't wreck the pickup!" she said, as they grabbed the keys and hustled out the kitchen door.

In Moberly, Chase waited in the pickup as Sam, Brian and T.J. scrounged around Harvey's Appliances. The young owner of the store, Harvey Woodson, impatiently drummed his fingers on a desk.

"All right, Curly, Moe and Larry, are you going to just look or are you going to buy something? It's closing time!"

"You don't have much of a selection," T.J. noted. "Back where I come from, most stores carry a half dozen brands of televisions."

"What's wrong with Rudolfo televisions? We sell a lot of them."

"For one thing, I've never heard of them," T.J. said.

"They come from Warsaw."

"Poland?" Sam asked.

"No! Warsaw, Indiana. I only sell American products."

"Does it have on-screen programming?" Sam asked

"What's that?"

"What about split screens?" asked T.J. "Or multiple language support?"

"Look, if you want a computer, buy a computer. If you want a good, basic, no-frills television set at a great price, buy this Rudolfo."

T.J. looked at the sticker. "I've got news for you, Harvey. The price is not so great. I could buy an RCA or a Motorola for this, and have enough left over to—"

"All right. We've talked enough. What's it going to be, sports? You gonna buy it?"

"We don't have much choice," Sam suggested. "We've got to get back to the ranch."

"All right," Brian said. "What kind of warranty do we get on this Rudolfo?"

"It expires about the time you put it in your pickup."

"Great doing business with you, Harvey," T.J. said. "I haven't been fleeced like this since I paid two hundred bucks for prize fight tickets and the fight ended in forty seconds of the first round."

As T.J., Sam and Chase lifted the television into the pickup, Brian started off down the street.

"Where are you going?" Sam asked.

"I noticed a tavern a couple blocks away. I'm going to check out the women. I'll be back in the morning."

"Are you nuts?" T.J. said. "What happens if Rock and Freud notice you're gone?"

"Good question. Make sure it doesn't happen."

As Brian approached Mandy's Tavern he could hear a juke-box playing "Ruby, Don't Take Your Love to Town." Inside, townsfolk were scattered throughout the joint. Two shapely young women coddled drinks at the bar. They seemed to be in their early twenties. And alone.

Brian appropriated a stool. "Mind if I join you, or is this a private orgy?"

"Private," said a brunette.

"But you can join us," said a blonde with dazzling blue eyes.

"Karie, behave yourself," the brunette told her. "He might think we're really into that."

"Shame on me," Brian said. "You ladies come here often?"

"Sometimes. On the weekends," noted Karie. "Haven't seen you before."

"New in town."

"What would you like?" asked a middle-aged bearded bartender.

"I think I have it," said Brian. "But give me a Bud anyway."

"Plan on staying here long?" the brunette asked.

"As long as it takes. You know, I have this problem. I don't have any place to stay tonight. What do you think I should do about that?"

"There's a motel down the street," noted the brunette. "Ask for a room that has a lock on the door and a mattress that doesn't sink in the middle."

"Sounds like you've been there before," Brian noted.

"You might say that. I worked there as a maid."

"Oh. Right."

The blonde moved closer to Brian. "I might know some-place you could stay. We can talk about it."

"By all means."

Karie nodded toward the door. "Get lost, Cindy."

Brian smiled. "You heard her. Get lost, Cindy."

Irene was aghast when T.J., Sam and Chase returned to The Homestead carrying a television set.

"Are you crazy? Rock will kill us! He was very definite. No televisions! They interfere with your concentration."

"I go crazy when I don't have my daily fix of television," T.J. muttered. "I get mean. Want to do all sorts of nasty things to the cook."

"Do you need help carrying it?" Irene asked.

"No thanks. We can manage," Sam said.

Margaret looked up from the book she was skimming in the living room. "Wow! A Rudolfo! Always wanted a Rudolfo television but I could never afford one."

"She's kidding, isn't she?" T.J. asked Julie.

"I don't think so," Julie said.

Edgar's reaction to the new arrival was different. "Oh, Lord. You're bringing the symbol of the decline of civilization right into our residence. Personally, I like Ernie Kovacs' description of television: A medium, so called because it is neither rare nor well done."

Margaret agreed to let them put the television set in her room, since it was on the first floor and it would be convenient for the rest of the team.

30

EARLY SUNDAY MORNING, Brian climbed into Karie's Lexus and she drove a few miles down the road, dropping Brian off a short distance from The Homestead.

"Will I see you again?" she asked.

"Depends. Do you watch much television?"

"Who do you think you're kidding? What would you be doing in Moberly if you're on television?"

"I haven't the faintest idea." He kissed her. "You're a fine lady, Karie."

"You're not so bad yourself, Frankie."

The Lexus roared off and Brian headed toward The Homestead, using trees as cover in case Rock or Freud was prowling around the grounds.

Brian ducked inside the kitchen door just as Irene opened it to put some garbage out.

"Brian! Where have you been?"

"Couldn't sleep so I took a walk. What's for breakfast?"

Hitting the books and a game scrimmage filled the daylight hours on Sunday. In the evening, Rock and Freud plotted strategy in the den as players alternated studying with trips into Margaret's room to watch a few minutes of television.

A STRATEGY SESSION ON Monday was followed by speed drills to determine how the Brains performed under pressure. It was a disaster. In the afternoon, Rock retired to his room to brood. Most of the players were lounging around the living room when the front doorbell rang.

A delivery man handed over a bouquet of red and yellow roses and baby's breath to Brian, who answered the door.

"One of my ladies must have penetrated Rock's barrier of secrecy."

Annie inspected the card that came with the flowers. "These are for Julie, you ninny."

Julie rushed to the door. "For me?" She tore open the card. It was signed "Love, David."

"Wasn't that thoughtful!" she said.

"He doesn't miss a trick," Sam muttered.

T.J. looked up from the book on Middle Eastern culture he was skimming. "How did he know where you are? No one is supposed to know!"

"He's very resourceful. Maybe Henry's bus company told him."

Henry wandered in from the kitchen with a cup of hot chocolate. "The company doesn't know where we are. Rock wouldn't let me tell them our destination."

"Something is fishy here," Sam suggested. "Let's take a closer look at that stuffed bear David sent you."

"What? Why?"

"Because that may be the answer to this puzzle."

"Sam, you don't honestly believe David would do something underhanded to keep track of me?"

"He found you, didn't he? Show me the bear. And Annie, get a knife out of the kitchen. I may need to perform a little surgery."

"Oh, no! You aren't going to touch my bear!"

Annie retrieved a knife from the kitchen and Juanita fetched the bear from Julie's room.

Julie hugged the bear to her bosom. "I am *not* going to let you harm this innocent little bear, Sam Winslow. Maybe we should use that knife on your private parts instead!"

"Things are getting nasty," T.J. commented. He pulled up a chair so he could be closer.

Sam took the knife from Annie. "We've got to find out if this is an innocent little bear—or a trojan horse. We won't harm the bear. I'll make a cut along the back of his neck. It can be easily repaired."

"You're going too far this time, Sam Winslow!"

"Don't holler when I'm performing surgery. This is a delicate operation."

Julie covered her eyes as Sam made a cut along the neck. Then he reached down inside the bear and felt around.

"I told you Sam! It's an innocent little bear. You really screwed up this time!"

Sam pulled his hand out of the bear. In it was a small gadget.

"I'd be willing to bet this is a GPS device David put in the bear so he could track you. He sure trusts you, Julie. If you marry him, will he have detectives following you everywhere you go?"

Julie was confused. "David wouldn't do that. There must be some other explanation."

"Then how did he know where you were?" asked Annie.

Julie didn't answer. She looked crushed. Sam put his arms around her. "It's all right, Julie. You couldn't have known he would do something like that."

As most of the Phils cracked the books or napped in the living room late Monday evening, T.J. switched channels on the television in Margaret's room until he found a show that looked interesting. "Late Night Edition" was just coming on. The graphic appearing behind Percy Smathers read, "ON THE TRAIL OF THE PHILS."

"Percy's leading off with us again!" T.J. announced. The players gathered around the television set as Percy introduced the show's first segment.

"ROCK NELSON AND HIS CHICAGO PHILOSOPHERS ARE IN HIDING BEFORE THE BIG GAME, BUT 'LATE NIGHT EDITION' IS HOT ON THEIR TRAIL. SINCE WE ANNOUNCED A THREE HUNDRED THOUSAND DOLLAR REWARD FOR ANYONE WHO TELLS US WHERE THE PHILS ARE HIDING, THOUSANDS OF PEOPLE HAVE CALLED IN TIPS.

"HERE'S WHAT WE KNOW SO FAR. THE DAY AFTER THEIR PLAYOFF VICTORY, THE PHILS LEFT CHICAGO BY BUS FOR A SECRET HIDEAWAY. WHERE DID THEY GO? WE HAVE FOLLOWED UP MANY LEADS.

"RUDY KELLOGG, A GAS STATION ATTENDANT ON HILTON HEAD ISLAND OFF THE COAST OF SOUTH CARO-LINA, SWEARS HE SAW CHASE AND MARGARET ON THE ISLAND YESTERDAY MORNING."

Film of Rudy rolled ...

"IT WAS THEM. I KNOW IT WAS. CHASE HAD THE LOOK OF A KILLER AND MARGARET ACTED WEIRD, LIKE SOME-ONE WHO'S TWO FRUIT LOOPS SHORT OF A BOWL, AND THEY COULDN'T FOOL ME EVEN THOUGH THEY SIGNED IN AT THE HOTEL AS MR. AND MRS. JAMISON. THEY CLAIMED THEY WERE ON THEIR HONEYMOON, BUT I KNEW THEY

WERE REALLY PHILOSOPHERS IN HIDING. SO DO I GET THE
REWARD FOR SPOTTING THEM?"

"MEANWHILE, A SURVEILLANCE CAMERA AT A BANK
IN JACKSON HOLE, WYOMING REVEALED THAT THREE MEN
AND A WOMAN DRESSED UP AS CHICAGO PHILOSOPHER
PLAYERS HELD UP THE BANK. POLICE DON'T THINK THEY
WERE THE REAL PHILS, ALTHOUGH THEY HAVEN'T RULED
THAT OUT ENTIRELY.

"OUR FAVORITE SIGHTING GOES TO MARVA HILLIARD
OF COOS BAY, OREGON, WHO TOLD THE *NATIONAL EXPOSER*
THAT ALIENS WHO LANDED IN A UFO CONFIDED TO HER
THAT THE PHILS WERE EN ROUTE TO THE PLANET REGINA
TO PREPARE FOR THE BIG GAME.

"AND SO THE QUESTION REMAINS: WHERE ARE THE
PHILS HIDING? WE'LL FIND THEM. AND IF YOU HELP US,
YOU COULD WIN A COOL THREE HUNDRED THOUSAND DOL-
LARS IN CASH! JUST CALL THIS 800 NUMBER. OPERATORS
ARE STANDING BY."

"I don't know which is harder to believe," Edgar said.
"That we flew to the planet Regina together or that we went
to church together."

"I could use an extra three hundred grand," T.J. mused.

"Oh, no," Julie snapped. "Let's nip this in the bud. We
are *not* going after the three hundred thousand. Rock would
kill us."

"Now, hold on," Edgar said. "The lad for once has an
interesting idea. Suppose we collect the three hundred grand
and ruin the credibility of 'Late Night Edition' at the same
time. When Rock is relatively sane, he wouldn't object to
that."

"You have a devious, conniving mind," Annie said.

"Of course he does," T.J. noted. "He worked for the government."

"*My* skills might be helpful," Chase, the former con man and burglar, suggested.

"I don't know," Margaret said. "It might be too much for me. After all ..."

The others finished the sentence: "I'm seventy-two years old!"

Margaret glared. "Well, I am!"

"Do you think we could pull it off?" Brian asked Edgar.

"Of course! Why, when I was in the State Department, we pulled off bigger scams than this and got away with it! Remember Iran-Contra? With Chase's help, and help from all of you, I think we could do it."

"We *might* be able to con them out of the three hundred grand," Julie conceded. "But we'll have to do it quickly, so Rock doesn't find out."

Sam smiled wistfully. "I think I used those words on our last date, when I was trying to seduce you."

"Let's hope this operation is more successful," Brian suggested.

31

DURING A GAME SCRIMMAGE Tuesday, Rock asked Margaret to name, in order, the world's four most populous countries. As Margaret pondered the question, Henry passed through the living room on his way to the front door.

"China, India, the United States and Indonesia," he said. "What did I win?"

"A free trip to the hospital," Margaret growled.

"Oops. See you later," Henry mumbled, as he ducked out the door.

Rock turned to Freud. "Are you sure it's too late to sign him up?"

After dinner, Freud and Rock retreated to their rooms—Freud to sleep and Rock to brood—and the Phils gathered in Edgar's room on the second floor. Glory curled up near the fireplace for a nap.

"Why does your room have a fireplace and ours don't?" Brian asked.

"I *always* have a fireplace," Edgar said. "That's the way things are. It's in my contract."

"So, have you decided how we're going to sandbag 'Late Night Edition'?" Julie asked.

"I prefer not to call it sandbagging. Words like that get you in trouble. In Washington, we didn't 'sandbag' the press or the opposition party; we used a combination of disinformation and creative storytelling to manipulate a situation to our advantage."

"You sandbagged them," T.J. said.

"Yes, well, I suppose we did. This is a relatively easy operation. When we plotted to overthrow governments, that was tricky. I remember the volatile situation in Chile—"

"Forget Chile," Margaret said. "How are we going to pull this off, Edgar?"

"Oh, yes ... well, we need to make a few preparations. I figure we can carry out the operation Wednesday evening."

"Tomorrow? On New Year's Eve? That doesn't give us much time."

"We can't wait any longer. Friday, we fly to Seattle. By then everyone will know where we are."

"What's the plan?" Sam asked.

"Well, we'll call 'Late Night Edition'. We'll offer proof that we know what we're talking about. We'll agree to reveal the Philosophers' whereabouts only if 'Late Night Edition' carries it in a live telecast Wednesday evening. And, finally, we'll insist 'Late Night Edition' transfers the three hundred grand into a secret overseas bank account *before* the show airs."

"How can we set up a secret account so quickly?" Brian asked.

"I just happen to have one," Edgar admitted.

"When do we contact Percy?" Julie asked.

"I'll borrow Irene's pickup and drive into town tonight with T.J. He says he's familiar with St. Louis and has friends there. While I call Percy's gang, T.J. will make a phone call or two to his pals.

"Wednesday evening, after Rock is barricaded inside his room, we'll all head out on the bus. Probably about eight."

"Bound for St. Louis?" Julie asked.

"Right. That's where the Phils are hiding out in an establishment that has a rather shady reputation."

"You're talking about a whorehouse?" Sam asked.

"Precisely."

"But how do you know where a whorehouse is in St. Louis?"

"That's where I come in," T.J. said. "I'll call some of my old college buddies in St. Louis who will find a house we can use, hire a few women and set up everything."

"They need to rent a van for us, too," Edgar noted. "The van will shuttle us between the bus and the house. I don't want Percy's crew to see the bus. If they follow us, they'll be looking for a van."

"It might work," Margaret said.

"You worry me, Edgar," Juanita remarked. "You're too good at this."

Edgar smiled. "Your taxpayer dollars at work."

"When you're in Moberly tonight, will you do a favor for me?" Julie asked. "Find a truck driver going on a long haul and tape this to the side of his truck." She handed Edgar the GPS tracking device David had hidden inside the stuffed bear. "I don't want David knowing where we are."

"Right!" Sam said. "He's such a sleazeball he'd probably try to collect the three hundred grand."

"Leave it to us," Edgar said. "T.J. and I will take care of it."

32

On Wednesday, Rock called another game scrimmage. Freud asked the Renaissance Man and Woman, Edgar and Juanita, "What did it mean if a cowboy 'didn't know his cans'?"

Neither player hit the buzzer.

"C'mon, Woodford," Rock scowled. "You ought to know this!"

Edgar shrugged. "The subject never came up at the Harvard Club or the State Department."

"Enlighten these poor ignorant souls," Rock told Freud. "What's the answer?"

"Cowboys on the range usually didn't have much reading material, so they memorized the ingredients on food cans. A cowboy who didn't know his cans had not memorized the labels."

Brian was flabbergasted. "That morsel of information ranks right up there with making words out of alphabet soup."

"What did you say, mister?" Rock demanded.

Brian grimaced. "I said I want to learn my cans before the big game."

"Damn right!" Rock bellowed.

AFTER PRACTICE, ROCK RETREATED to his room and locked the door, as usual. The Philosophers finished off dinner quickly, then prepared to move out for their New Year's Eve outing, with Henry driving the bus.

"I don't understand," Henry grumbled. "Are you sure this has Rock's approval? If it doesn't, I'm in deep trouble."

"Of course it does," Edgar assured him. "He asked us to drive to St. Louis on a top-secret mission."

"Maybe I'd better ask Rock," Henry said, as he started off toward the coach's room.

Edgar grabbed him by the arm. "Rock is in no mood to be bothered. Besides, I told you. This is a *secret* mission. He would deny everything."

Not all the players were needed to pull off the scam, but all insisted on going along, leaving only Rock, Freud and Irene at The Homestead.

The bus stopped at Farley's Drugstore in Moberly, where T.J. called his friends to get the address of the house. He told them to park the van two blocks east of the house. Edgar purchased four cheap cell phones.

The bus rambled south along state road 63, then merged onto Interstate 70 and rumbled east toward St. Louis.

Annie gazed out a window at the passing landscape. Only a distant floodlight mounted on a farmhouse and the headlights of cars cruising along the interstate alleviated the darkness. "This must be how soldiers feel when they take off on secret missions," she suggested.

"What is she talking about?" Henry asked. "Are we doing something that could get us killed?"

"Of course not," snapped Edgar, who was riding shotgun in the seat nearest Henry. "It could land us in jail a few years. Nothing serious."

"*Jail?* What the hell am I involved in?"

"Keep your eyes on the road," Chase said. "The less you know, the better."

"Jail would serve you right," Margaret grumbled, "You tried to show me up when you answered that question about populated countries. Anybody can get one or two questions right. It's doing it under pressure that separates the pros from the amateurs."

"Besides." Brian said, "she's seventy-two years old."

Margaret smiled. "Not any more, loverboy. Today is my seventy-third birthday!"

The team burst into song, singing happy birthday to Maggie.

The live "Late Night Edition" broadcast was scheduled to begin at 10:30 P.M. At 10:15, Henry parked the bus behind a white van on West Kingsbury Avenue on the west side of St. Louis. He became noticeably nervous when Edgar insisted he be ready for "a fast getaway". If Rock had sanctioned the outing, why would a fast getaway be necessary?

Edgar gave three of the cell phones to Margaret, T.J. and Chase. Margaret and Annie stayed behind with Henry in the bus. The other seven players piled into the van, with Chase at the wheel. A block from the house, Sam, Edgar and Juanita got out of the van. The others waited in the van.

Sam, Edgar and Juanita strolled down Kingsbury Avenue and approached Diane Mercross, the "Late Night Edition" temptress who had tried to compromise Sam. Diane was staked out in front of a large brick ranch-style house. Two camera crews were deployed nearby, not far from two remote broadcasting vans.

"It *is* you!" Diane exclaimed. She motioned in the direction of a bush. Percy Smathers stood up, brushed himself off and approached them.

"I'm relieved to see you. I feared this would be another wild goose chase. We've had all sorts of crank calls about where you were hiding out. One guy who called this afternoon claimed to be Julie's financé. He said the Phils were on an interstate, apparently staying on the move in a motor home to avoid being seen. Said he was tracking you with GPS technology."

"Obviously, a poor deranged soul," Sam suggested.

"Are you ready to transfer the money?" Edgar inquired.

"Yes. So what's the setup?"

"Like I told you on the phone," Edgar said. "The Phils are holed up in that house. You've got an exclusive. No one else knows."

Just then the white van pulled into the driveway and Julie, Brian and T.J. got out and headed toward the house. Then Chase drove back the van down the street.

Percy's adrenaline kicked in. "This is terrific. At 10:30, we go on the air. Two minutes later, I want team members to come out of that house. Use any excuse you need to—shout 'fire', 'police!', anything."

"Of course, Percy. No problem," Sam said.

"Transfer the money *now*," Juanita insisted. "It's not that we don't trust you …"

"Yes, it is," Edgar said. "Do it *now*! Transfer the money to this account."

He handed a slip of paper bearing an account number to Diane Mercross. She stepped into one of the "Late Night Edition" remote vans and entered the data on a laptop computer. Two minutes later, she exited the van.

"Its done," she said.

Edgar used a cell phone to call Margaret, who was sitting in the bus next to Annie.

"See if the money is in," Margaret told Annie, whose laptop was connected to the Internet via a wireless connection.

"Affirmative," said Annie.

"It's in!" Margaret told Edgar.

"Now keep your part of the bargain!" Percy told Edgar.

"It's show time!" Edgar declared.

"Thanks," Percy said. "This is terrific. A world exclusive! We've been promoting it all day. Our ratings will go through the roof! ... One minute to air time! Get ready! Throw the floodlights on the house!"

Suddenly the house was bathed in light.

With Percy's attention focused on the house, Edgar, Sam and Juanita slipped away and started walking back down Kingsbury Avenue.

At precisely 10:30, Percy went on the air live.

"GOOD EVENING FROM ST. LOUIS, MISSOURI. I AM PERCY SMATHERS, YOUR HOST FOR 'LATE NIGHT EDITION', AND ON THIS NEW YEAR'S EVE, WE ARE PRESENTING THE EXCLUSIVE STORY THE WHOLE WORLD HAS BEEN WAITING FOR ..."

BACK AT THE HOMESTEAD on the outskirts of Moberly, Rock tired of pacing the floor, but he knew it was no use trying to sleep. He had slept very little in recent weeks—and when he did, he dreamed about weird things, like huge whales and Hacker coach Bronco Griffin.

He unbolted his door and ventured into the living room. No one was there.

The players must be studying in their rooms, he decided. He started toward the kitchen, but stopped when he heard noise coming from Margaret's room. He knocked, but Margaret didn't come to the door. He opened it.

Margaret wasn't there, but a television set had been left on. *A television set?* Rock had ordered all televisions removed from the house, yet Margaret had one in her room. What was going on? Heads would roll over this!

Rock plopped down on the bed and picked up the remote control. He switched from channel to channel … from news shows to "The Tonight Show", from college basketball games to David Letterman, from cooking shows to "Late Night Edition" … Wait a minute … What was happening on "Late Night Edition"?

Percy Smathers, stationed near a large ranch-style house, mentioned something about the Phils. What was the sleazy old goat up to now?

"'LATE NIGHT EDITION' HAS UNCOVERED THE SECRET HIDEAWAY WHERE THE CHICAGO PHILOSOPHERS HAVE BEEN HOLED UP. COACH ROCK NELSON INSISTED HIS TEAM PREPARE FOR THE BOWL AWAY FROM THE GLARE OF PUBLICITY AND THE FANATICISM OF FANS, SO THIS IS WHERE HE BROUGHT HIS PLAYERS, TO THE HOUSE YOU SEE LIT UP BEHIND ME."

At that moment, people scurried out of the house and cameramen used telephoto lenses to film them.

"HERE THEY ARE NOW, THE CHICAGO PHILOSOPHERS!"

Diane Mercross hurried up the pathway leading to the house and stuck a microphone in front of a shapely brunette clad in nothing but a blue velvet bathrobe.

"YOUNG LADY, WERE YOU VISITING ONE OF THE PHILOSOPHERS TONIGHT?"

"PHILOSOPHERS? I DON'T THINK SO. LET'S SEE, THERE WAS AN AUTO MECHANIC, A DRUG DEALER ..."

Diane swallowed hard. "OBVIOUSLY, SHE HANGS OUT IN A DIFFERENT PART OF THE HOUSE. HERE'S ANOTHER YOUNG LADY. PARDON ME, MISS ... ARE YOU WITH THE PHILOSOPHERS?"

The young woman scowled. "WHAT'S GOING ON? YOU JUST CAUSED ME TO LOSE FIFTY BUCKS."

Diane was dumbstruck. "OH, MY GOD. HAVE THE CHICAGO PHILOSOPHERS BEEN HOLED UP IN A HOUSE OF PROSTITUTION?"

The girl looked around. "HAVE THEY? WHERE?"

"HERE! AREN'T YOU GIRLS HOOKERS?"

"WE PREFER TO THINK OF OURSELVES AS BUSINESSWOMEN WHO CHARGE BY THE HOUR. LIKE LAWYERS"

"BUT WHERE DID THE PHILOSOPHERS GO?"

"WHAT PHILOSOPHERS?"

"YES, WELL, UH ... BACK TO YOU, PERCY."

Flustered, Percy faced the camera. "THANK YOU, DIANE. WE'LL BE RIGHT BACK AFTER THESE COMMERCIALS."

IN ST. LOUIS, PERCY DESPERATELY attempted to figure out what was going on.

"Where are Edgar, Sam and Juanita? They've got my three hundred grand! And where are Julie, Brian and T.J.? I saw them go inside!"

The crew professed ignorance.

"Find them!" Percy ordered two assistants. The young men ran up the sidewalk and into the house.

"I think we've been had," Diane Mercross said.

"But six of the Philosophers were here five minutes ago! I talked to three of them! I *know they're here*. Find them!"

BACK AT THE HIDEAWAY, Freud was headed for the kitchen in search of an evening snack when he heard noise coming from Margaret's room and noticed the open door. As he moved closer, he was stunned to see Rock sitting on the bed watching television.

"What's going on, Rock?"

"You gotta see this! Percy Smathers and his moronic crew think we're holed up inside a whorehouse near St. Louis. They've got egg on their face on this one!"

PERCY SMATHERS WAS SO CAUGHT up in the commotion that he didn't realize he was on the air again.

One of his assistants opened a window in the house and called out, "THEY AREN'T HERE, PERCY! THIS IS JUST WHAT IT LOOKS LIKE! *THESE GIRLS ARE HOOK-ERS!*"

"*BUSINESSWOMEN,*" corrected one of the girls.

"FIND THE TEAM!" Percy ordered. "THEY WERE HERE FIVE MINUTES AGO. THEY COULDN'T HAVE GONE FAR! TRACK THEM DOWN BEFORE I MAKE A COMPLETE JACKASS OF MYSELF!"

"TOO LATE," Diane Mercross said. "YOU'RE ON THE AIR."

"WHAT?" Percy tried to save face. "WELCOME BACK TO ST. LOUIS. THE CHICAGO PHILOSOPHERS WERE HOLED UP IN THIS HOUSE UNTIL A FEW MINUTES AGO, BUT APPARENTLY THEY SAW US COMING AND HIGHTAILED IT OUT THE BACK DOOR. WE ARE TRYING TO TRACK THEM DOWN

AND SORT OUT THIS MESS. WE WILL KEEP YOU POSTED. FOR
NOW, LET'S GO BACK TO OUR STUDIOS IN CHICAGO."

The Phils who were in the St. Louis house—T.J., Julie and
Brian—had scrambled out the back door during all the com-
motion and ran through a neighbor's yard to Washington
Avenue, the street that ran parallel to Kingsbury Avenue.
Chase was waiting for them there with the van.

"Haul ass!" Brian shouted, as the trio of teammates
jumped into the van.

With brakes screeching, Chase hightailed it back to
Kingsbury Avenue, where the bus was waiting. He parked
the van in a driveway. Moments later, Sam, Edgar and Juanita jogged back from their encounter with Percy.

"Let's get out of here!" Edgar told Henry.

"Why? Did you rob a bank?"

"No, but we bagged three hundred grand for a few minutes work—"

"Wow!"

"—and five grand of it is yours if you get us back to The
Homestead fast!"

"Hang on to your seats!" Henry pressed down the gas
pedal. "Like I said, this bus has a jet engine."

The bus barrelled around a curve, brakes squealing.

"Not so fast," Sam cautioned. "We don't want to get
arrested."

"What do you think?" Annie asked Edgar. "Did we pull
it off?"

"You were all magnificent. It was perfect! We got the three
hundred grand and succeeded in making Percy Smathers
and 'Late Night Edition' look like fools in front of the entire
world. All in all, it's been quite a New Year's Eve!"

BACK AT THE HIDEAWAY, ROCK and Freud tried to make sense of what they had just seen on television.

"Somebody set Percy up," Freud said. "He's had it coming for a long time!"

"But who?"

"I think our players did it."

Rock shook his head. "No way. They're here!"

"It wouldn't be the first time they took off without your permission."

Rock growled, "Are the players in their rooms?"

Freud quickly searched the house. Three minutes later he returned to Margaret's room.

"I can't find any of them!"

Rock wearily shook his head. "Do they *ever* hit the books? Am I the only one who knows the biggest game of our lives is coming up?"

"They sure get around, don't they," Freud mused. "They never cease to amaze me!"

Rock smiled slightly. "I wish they'd put some of that energy into their practice sessions. ... Don't let them know we found out about this."

"You aren't going to break their necks?"

"No. You say if I want to win the Brains Bowl, I've got to cut them some slack. So I'm all right with this. I can deal with it. But if we *lose* the bowl, I'll break their necks and yours, too. That's fair, isn't it?"

33

ON THURSDAY—NEW YEAR'S DAY—the team jogged and chopped wood. Then Rock gathered his crew in the living room.

"I couldn't find you last night," he began gruffly. "I assume you were at a church function."

"Oh, yes!"

"Absolutely!"

"They had a potluck supper at George and Mollie Relford's home!" T.J. added.

Rock flinched. T.J. was laying it on a little thick. "All right. Now, as you know, we fly to Seattle tomorrow morning. This is our last day here. You should be in top form by now. You should know everything you need to know. You should be functioning like a well-oiled machine." He shook his head. "If I believed that, I'd be crazier than people say I am. We've still got a lot of work to do. Make every minute count between now and game time!"

THE PHILS STUDIED HARD during the day. That evening, with Rock barricaded in his room, they gathered around the living room to study. At 10 P.M., Irene and Henry bustled in from the kitchen carrying trays of cookies and bottles of champagne and soft drinks.

"I thought you might enjoy a little New Year's celebration," Irene said.

The weary Phils broke into broad smiles.

Brian grabbed a handful of chocolate chip cookies. "Despite the coaching staff's failure to allow my women friends to join us, this has been an adventure I won't forget."

"And your women friends appreciated it, too," suggested Juanita.

"Edgar enjoyed it here," Annie said mischievously. "Am I the only one who's noticed that he's smitten with Irene?"

Edgar blushed. "I am not smitten with anyone. Mrs. Harper happens to be a fine lady who seems to enjoy my company."

"Well, I don't know if I'd go that far," Irene said, smiling.

A few minutes later, Sam barged into the kitchen looking for more cookies and found Julie nibbling on chocolate frosting she had scraped off a yellow cake.

"Oh-oh," Sam said. "We have a felony in progress. Grand theft frosting."

She smiled slyly. "Well, if it isn't David Number Two."

He pulled up a chair and helped himself to a spoonful of frosting. "I didn't think you heard my suggestion about changing my name."

"I heard it. … Maybe David Number One should change his name to Sam."

"Then you'd be engaged to Sam."

"Yes, but he'd be back in Philadelphia."

"You seem very relaxed, Julie. Have you been nipping at the champagne?"

She smiled slyly. "Why do you ask? Because you think if I get drunk again, I'll crawl all over you?"

"That's not a bad idea."

"You're wicked, Sam Winslow. Or David Winslow. Or whatever your name is ... " She had scraped so much frosting off the cake, she decided she might as well cut into it and have a piece. "Hard to believe this is all going to end in a few days."

"You seem different. Since we got to know each other, you're having second thoughts about David, aren't you?"

"What? No! ... well, maybe ... I don't know. Right now, I can't think clearly about anything. I have trouble remembering *my* name."

"Should we talk about it?"

"No! We'd better get back to the party. They're probably wondering where we are."

Sam and Julie rejoined their teammates in the living room.

"I feel guilty about the loot we got from Percy," Juanita said. "I don't feel right taking the three hundred thousand."

"In case you haven't heard," T.J. said, "we aren't keeping the money. We're giving it to charity—Henry's five grand, too. We figured the satisfaction we got from sandbagging 'Late Night Edition' was enough."

"What charity?" asked Margaret

"The Brian Marshall Home for Unwed Mothers?" suggested Juanita.

"No," T.J. said. "A half dozen charities that are a little more needy than that."

"The last week and a half has been fun," Annie said.

"Aside from T.J. mooning the residents of Moberly on our way back from church, everything went rather well."

"I wasn't mooning them," T.J. insisted. "Some old lady got hold of my pants when we left the church and tried to pull them off me."

"Happens to me all the time," commented Brian.

Before long, the supply of cookies was exhausted, the two bottles of champagne had been drained, and the players retreated to their rooms to catch a few hours sleep.

IV

Showdown
in Seattle

FRIDAY, JANUARY 2 - SUNDAY, JANUARY 4

34

THE PACE OF LIFE at the Moberly homestead noticeably quickened on Friday, the second day of the new year, as the Philosophers packed their belongings and prepared to leave for Seattle. Edgar noticed Irene and Glory watching the commotion from afar.

"Get your things together," he told Irene. "We leave in an hour."

"Me? I'm not going with you."

Edgar came over, put an arm around her shoulder and gave her a gentle shove toward her bedroom. "Oh, yes you are. You're a part of this now. We had an incredible season and now we're in the Brains Bowl. You don't want to miss that, do you?"

"But Edgar ... I can't pack up and go with you on the spur of the moment."

"We have *less* than an hour," Juanita pointed out, on her way to her room. "You'd better get moving."

"But what about Rock?" Irene protested. "He wouldn't like it if I went along."

"Don't worry about Rock," Edgar said. "He's such a wreck he probably won't notice you're on the bus."

"Or, he might put you in the starting lineup," Annie suggested.

"No more excuses," Edgar said. "You're a part of all this now."

A glint of excitement came into Irene's eyes. "All right, I'll do it. I've become attached to all of you. I feel like I *am* part of the team. But I can't leave Glory behind!"

"Bring her along," Edgar said. "Now, hurry! We leave in an hour."

"*Less* than an hour!" Annie snapped.

As Henry loaded baggage under the bus, the Phils took a last look at The Homestead.

"I'll miss this place," Julie said.

"We had a good time," Juanita chimed in.

"Enough sentimentality," Henry grumbled. "Let's roll!"

Rock boarded the bus and surveyed the seats to make sure his players hadn't gone A.W.O.L. again. The players were all present and accounted for—but what were Irene and her cat doing on the bus?

"Did they kidnap you?" he asked Irene.

"I came willingly. I wanted to see you play in the Brains Bowl."

"All right." He turned to Freud. "Any other stowaways I should know about?"

"None I'm aware of. With this group, I can't be sure."

"Who said the cat could come along?"

"Edgar."

"I thought he hated cats."

"Not any more. I think the cat adopted him."

Rock shook his head. "The world keeps getting weirder and weirder."

Nervous and weary, Rock slumped in a front seat.

He had noticed a change in the team's spirit. They were less stressed and more optimistic. All of which was fine if they didn't forget what it was all about: giving everything they had to win the Brains Bowl.

Rock also realized he was just as obsessed with winning as ever. Well, that was what he was paid for. If he went too far, Freud could pull him back on the ship. That was what Freud was paid for.

So be it.

> As time grew near, Ahab neither shaved, supped, nor prayed.

AT ST. LOUIS-LAMBERT International Airport, Henry parked the bus near a jet Ben Sloan had chartered to fly the Phils to Seattle. The players savored their last few hours of privacy because they knew that when the jet landed, they would be catapulted into the thick of the Brains Bowl madness—all the more intense because of speculation about where the team had hidden out the last week and a half.

T.J. seemed particularly morose. Juanita asked him why.

"I'd be happier if Kathy was going to be in Seattle."

"Have you decided not to marry the girlfriend back in Detroit?" she asked.

"That's right."

"Your lovelife is more screwed up than 'The Young and the Restless'," Annie commented.

"It's more like 'The Amateur Hour'," suggested Brian.

"And yours is like 'Trixie Does Texas'," Julie told him.

"It was a couple weeks ago. Then I hit a speed bump in Missouri. Now I'm ready for the open road again—no speed limit."

"God help us all," muttered Annie.

"Amen," said Brian.

Henry helped the Phils gather their luggage after they climbed down off the bus. He waved as they headed toward the terminal. "Good luck!" he said.

"You'd better grab your bags if you're coming with us," Juanita called back to him.

Henry looked shocked. "What? Nobody said anything about that."

"Get a move on," Brian hollered. "We can't hold the plane for you."

"But ... Rock doesn't want me to go!"

Rock turned around. "The cat is going. You might as well go, too. Get moving!"

"Yes, sir!"

As the jet descended near Seattle, the Phils could see Puget Sound, the skyscrapers downtown and towering mountains in the distance.

After a rough landing, the players filed into the terminal. A handful of loyal fans spotted them. Then word of their arrival spread like wildfire throughout the terminal.

Reporters for "Late Night Edition", the Associated Press, ESPN, Fox Sports and the Seattle and Chicago newspapers had been camped out at airports and major hotels in the Seattle area for three days awaiting the arrival of the Phils.

Rock, totally preoccupied with preparations for the game, led his crew on a relentless march from the plane to a waiting bus. He did not hear questions shouted by reporters. He did not see the exuberant welcome from Chicago fans who had made the pilgrimage to Seattle.

Carl Norton, an Associated Press reporter, realized Rock

was on another plateau. He focused on the players. "Brian!" he shouted. "Where were you and the team holed up?"

"We weren't holed up," Brian said. "We just had a hard time finding this place."

"Stop the bull!" yelled Percy Smathers. "Where have you been the last ten days?"

Juanita smiled. "Like the lady in Oregon said, we were beamed up to the planet Regina. Nice place. You ought to see it."

"I want my three hundred grand back!" Percy insisted.

"What three hundred grand?" Edgar said. "We've been out of touch with civilization. What are you talking about?"

"I'm going to get you!" Percy yelled.

The players marched on toward the team bus Ben Sloan had chartered.

THE BUS DROPPED THE PHILS off at a back entrance to the Alexis Hotel, a luxurious European-style establishment housed in a charming older building a block from the waterfront on First Avenue. Because the hotel was small and expensive, Freud thought the team would have more privacy than it would in a large hotel. The owners were skeptical about housing the Phils, fearful that players like Chase and Margaret would damage the establishment's fine reputation, but Freud convinced them the Phils were relatively refined and cultured. ("I lied through my teeth," he told Rock.)

Freud signed the team in, then bellboys showed the players, coaches, Irene and Henry to their spacious rooms.

"It's 3 P.M.," Rock said, when the players stepped out of the elevator. "We'll meet in the suite at the end of the corridor for a team meeting at 6 P.M."

Rock and Freud stayed in executive suites with living rooms that included sofas, dining tables and desks. Brian was given a spa suite, Margaret an Alexis Suite with a powder room and jetted tub, and Edgar an Author's Suite complete with designer bookshelves, a jetted bathtub and, of course, a wood-burning fireplace.

Juanita passed Edgar's room as Edgar unlocked the door and she noticed the fireplace.

"That's disgusting. I'm lucky if I get ice water and a soft bed."

"Age and rank have their privileges," Edgar noted.

Glory ran over to the fireplace and made herself comfortable.

The other players stayed in King Deluxe Guest rooms and Irene and Henry were assigned Alexis Queen Guest rooms. All rooms included desks and high-speed Internet service, though Rock had ordered all televisions removed. Some rooms had a view of the city, others of the interior courtyard.

AT 6 P.M. THE TEAM filed into the suite for its meeting with Rock.

"All right. Listen up, you meatballs. The game is only two days away. We've come a long, long way. What you do between now and game time is important. Avoid distractions, keep your thinking clear and finish cramming for the game."

"Darn," said Margaret. "I just signed up for a bus tour of Seattle."

"There will be none of that until the bowl is over," Rock declared. "We are all required to attend the League Commissioner's Party on Saturday night. I suppose they were afraid no one would show up if it wasn't mandatory—he doesn't have a lot of friends. So be there! Dress appropriately!"

35

THE PHILS DINED IN THE hotel's restaurant, The Library Bistro & Bookstore Bar, on Saturday morning, making a point of avoiding fans and reporters. Later, they crammed for the game like undergraduates facing do-or-die final exams. As evening approached, they retreated to their rooms, where they showered and dressed for the Commissioner's Party.

The men traded tuxedos until each found one that fit—all except Edgar, who always carried a tux with him. The women allowed themselves an hour to bathe and fix their hair.

"All right, who stole my corsage?" demanded Margaret.

"Is that what this is?" Brian said. "I thought it was a boutonniere."

Margaret tromped into Brian's room, swiped the corsage off the lapel of his tux and marched back to her room.

"You're welcome!" Brian called after her.

Annie wore jeans under her auburn gown. Freud explained that was not a good idea.

"This gown isn't *me*, Freud," she complained. "I gotta be me!"

T.J. caught a glimpse of Annie in the hallway, did a second-take, and burst out laughing.

"All right, shorty," Annie said. "What's so funny?"

"Nothing. Nothing at all," T.J. said.

Chase headed for the meeting room wearing a tux and baseball cap. "Nice duds," he told Annie, as he passed her.

"Thanks, Chase. You've got class!"

But Freud insisted she ditch the jeans and Chase get rid of the baseball cap. They did.

Sam arrived in the meeting room looking stylish and handsome, but also worried. "I ought to be booking it. I don't want to make a fool of myself in the bowl. They expect a billion people to be watching around the world."

"Holy smoke," Margaret said. "That many?"

"Thanks, Sam," Freud mumbled. "I had convinced Margaret it's just another game."

"Yes, and the Lamburghini is just another car," Edgar said.

Rock wandered in dressed in a tux, but his beard was stubby and his hair unruly, His shirttail hung over his pants. He obviously was not interested in winning any "best dressed" awards.

"What's the matter, Coach? Were all your sweatshirts dirty?" Brian called out from the back of the room.

"Who said that?" Rock roared.

"Damned if I know," Brian muttered.

"Behave yourself, mister. And that goes for all of you!"

Rock took a good look at his Philosophers. It was the first time he had seen them when they didn't look scruffy. They had worn sweatpants for the team picture.

"If I had anything to say about it, you wouldn't be going to this shindig tonight," the coach said. "You'd be hitting the books! But the league says we've all got to go, so we will. I'm allowing you one drink from the bar, that's all. I want you sober for the game. Try not to embarrass me or the team. And if the commissioner asks you to dance, do it!"

"That's where I draw the line!" T.J. said.

"Do you think he can tango?" asked Edgar.

"I was talking to the women, you idiots!"

"By the way, T.J." Edgar said. "I almost forgot. You were out of your room when the desk clerk tried to reach you so he called me. There's someone downstairs waiting to see you. I think her name was Karen, or Kitty …"

"Kathy?" T.J. asked excitedly.

"That's it."

T.J. ran for the elevator.

T.J.'s eyes swept across the lobby, but Kathy was nowhere in sight. What if she had left? He was about to check out the restaurant when someone tapped on his right shoulder. He turned, and there she was, the slender sexpot of a librarian from Chicago. She was wearing a white blouse and gray slacks.

"Kathy! You came to Seattle!"

"Well, I wasn't doing anything else this weekend."

T.J. leaned over and kissed her. "I was hoping you'd show up."

"What are you dressed up for?"

"The Commissioner's Party is tonight. And you're going with me!"

"Forget it. I can't go looking like this."

"C'mon." T.J. grabbed her by the hand and led her to the elevator.

On the third floor, T.J. explained to Annie, Julie, Juanita, Margaret and Irene that Kathy needed a gown to wear to the party.

"You're about my size," Juanita said. "Come with me."

Fifteen minutes later Juanita appeared outside T.J.'s room. When she moved aside, he could see Kathy, wearing a flowing baby blue satin gown. She had ditched the glasses and her hair fell teasingly to her neck.

"You're beautiful," T.J. said, taking Kathy in his arms and kissing her again.

"Aw, horse feathers," Margaret muttered. "Can't you do that stuff behind closed doors?"

Brian stopped outside T.J.'s room and noticed Kathy. "Holy Moses. You mean you hid all that on our date? For me, you dressed like a homeless woman."

"Get out, Brian," snapped T.J.

"Remember to have the gown back by midnight or you turn into a pumpkin!" Juanita warned Kathy.

THE COMMISSIONER'S PARTY—ranked as the big social event associated with the Brains Bowl—was held on the grounds of Seattle's seventy-four acre Civic Center, a group of buildings in a park-like setting that was a remnant of the 1962 Seattle World's Fair. The party allowed the commissioner to bask in the limelight as the league put its best foot forward.

The Phils arrived at the party in four limousines. The entourage included the nine players, Rock, Freud, team physician Archie Bolton, Kathy Lamaster, Irene Harper, Henry Clover, Ben Sloan and Sloan's attractive young wife, Melony.

Shortly after arriving, several players headed for the bar to fetch their one and only drinks. Brian was wrestling with the problem of how to make his bourbon and water last through the evening when he noticed Chase approaching with a gallon jug.

"Fill it up!" Chase told the bartender.

"Don't you think that's stretching the one-drink decree a little far?" Brian asked.

"The coach said one drink from the bar. This is mine."

The Phils broke up into small groups and circulated around the ballroom.

"Why have you worked so hard to get to the Brains Bowl?" Jeff Van Widingham, a computer company CEO, asked Margaret. "It can't be easy for a senior citizen."

"I want to win this one for all senior citizens," Margaret said. "I want to show people it's a mistake to put us out to pasture and ignore us."

"And what about you?" Van Widingham asked T.J., who lingered nearby with Kathy. "Why have you worked so hard to get to the Brains Bowl?"

T.J. pondered the question. "Other than the obvious reason—that Rock would kill me if I didn't—I would say I wanted to show what young people can do so we can put the old folks out to pasture and ignore them."

"What?" Margaret bellowed.

The CEO wandered off to meet other guests.

"T.J.!" Kathy said. "Why did you say that?"

"I was joking!" T.J. mumbled.

Juanita approached, gin and tonic in hand. "Getting us more bad publicity?" she asked T.J.

Margaret grimaced. "When the commissioner gets wind of what T.J. said about senior citizens, he'll fine him about five grand. ... Oh, look. Van Widingham is talking to a reporter and pointing at T.J."

"Oh-oh," T.J. said. "C'mon, Kathy. Pardon us while I try to mend a few fences."

T.J. and Kathy headed off in the direction of the CEO and the reporter.

After paying their respects to League Commissioner C.G. Thornton and his wife, Edgar and Irene retreated to a table at the far side of the room. Edgar looked like a distinguished government official, comfortable in a tux and confident he could control any situation. Irene wore a sequined violet gown.

"You look lovely tonight," Edgar told Irene.

"Thank you, Edgar. … Your glass is empty."

"Rock is allowing us one drink. I've had mine. I'd kill for another one."

Irene smiled. "Ironic, isn't it. You're allowed one drink and you're dying for more. I can have all the drinks I want, but I don't drink liquor."

Edgar's face brightened. "Let's head over to the bar, dear. Maybe we can think of a way to remedy this dastardly situation. For starters, order a vodka martini and I'll take it off your hands."

Percy Smathers, Diane Mercross and a "Late Night Edition" cameraman slipped into the ballroom. Percy nodded toward the group where Rock was socializing.

"Don't take your eyes off Rock," he told the camerman. "Get everything he says on video. The old fool attacks people and slanders them every time he opens his mouth. Shoot it for me!"

"What's the purpose?" Mercross asked Percy.

"I'm going to hang the old reprobate using his own words. I'll edit the video and during the Brains Bowl we'll show it on the big board. Rock will be completely humiliated. All *you* need to do is make sure the technician who puts video up on the Brains Board shows it at the right time."

"How do I do that?"

"Seduce him, bribe him ... I don't care. Just get it done!"

Rock and Freud mingled with league personnel and the coaching staffs of teams which hadn't made it to the Brains Bowl.

Python McGruder, head coach of the Atlanta Opportunists, told Rock he had heard the crack Rock made about the 'Tunists not winning a game since the Atlanta library had burned down in *Gone With the Wind*. "For your information, Rock, we've won at least three or four games since then."

"Congratulations," Rock mumbled.

"No offense taken. Do you think you have much chance of beating the Hackers?"

"Sure," Rock said. "I'm just not sure *how* we're going to do it."

"A lot of teams have that problem. The Hackers walloped us by thirty-four this year. They would have won by more, but I faked a heart attack in the fourth quarter and their players took pity on me."

"Heart attack, eh?" Rock grumbled. "I'll remember that."

Purly Simmons, head coach of the Kansas City Populists, bumped into Rock, spilling some of her manhattan on him.

"Sorry, Rock." She brushed the liquor off his tux.

"Humph," grumbled Rock.

"By the way, I've been talking to your assistant coach and I might steal him away from you. His insights into the game are very perceptive."

"Freud's contract has another year to run."

"Not Freud. Your other assistant." She nodded toward Henry, who was conversing with coaches from other teams.

"Go for it," Rock said. "But he'll want a good salary."

In a far corner of the ballroom, Sam and Julie sipped Pepsis. Julie wore a royal blue strapless gown.

"I realize we haven't known each other long, Julie, but we've been through a lot together. We've had more fun than you ever had with that stuffed-shirt juvenile rocket manufacturer who tried to spy on you. You know you don't want to marry him. You've got to break off your engagement!"

"Sure, I have some doubts, but—"

Sam moved closer. "Open your eyes, Julie. You aren't in love with David. When you and I are together, it's like I've known you forever."

She sighed. "Don't push me on this, Sam. I need to think about it." She turned to go and was stunned to see ... *"David! What are you doing here?"*

A young man about six-feet tall with brown curly hair approached. He was wearing a tux and was built like a football player.

"I knew somebody who knew somebody who had tickets. Well, aren't you glad to see me? How about a kiss?"

"No, thanks," Sam said. "We haven't been introduced. I'm easy, but I'm not *that* easy."

"I know you! You're that guy who was out partying with Julie."

Sam shrugged. "Yes, well, Julie asked me out and I didn't want to turn her down. Would you turn her down?"

"No. But why would she ask you out?"

"She's been through a lot. The pressure … the hype … the stress … Isn't that right, Julie?"

"That's right! I desperately wanted to escape from the madness, and Sam was there when I needed him. You know, David, you hardly ever wrote or called."

"I'm sorry. I was busy."

"Building war toys for kids?" Sam asked.

"That's right."

"Well, while you were building rockets and trying to keep me on a leash by using a GPS tracking device," Julie noted, "I was having difficulty coping. And I got to thinking. Is that what it would be like if I married you? You wouldn't have time for me because you were churning out war toys for children?"

"How can you sleep at night?" Sam interjected.

"I sleep just fine. Look, Julie, I'm sorry I neglected you and I'm sorry about the GPS device. It won't happen again."

"An apology isn't good enough," Sam declared.

"Will you shut up, Sam?" She turned to David. "No, it won't happen again, because I think it's best that we don't see each other any more. I was swept off my feet by your good looks and your success in business, but it's obvious we don't have much in common. It's best we end our relationship now, before I end up as a proper little housewife in a proper little home in a proper little suburb of Philadelphia." She extended her arm for him to shake. "Goodbye, David."

David ignored the outstretched hand. "If that's the way you want it, goodbye, Julie. There are plenty of other women who will marry me."

David stomped off. Sam called after him, *"yes, but do they know how you made your money?"*

Sam sipped his Pepsi as he watched David head for an exit. "I like the way we handled that."

He noticed Julie was crying. He reached up and brushed away the tears. "He's not worth crying over," Sam said.

"I know."

"But you're still crying."

"I know."

Brian watched all this from afar. Here he was, at the Commissioner's Party without a date. Sam's and T.J.'s companions were knockouts. Where was the justice in it?

"Give me another swig," Brian told Chase.

Chase refilled Brian's glass.

Brian noticed Percy Smathers hovering around a far corner of the ballroom. "What's that scandal mongerer doing here?"

"Gathering more ammunition to attack us," Chase suggested.

Diane Mercross, drink in hand, sidled up to Percy. The tabloid journalist was a knockout in her gold satin strapless gown.

When Percy wandered over to gab with Bronco Griffin, Brian approached Diane.

"Things are looking up," Brian told her. "What brings you here? Looking for new victims to humiliate?"

"Not tonight. I'm off duty." She flashed a beguiling smile.

"Do you and Percy have a personal relationship?"

"Yes. He tells me where the sleaze is and I dig it up."

"Nothing romantic?"

"You can't be serious. He's a confirmed workaholic. No heart. No morals. Not my type."

"You deserve better."

"I know. Who did you have in mind?"

"You're looking at him."

"You have a reputation as a womanizer."

"You and your depraved boss gave me the reputation. I'm just a simple Californian who happens to like women. And I treat them right."

"I'm beginning to see you in a different light, Brian. One or two more of these"—she held up her scotch—"and you'll look even better."

"Time for another visit to the bar."

Henry was deep into a glass of whiskey when Brian and Diane arrived at the bar.

"How is it going?" Brian asked.

"Not bad. I just gave up bus driving. You're talking to the new assistant coach of the Kansas City Populists."

"No kidding! Congratulations."

"Isn't that Percy's girlfriend?" Henry whispered.

"No!" Diane declared. "I'm his assistant."

"Aren't words wonderful," Henry mumbled. "They can cover up a multitude of sins."

"Read my lips: I am *not* Percy's girlfriend!" she snapped indignantly, as Brian whisked her away from the bar.

"I don't think I like him," she said.

"Henry's all right. He's very protective of our team. I think he was afraid I'm sleeping with the enemy."

"And are you?" Diane asked, teasingly.

"Not yet. But I'm working on it."

Assistant Commissioner Blaine Vincent asked that guests be seated, and after a few introductory remarks, players and coaches from both teams were introduced. Then Commissioner Thornton delivered a short speech on the Brains Bowl, sportsmanship and players' demands for "excessive salaries". Vincent hastily reminded the commissioner it was neither the time nor the place to alienate the players.

Awards were presented for best individual and team performances during the year. The Hackers won nine awards. The Phils hauled in seven. Rock didn't pay much attention. He had his eyes on the Einstein Trophy, which would be presented to the winner of the Brains Bowl.

At 10:30, Rock rounded up his team.

"Let's blow this joint," he said. "Get back to the hotel. Crack the books, then get some sleep. We've got a big day tomorrow."

Most of the players returned to the limousines for the ride back to the hotel. Brian slipped away with Diane Mercross.

SAM AND JULIE STROLLED around the civic center grounds before leaving. The late-evening air was chilly.

"You've been unengaged for two hours," Sam noted. "Any idea what you'll do with the rest of your life?"

She smiled. "I don't even know what I'll do after the game tomorrow."

"Me either. We can take our time deciding. Freud says we'll get truckloads of offers from Brains teams and universities. ... Joining the Phils for the playoffs was the best thing that ever happened to me. It's been quite an experience ... and I met you."

Julie sighed. "Meeting you has changed my life, too. I was engaged, relatively happy, everything was going along smoothly. Now my life is in turmoil."

"I know. Isn't it great?"

"You are impossible."

"I've been told that before."

"We should get back to the hotel," Julie said.

The limousines had departed so they hurried toward a row of taxicabs.

"Our relationship required a lot of work," Sam noted. "It got off to a rocky start—the screaming in the elevator, the way you crushed my ego on our first date, the way you drove me crazy every time we were together."

"But you didn't give up."

"I knew we were meant to be together."

"I think there's another reason. You have difficulty recognizing rejection."

"I know. ... You have difficulty recognizing love."

"I know."

36

SAM PARTED WAYS WITH Julie at the door to her room.

He slipped off his tux and for a half hour tried to study. Then he turned out the lights, plopped into an armchair and gazed out the window. He knew he wouldn't sleep because Julie and the Brains Bowl were rocking his world. After several minutes of restless daydreaming, he put on a gray knit shirt and workout pants, fetched his coat and left the hotel.

A cold drizzle pelted the sidewalk as he meandered through the streets of downtown Seattle. There was so much to think about, so much to get straight in his mind. He also felt burdened by guilt because he knew he should be preparing for the big game.

A few minutes later, he realized he had traveled in the direction of the huge Emerald City Dome where the game would be played. He wandered inside, passing a few cleaning people, and continued on until he reached the playing floor.

The huge facility mesmerized him. The endless rows of seats soon would hold eighty thousand screaming, fanatical fans. Up high, scattered around the circumference of the dome, were luxurious box seats. VIPs paid thousands of dollars to watch the game from there.

Sam's eyes drifted to the playing area, where a professional basketball game had been held earlier in the evening. Workmen had not yet converted the floor from a basketball court into the playing area where Brains teams would compete the next day.

A stray basketball caught Sam's eye. He picked it up, dribbled toward one of the baskets and began shooting. Soon—to the amazement of the cleaning crew—he was doing his own play-by-play ...

"And the bounce pass goes to Sam Winslow, who dribbles, fakes and sinks a twenty-foot jump shot!"

Only he missed.

Sam heaved shots up to the basket for several minutes. Then, he noticed someone watching him from the shadows.

It was Rock.

The Phils coach was decked out in a sweatshirt and workout pants. He looked weary. He slowly made his way to the basket where Sam was shooting.

"Uh ... sorry, coach," Sam said. "It's just that I'm kind of a basketball nut, and I always wanted to shoot baskets in an arena this big."

Rock didn't say anything for a few moments. Then he took the ball from Sam. "Me, too, kid," he mumbled.

Rock shot a fifteen footer than fell short. Sam missed on a jumper from the free throw line.

"I hope we do better than this tomorrow," Sam said.

Sam scored on a twenty-footer, then tossed the ball to Rock, who sank a jump shot from the side.

"Maybe it's a good thing you're on the team, Winslow. Compared to you, I look pretty normal."

Sam leaped for a rebound, but Rock scooted in and snatched the ball away from him.

"You've got to hustle, kid! Whatever you do in life, give it everything you've got!"

Sam hit a hook shot from the foul line. "I know that's my problem. Sometimes I don't put everything into what I'm doing."

Rock hit on another jump shot. "I never had that problem, kid. People say I go too far. Maybe they're right. But I know you've got to work hard—very hard—to get what you want in this crazy world."

Sam sank an eighteen-foot jump shot.

"Not bad for a guy who didn't have a job a month ago," Rock mused.

The coach sank a ten-footer.

"Not bad for a college dropout," Sam noted.

Out of breath, Rock looked on as Sam took a few more shots. Then he said, "Get some sleep, Winslow. We've got a big day coming up."

Sam headed toward an exit. When he looked back, Rock still stood on the court, gazing into the far corners of the huge arena. The coach seemed awed, confident and scared—all at the same time.

"Are you coming, Rock?" Sam asked.

"In a few minutes. ... It's hard to believe we really made it here."

37

PERCY SMATHERS WAS EDITING video tape when Diane Mercross arrived at the "Late Night Edition" regional office in Chicago Sunday morning.

"You've got to see this," Percy told Diane. "It's beautiful. It will get Rock banned from the league!"

"Wonderful," she mumbled. "Just think what you could accomplish if you put your talents to constructive use."

"That's what I'm doing," Percy said. "Look at this."

Diane watched as tape of Rock at the commissioner's party appeared on the editing machine monitor. Rock's colorful comments supplied the audio:

> "When I retire from coaching, I might become the league commissioner. It's an easy job. All you do is hand out fines and seduce the coaches' wives when the coaches aren't looking."
>
> * * *
>
> "I wouldn't say referees are corrupt. The league would fine me if I did. Referees are blind, ignorant and prone to accepting bribes. But corrupt? No way."
>
> * * *
>
> "Television reporters are like snakes, waiting to attack you, then crawling back into the shad-

ows to wait for their next prey. The only way to stop them is to chop off their heads."

* * *

"My number one goal is to win the Brains Bowl. Number two is to wipe Percy Smathers off the face of the earth. If we lose the Brains Bowl, Percy moves up to number one."

* * *

"The Mob doesn't own the Phils. Ben Sloan owns the Phils and the Mob owns him. ... *Hey, stop that cameraman! I was joking!*"

"Did you find someone who can put it up on the Brains Board for us when the time comes?"

Diane sighed. "Yes. He wants ten grand or a night in the sack."

"You should make the sacrifice so I don't need to pay the ten grand."

"He wants a night in the sack *with you*."

"What kind of sick pervert is he?"

"I see. It's all right if I sacrifice myself, but for you, it's out of the question."

"Just give him the ten grand. I'll have the tape ready in a half hour."

Percy left a half hour later. Diane decided to have a talk with one of the film editors before she headed over to the Brains Bowl.

38

There she blows!—There she blows! A hump like a snowhill!
It is Moby Dick!

A COOL RAIN SPLATTERED SEATTLE streets as Sunday dawned.
The city's hotels, motels and restaurants bulged with Brains
fans and sports reporters eagerly anticipating the big game.

At the Alexis Hotel, uncharacteristically quiet Phils gathered for breakfast in the Library Bistro. While indulging
in buttermilk pancakes and Brioche french toast, they pondered how to hit their buzzers faster by cutting down on
precious milliseconds. They assumed the other players were
still in their rooms.

Sam had plunged deep into Paul Johnson's *A History of the
American People* when the ringing of his telephone rattled
his fragile nerves.

"Mr. Winslow, we have orders not to bother the players
unless it's important, but we thought you might want to take
this phone call. It's from someone who claims to be your
brother, Joe."

"I'll take the call."

"*Hey, little brother! Are you nervous about playing in the big game?*"

It was a stupid thing to ask a rookie who was about to compete in front of a billion people.

"Yes. Next question?"

"I wanted to tell you we are here."

"Who's here?"

"Dad, mom and me. We're at the Seattle airport. We flew in to see you play."

"How did you get dad and mom on an airplane?"

"I told mom you were going to hell—dating scantily-clad women who get men drunk and haul them off to their rooms."

"Thanks a lot. How did you get dad on the plane? He hates to fly."

"I told him there are scantily-clad women here who get men drunk and haul them off to their rooms."

"That figures."

"Well, I gotta go. Dad's wrestling with a luggage handler because he thinks the kid's trying to steal our bags. ... By the way, Sam, I don't like to complain, but did you get us good seats? In Chicago, they stuck us so far back we passed a 'Welcome to Canada' sign on the way to the rafters."

"This isn't a good day to mess with my mind, Joe. Management decides where the complimentary seats will be. Players don't have anything to say about it."

"All right, little brother. Just thought I'd ask."

At noon, the Phils gathered in the Library Bistro for lunch. Freud noticed Chase carried a copy of *Playboy*. "Doing a little last minute studying?"

"You bet," Chase said. "Motivation."

"Where are Margaret and Brian?" asked Julie.

"Must be in their rooms," Freud said. "Better go get them."

Annie headed off to Margaret's room while Edgar checked out Brian's.

Five minutes later, they returned to the Bistro.

"Margaret didn't come to the door," Julie said.

"Brian didn't either."

"It's all beginning to make sense," T.J. mused. "They're having an affair! This explains why Margaret is going crazy."

"Perhaps we shouldn't jump to conclusions," Freud suggested. "We've got to find them. Does anyone know where they could be?"

Moments later Brian entered the restaurant still wearing the tux he had worn the night before.

"Where have you been?" Julie demanded.

"I took a little detour on the way back from the commissioner's bash."

"I bet the detour was named Diane Mercross," Annie noted. "I saw them together at the party."

"You went home with that hatchet woman?" Juanita asked.

"She's not that bad. She's a decent person who made the mistake of hitching her wagon to Percy's sleazemobile, that's all. ... When she left her apartment this morning, she didn't wake me."

"Get your mind back on the game," Freud told Brian. "We need to find Margaret—*fast!* Sam, call the hospitals. Julie, call the taxi companies."

"Margaret mentioned her husband was buried in a cemetery somewhere around here," Annie recalled. "Maybe she visited the grave site."

"Get on your computer and find out where he's buried!"

Freud ordered. "Where's Henry? Tell him to be ready to go. He'll need to find Margaret and bring her back."

"He must be upstairs," said Chase.

"Unless *he* ran away with Margaret," T.J. suggested.

As Annie searched the Internet for the cemetery site, Sam called hospitals and Julie called taxi companies from their rooms. The other players and Freud waited in the hotel lobby.

Henry hustled in wearing a black leather jacket. "What's the emergency?"

"Margaret is missing," Freud said.

Annie ran into the lobby. "An obit on the web says her husband, Bernard, was buried in a Riverton Heights cemetery."

"She might be there," Freud told Henry. "Find her and bring her back!"

"No problem," Henry said. "Where's Riverton Heights?"

"Just north of the Seattle-Tacoma International Airport," Annie said.

"Get moving!" Freud told Henry. "Annie will track down directions to the grave site and give them to you over your cell phone."

Freud gave Henry the keys to a Chrysler the team had rented and Henry bolted out the door.

"This might be the little shove that sends Rock over the cliff," Brian mused.

Later that afternoon, Freud knocked at Rock's door. After a few moments, Rock opened it. The coach was dressed but his hair was dishelved and he hadn't shaved in about three days.

"You're a mess, Rock. You can't coach in the Brains Bowl looking like that."

"Who cares how I look? It's winning that's important."

He caught a glimpse of himself in the mirror. "Holy crap. Is that me?" He combed his hair. "Did I look like this at the commissioner's party?"

"Pretty much."

"You're fired."

"Should I stick around for the game?"

"Yeah."

The coach shaved, then slipped on a jacket. "Is the team ready?"

Freud hesitated. "More or less."

WHEN THE PHILS GATHERED OUTSIDE the hotel to board the bus that afternoon, Annie told Freud that Henry had arrived in Riverton Heights but he was still looking for the cemetery and there was no sign of Margaret. She would keep in contact with him using her cell phone.

Rock claimed a seat near the front in the bus and didn't seem to notice at first that Freud—not Henry—was driving.

Three blocks into the trip, Rock grumbled, "Where the hell is what's-his-name?"

"I sent Henry on an errand," Freud said.

"You know how to drive this thing?"

"I guess we'll find out," Freud mumbled, as he narrowly missed sideswiping a Volkswagon.

"You're doing this to aggravate me, aren't you?"

"Rock, I would never do that!" Freud said.

"I would!" Brian piped up from the back of the bus.

Rock didn't seem to hear him.

At the Emerald City Dome, players filed into the stadium.

"Where's Margaret?" Rock demanded.

Freud swallowed hard. "I think she took off to see her husband's grave. I sent Henry to bring her back."

"She isn't here? Lord almighty. ... When did you plan on telling me one of my starters is missing?"

"I figured you'd notice it eventually."

"You'd better hope she shows up fast, or there will be three people in the grave. Margaret, her husband, and you! Got it?"

"Yes, Rock."

As, the Phils headed for their locker rooms they could hear noisy fans rocking the rafters. Players changed into game uniforms, then gathered in the men's locker room.

Rock emerged from the coach's room looking weary and tormented. Bags as big as tires hung below his eyes. He strode slowly to the center of the room. His natural instinct was to unleash the furies of hell and whip his team into a frenzy that would carry it to victory, but Freud insisted an outburst like that would send the troops over the edge. Struggling to control his emotions, Rock addressed his crew in a harsh whisper that soon rose to a mighty roar.

"Y'know, when I was a kid in high school, the football coach said I was too small to make the team. But every day, I practiced with the squad, and every night I stayed late kicking field goals. One day, late in the season, it rained as I kicked three-pointers, and the coach—old Abe Thurmond—trotted onto the field and said he reckoned he could use me since I worked harder than anyone else on the team. But he didn't play me that week, or the next. Not until the last game of the season. We were battling for the league championship. Our kicker was having a lousy game, and we trailed by a point with three seconds left. Abe sent me in to try a field goal from twenty-seven yards out. Everything was on the line, but I was rarin' to go. And I gave it everything I had."

"You kicked the field goal?" T.J. asked.

"No. The center screwed up the snap."

Rock paused and let his words sink in.

"As a motivational story, that sucks," Brian commented.

"No, I didn't kick the field goal. I scooped up the ball and started running. Ran like hell. Before anyone realized what happened, I was in the end zone. We won the game. And it was the greatest feeling in the world … until now. Until we made it to the Brains Bowl.

"Winning requires guts and determination. You've got to give the game—any game—everything you've got. When fate calls—when your Abe Thurmond taps on your shoulder and says, 'I'm sending you in, kid'—you've got to be ready.

"We fooled the idiot experts and made it to the Bowl, but that isn't enough. No one cares about the team that loses. To prove ourselves, we've gotta *win*.

"You are up against the toughest, smartest, most infuriatingly arrogant team in the league. If you show any weakness, the Hackers will pound you into the ground.

"Stay with them and seize every opportunity! We've got to wipe that stupid grin off coach Bronco Griffin's ugly face once and for all.

"Sure, it's rough. You're tired and irritable and cranky. You fall asleep at meals, and you've got dispositions like garbagemen working in a blizzard. But you can't fall apart on me now. You've got to win one more time.

"Freud tells me Margaret is A.W.O.L. Until she gets here, I'm moving you over to R.M., Edgar. You will start at the world slot, T.J.!"

T.J.'s eyes opened wide. "I'm starting? *In the Brains Bowl?*"

"Like I said, kid … when fate taps on your shoulder you've got to be ready!"

The other players congratulated T.J.

Rock resumed his pep talk. "Just remember: millions of people wish they were in your shoes. *We can win! You can be heroes! We can be the Brains Bowl champions!*"

"*We can do it!*" Chase said.

"*We can do it!*" the others shouted, as they jogged toward the playing area.

"If T.J. screws up," Rock told Freud, "it's another nail in your coffin."

WHEN THE PHILS EMERGED from the bowels of the stadium and stepped onto the playing floor, an enormous cheer erupted from the crowd.

Percy Smathers and Diane Mercross watched the spectacle from the press section.

"You have the video tape and you've arranged for the technician to load it. Right?"

"Yes, Percy. Are you sure you want to do this?"

"Absolutely."

Lights dimmed, music erupted and spotlights focused on the playing floor as players from both teams were introduced. The singing of the national anthem followed.

The rowdy crowd quieted down as head referee Lester Block approached the Hot Zone for the Shakespearean tipoff:

"For four points: identify this passage!"

On the Brains Board appeared the quotation:

This above all—to thine own self be true,
And it must follow, as the night the day,
Thou canst not then be false to any man.

Hacker world specialist Wolfgang Heller slammed his buzzer first. *"Hamlet!"*

"WAY TO GO WOLFGANG!" read the Brains Board message. In this game, the board would encourage players on both teams, since neither was the home team.

The Hackers had wasted no time putting points on the board.

Edgar Tolin Woodford and Leroy Hollinger rode to the Hot Zone for an R.M. faceoff.

Hollinger, a former pastor, smiled benignly. "You might as well get out of here and go home, Woodford. God is on *our* side."

"That's not what He told me. He plans to punish you for leaving the church. Didn't say what kind of punishment ... floods? famine? pestilence? Who knows?"

Hollinger looked shaken.

Lester Block posed the question: "For three points: This man, often considered the father of quantum mechanics, devised the Uncertainty Principle that turned traditional physics on its head. Was it (a) Albert Einstein (b) Lee De Forest or (c) Werner Karl Heisenberg?"

Edgar and Hollinger seemed to hit their buzzers at the same time. The light in front of Edgar's desk lit, indicating the computer had determined Edgar hit his button first.

"Interesting question," Edgar commented. "I once knew a minor diplomat from Austria with the same name. Short little man, had a nasty habit of bumming cigars off me."

"Do you want to answer the question?" inquired Block, losing patience. On the sidelines, Rock was going crazy.

"Of course," said Edgar. "C—Heisenberg."

"WAY TO GO, EDDIE!" flashed the Brains Board.

"I told them not to call me Eddie," Edgar mumbled.

The Phils trailed, 4-3.

The world specialists, T.J. Collins and Wolfgang Heller, moved to the Hot Zone. Heller, who led the league in scoring during the regular season, came to the Hackers from the Stuttgart Professors, the most successful Brains team in Germany.

"Why am I competing against a second-stringer?" Wolfgang wondered aloud.

"Why am I competing against a bum who can't find his way to a barbershop?" asked T.J.

The head referee intervened: "For two points: for whom were the Philippine Islands named?"

T.J. slipped lower in his seat as Wolfgang confidently smacked his buzzer. "King Philip the Second of Spain."

"WONDERFUL, WOLFGANG!" declared the Brains Board. The Hackers led, 6-3.

In Riverton Heights, Henry located the entrance to the Last Resting Place Cemetery. There was one small problem. The cemetery was home to hundreds of burial sites. Where was Bernard's grave?

Henry drove into the cemetery and a few minutes later came to a screeching halt. He nearly hit Margaret, who was shuffling along near the gravel path. She looked as though she had been battered by a tornado.

"What the hell are you doing?" she growled. "Where did you learn to drive?" She adjusted her glasses and took a closer look. "Oh, it's you. I should have known."

"Get in Margaret! The Brains Bowl is starting and Rock

and Freud are probably having heart attacks because you aren't there."

She climbed into the front seat. "Guess I lost track of time. ... Well, what are you waiting for?"

"Buckle your seat belt!" Henry pressed the accelerator, throwing them both against the backs of the seats.

"Take it easy, hot shot! I'm seventy-three years old, you know!"

"Yeah, the whole damn league knows," Henry grumbled.

He picked up his cell phone and called Annie.

"I've got the cargo and I'm heading for port," Henry said.

Annie strained to hear over the noise in the stadium. "Run that by me again. What cargo?"

"I've got Margaret and we're on our way back."

Annie could hear Henry shouting at Margaret to get her hands off the steering wheel. "She's a handful," he told Annie. "Can I knock her out?"

"Don't give her any medicine! She's got to be alert so she can play!"

"I wasn't talking about medicine. I was going to knock her out."

"Who the hell are you, anyway?" Margaret yelled at Henry, as he hung up.

ANNIE INFORMED ROCK AND Freud that Margaret was on her way to the stadium.

The quotation specialists, Julie Howard and Maxwell Tweed, rode out to the Hot Zone.

"You remind me of a spy I seduced in the line of duty a few years ago," noted Tweed, the former F.B.I. agent. "Unfortunately I had to kill her."

"How did you do it?" Julie asked. "With your body odor?"

"What?" responded Tweed, with eyes bulging.

The head referee interrupted. "For three points: identify the poet who wrote these lines."

On the Brains Board appeared the quotation:

Stone walls do not a prison make, nor iron bars a cage.

Tweed whacked the buzzer with a vengeance. "Richard Lovelace," he said.

Chicago fans groaned. Hackers on top, 9-3.

"THE PHILS' JITTERS AND INEXPERIENCE ARE TAKING THEIR TOLL," Moose Harrison noted. "LET'S SEE IF SAM WINSLOW CAN STOP THE HACKERS' MOMENTUM. THERE'S A LOT OF PRESSURE ON SAM, WHO A MONTH AGO WAS HANGING OUT IN FRANKLIN, INDIANA, WITH-OUT A JOB."

Sam and the Hacker history ace, Cynthia Medlow, traveled to the Hot Zone. Cynthia's curly brown hair seemed to say "come hither" but her cold blue eyes warned "don't tread on me!"

"Have you read my latest book, Winslow?"

"No."

"It's called *How to Be a Brains Player.*" She held up a copy. "It might help you. I watched your last two playoff games and you need all the help you can get."

"I can't believe you're using me and the Brains Bowl to plug your book!"

"Not at all. I'm just telling you it's been published. And it's twenty-four eighty-five."

"For two points," said Lester Block. "Who founded the Sierra Club? Was it (a) Theodore Roosevelt, (b) Harold Dwyer, or (c) John Muir?"

Cynthia hit her buzzer before Sam had time to ponder the question. "C. John Muir," she said.

"YES, CYNTHIA!" roared the Brains Board.

She flashed a cold smile at Sam. "You need to buy my book—fast!"

The Hackers led, 11-3.

> In the cheap seats, far from the stage, Mona Winslow grumbled, "I don't like that woman. She's a hussy."
>
> "It takes a while for Sam to get warmed up," Joe explained. "He'll do better."
>
> "I hope so."
>
> "Shhh," cautioned Fred. "We don't want anyone to know we're related to him."
>
> "What are you talking about? He's our son!"
>
> Fred slunk down in his seat. "A little louder, they could hear you in Russia."
>
> Joe squinted to see the playing floor through a pair of binoculars. "It's no use," he said. "For a good view, I'd need the Hubble Space Telescope."

The popular arts specialists, Brian Marshall and Jaycee Yancey, moved to the Hot Zone for their first faceoff. Yancey, a retired Army colonel, wore her old uniform.

"Doing anything after the game?" Brian asked.

"Don't waste your questionable charms on me. You are not my type. I hear you are lazy and self-indulgent. Did you ever serve in the military?"

"Do the Boy Scouts count?"

"No."

"For three points," said Lester Block, "identify the play in which The Auctioneer, The Crocodile God and Lem appeared, and name the playwright."

Brian beat Yancey to the buzzer. *"The Emperor Jones,* Eugene O'Neill."

"FABULOUS!" noted the Brains Board.

But the Hackers still led, 11-6.

In Chicago's Northwestern Memorial Hospital, Tina Meredith had taken the first few steps on the road to recovery, but it was a long road. Against doctor's orders, she was watching the Brains Bowl on television. Her replacement, Sam Winslow, was struggling and she feared the team was doomed without her.

Dr. Murphy, making his rounds, wandered into the room. "Tina! You can't watch the game!"

"This is my team, doc. Come hell or high water, I'm gonna watch it!"

Murphy's eyes drifted to the screen. "How are we doing?"

"Down five in the first quarter."

"Crap. I've got three big ones riding on the Phils." He pulled up a chair. "I'll keep an eye on you, make sure you don't get too excited. ... *Nurse!* Get me a hamburger and orange soda, will you?"

"Make that two," Tina said.

In the Emerald City Dome, a horn blew, signaling a Brain Buster three-on-three confrontation. Players waited expectantly to see who would compete. Moments later, Julie, Chase and T.J. were transported to the Hot Zone to face Maxwell Tweed, Jake Clayton and Wolfgang Heller.

A jumbled assortment of letters appeared on the Brains Board:

WKH FLYLO ZDU

The referee declared, "Solve this coded message using the Julius Caesar cipher."

Most of the players knew the Julius Caesar cipher could be cracked by moving ahead three letters in the alphabet to determine what a letter stood for, but Tweed figured out the solution first. "The Civil War!" he asserted.

"JUHDW!" noted the Brains Board. It decoded the message a few seconds later: "GREAT!"

"THE HACKERS HAVE TAKEN CONTROL OF THE GAME," Moose Harrison conceded. "THEY LEAD 15 TO 6. IF CHICAGO'S CARDIAC KIDS DON'T WAKE UP, THEY'LL FIND THEMSELVES SO FAR BACK THEY CAN'T PULL THIS ONE OUT."

Henry breathed a little easier after finding his way to Interstate 5. "We'll make good time now."

Margaret pointed to a road sign. "Right. We'll be in California before you know it. We're supposed to be on 5 north, going back to Seattle, you idiot!"

"Crap." Henry exited the southbound lanes of Interstate 5 at the next off-ramp and hooked up with the northbound lanes.

In the Emerald City Dome, Chase and Hacker sports whiz Crazy Jake Clayton traveled to centercourt.

"Fasten your seat belt, boy," growled Crazy Jake. "It's gonna be a rough flight tonight. Fog all over the place. Can't see a damn thing."

"Do you have any idea where you are?" asked Chase.

"Controllers in the tower often ask me the same thing. No, I don't."

"For two points," Lester Block said. "In 1921, the Chicago Staleys were champions in what sport?"

Chase knew the answer, but Crazy Jake beat him to the buzzer. "Football. The Staleys, later known as the Chicago Bears, won the first National Football League title."

Chase returned to the sidelines in a funk. It was a question about one of his hometown teams, but he had been upstaged by Crazy Jake. The Hackers led 17-6.

Rock confronted Freud on the sidelines. "We're getting murdered. The players need the fear of God pounded into them!"

"They'll crash and burn if you tear into them, Rock. They're stressed out. As Jake Clayton would say, just ride it out."

Rock surveyed his exhausted ragtag crew. "You'd better be right, Freud. If we lose, you'll be coaching in Antarctica next year."

"Antarctica? Hmm. That might not be so bad."

"Get outta here, scumbag ... *And where is Margaret?*"

Later in the first quarter, T.J. Collins and Hacker world ace Wolgang Heller met again at centercourt. T.J. could feel a billion eyes staring at him.

"Sorry to be the bearer of bad news, T.J., but your house burned down," Wolfgang said. On the Brains Board, video appeared showing a house in flames.

"You're a day late and a dollar short, Wolfgang. We used that prank on Baltimore in our last game. We used the same kind of special effects that made it look like a house was really burning."

"Special effects?" Wolfgang seemed puzzled. "No one said anything about special effects. Your house really is burning. I figured if you could get away with burning your opponent's house down, so could I."

"What?" T.J. took a closer look. "That isn't my house, you idiot. That's my neighbor's house!"

"Oops. ... Well, let's get on with the question, shall we."

"For three points," Lester Block announced, as the question appeared on the Brains Board, "where were the Bee Gees born? (a) Gibraltar (b) the Cayman Islands (c) the Isle of Man."

T.J., a Bee Gees fan, slammed his buzzer. "C—the Isle of Man!"

"That is correct," said the head referee.

A smile crossed T.J.'s face as Kathy blew him a kiss.

"That's your quota for the game," said Wolfgang.

On the sidelines, Rock slapped T.J. on the back. "That's the way to do it, kid!"

The first quarter ended with the Hackers on top, 21-12.

Two minutes into the second quarter, Julie and Maxwell Tweed returned to centercourt.

"By the way, Miss Howard. You might want to be nicer to me. The F.B.I. has a bulky file on you. We know you've been consorting with known felons and weapons manufacturers."

"Are you out of your mind? Chase Turnbull is my teammate and the weapons manufacturer is a friend who makes toys for children."

"So you admit it?"

"The only thing I admit is that you are an idiot!"

"For two points," said Lester Block. "Who said 'drama is life with the dull bits cut out'?"

Julie slammed her buzzer first. "Alfred Hitchcock!"

"OUTSTANDING!" declared the Brains Board.

Hackers led, 24-14.

The Renaissance Men—Edgar Woodford and Leroy Hollinger—squared off in the Hot Zone.

"For three points," Lester Block said. "According to the Bible, who succeeded David as King of Israel?"

Hollinger, the ex-preacher, smacked the buzzer vigorously. "Solomon!" he declared.

"RIGHT, REVEREND!" announced the Brains Board.

"That's really fair, people," Edgar complained, apparently to the referees. "Of course he would know the answer to a Bible question. He pastored a church before he was kicked out!"

"I wasn't kicked out!" Hollinger declared. "It was a misunderstanding about money missing from the collection plate!"

Edgar smiled. "I think agent Tweed and his buddies at the F.B.I. will be interested in checking that out."

Hackers in control, 29-17.

The history specialists, Sam and Cynthia Medlow, rode to centercourt.

Sam held up a copy of *PHILanderer*. "This is Brian Marshall's new book. He tells about his one-night stand with Cynthia Medlow. Read all the gory details. Twenty-four dollars. Available now."

"That's a lie. I never ... he never ... we didn't ... oh, forget it."

Lester Block declared. "For two points: Who is the American credited with inventing air conditioning? Is it A. Rudolph Trane, B. Willis Carrier, or C. Harry Ruud?"

Cynthia walloped the buzzer. "A. Rudolph Trane."

"WRONG!" blared the Brains Board.

"Chicago?" said the referee.

"Harry Ruud?" Sam guessed.

"WRONG AGAIN!" said the Brains Board.

"It was Willis Crane," the referee said.

On the sidelines, Rock pulled out a clump of his hair.

Brian and Jaycee Yancey returned for a popular arts question.

"Don't slouch!" Jaycee ordered. "Sit up straight! Give me a year and I could whip you into shape!"

"You are such a tease," Brian commented.

"For three points," said the head referee. "In 1976, Jack Nicholson won an Academy Award as Best Actor in a Leading Role. What was the film he starred in?"

Jaycee slammed her buzzer. *"One Flew Over the Cuckoo's Nest!"*

"HURRAY JAYCEE!" exclaimed the Brains Board.

"I'm not surprised you knew the name of *that* movie," Brian commented.

Hackers led, 32-17.

On the sidelines, Rock conferred with Freud.

"Our players still don't have their heads on straight," Rock lamented. "They should be focused on fighting the enemy, but Edgar looks like a love-sick puppy, Sam and Julie act like love-struck teenagers, and T.J. keeps eying some dame in the sixth row. This isn't a whaling boat, out to destroy Moby Dick. We're on a freakin' Love Boat!"

"Calm down, Rock. They're giving it all they've got."

Just then T.J. blew a kiss to Kathy.

Jake Clayton and Chase Turnbull returned to centercourt.

"Whoa!" exclaimed Jake. "We had a close call with a

flock of birds. If they get into your engines, you've got real problems!"

"You've got real problems anyway," Chase suggested. "How did you get a pilot's license?"

"License? I need a license?"

"For three points," said Lester Block. "Which team won the National Basketball Association title every year but one from 1949 to 1954?"

Chase pushed his buzzer. "The Minneapolis Lakers!"

"WAY TO GO, CHASE!" noted the Brains Board.

Hacker lead cut to twelve points, 32-20.

Late in the first half, Julie Howard and Maxwell Tweed met in the Hot Zone.

"TWEED SEEMS RATTLED," Moose Harrison pointed out. "HE SLAM-DUNKED JULIE THE FIRST TIME UP, BUT SHE DROPPED HIM IN THEIR SECOND FACE-OFF. TWEED HAS HIS HANDS FULL WITH JULIE."

"Haven't you gone home yet?" asked Tweed.

"You really are a blowhard," Julie said.

"For three points," announced the referee. "Name the source of this quotation about Columbia University."

On the Brains Board appeared the lines:

> "It is the foremost university. There are thirty-two hundred courses. You spend your first two years in deciding what course to take, the next two years in finding the building that these courses are given in, and the rest of your life in wishing you had taken another course."

Julie walloped her buzzer. "Will Rogers!"

"That is correct!" said the referee.

Chicago fans roared their approval.

As time ran out in the first half, Wolfgang outdueled T.J. by identifying the capitol of Ethiopia as Addis Ababa.

"THE HACKERS GO TO THEIR LOCKER ROOMS LEADING BY NINE AT THE HALF, 45 TO 36," Moose told his television audience. "THE PHILS HAVE BEEN HANGING ON FOR DEAR LIFE. THEY'VE GOT TO GET THEIR ACT TOGETHER IF THEY'RE GOING TO BEAT THIS DETERMINED AND EXPERIENCED HACKER TEAM."

Disappointed and nervous, Rock faced his troops in the locker room.

"This is it. We're in the middle of World War III, the fate of the world is at stake, and you'd better get your heads on straight while there's still time."

Freud grimaced, fearing an onslaught was imminent. Yet, Rock's voice seemed to soften.

"It's been a rough ride for us this year. Been kind of like *The Odyssey*, where Odie had to battle fearsome enemies for ten years just to get home after the Trojan War."

"Odysseus," Freud whispered. "Not Odie."

"Don't nitpick. The point I'm making is this: he gave it everything he had, it took him ten years, but he got home and he prevailed. Sure, Odie was strong, but he survived because he was wily. He knew how to outwit his enemies.

"That's what we've been doing. Sometimes maybe we weren't the best or the smartest team, but we found a way to win. And that's what we've got to do now, when we're nine points down.

"Freud says I'm obsessed. Says I push you too hard, and forget to tell you when you do something right. He may have a point. I'm proud of some things you've done. Other things, not so much. Like the partying around Chicago when you should have been working.

"Sure, I may go too far, but the rest of you don't go far enough. And, by the way, just so you don't think you put one over on the old man—I know what you did in St. Louis ... how you set up Percy Smathers." He paused and looked around the room. *"Show me some of that spirt and teamwork on the playing floor!*

"Our focus now must be on only one thing—winning this game. *If you push yourselves to your limits for twenty-four minutes, you will be the league champions! This is our chance to make history! We can win this game!"*

"Just twenty-four minutes!" Brian shouted.

"We can do it!" Julie said.

"Let's win this one for Odie!" Chase hollered.

Rock grimaced. "I think he missed the point of my story."

With a new intensity, the team jogged back to the playing floor.

Rock put Juanita into the lineup to open the second half at the Renaissance slot.

The Hackers' Jaycee Yancey nailed the Shakespearean toss-up, ("A man can die but once; we owe God a death," from *Henry the Fourth*.)

Julie faced Maxwell Tweed in a quotations faceoff.

"How did you know about my relationship with David, the toy weapons maker? Did you bug my apartment?"

"Don't be paranoid. That would require a court order."

"You didn't answer my question."

"I didn't, did it?"

Lester Block intervened. "For three points, who was newspaper editor William Allen White writing about in this obituary?"

On the Brains Board appeared the quotation:

> This person "contributed to the journalism of his day the talent of a meatpacker, the morals of a money-changer and the manners of an undertaker."

Julie slammed the buzzer. "It's a perfect description of Percy Smathers, but the obit appeared before Percy's time, so the answer is Frank A. Munsey."

"RIGHT ON, JULIE!" raved the Brains Board.

Hacker coach Bronco Griffin immediately protested. "She disparaged the character of Percy Smathers while giving the answer. Nail her for unsportsmanlike conduct!"

Block asked the three judges for a ruling.

They conferred briefly. A few moments later Block announced the decision.

"It seems Percy Smathers once referred to one of our judges as 'a windbag with the physique of an elephant and the spine of a jellyfish'. The judges say Miss Howard's description of Smathers was reasonable."

The crowd roared its approval as Smathers yelled from the press area, "I'm going to sue the judges *and* the Phils! I'll sue the whole lot of you!"

The Phils trailed 49 to 39.

Henry hurried into the stadium with Margaret a half step behind. She had changed into her uniform.

"Sorry, Rock. I had to see Bernard."

Rock was in no mood for explanations. "Just get in there and give 'em hell!" He pulled Juanita out of the game and sent Margaret in.

As Margaret hurried toward the playing court, Rock asked Freud, "Who the hell is Bernard?"

"Her husband. Died twenty years ago."
"Lucky bastard."

Margaret took over the Renaissance chair. Rock sent Annie in to take over the world position. Edgar headed for the sidelines.

Margaret was immediately transported out to center-court to battle Leroy Hollinger.

"Nice of you to show up," Hollinger said. "Shall we see if the church will recognize it as a true miracle?"

"The miracle is that you aren't in jail. By the way, God left a message on my cell phone for you ..."

"Yes?" said Hollinger, warily.

"He said 'put the money back in the collection plate!' "

"Will you people stop saying things like that? God works in mysterious ways, but he doesn't leave telephone messages!"

Lester Block read the three-point question: "Which of these is *not* one of the six official languages of the United Nations? a. Chinese b. Spanish c. Italian d. Arabic."

Hollinger smacked the buzzer, "Italian!"

"Correct!" declared the head referee.

Moose Harrison commented, "MARGARET IS BACK, BUT THE PHILS TRAIL 52 TO 39 IN THE THIRD QUARTER. THE HACKERS ARE TRYING TO PUT THE GAME OUT OF REACH."

Cynthia Medlow and Sam Winslow faced off over a three-point history question: "Two presidents died July 4, 1826 as the United States celebrated the fiftieth anniversary of the signing of the Declaration of Independence. Name the presidents."

Sam swatted at his buzzer. "John Adams and Thomas Jefferson!"

"WHAT A ROOKIE!" exclaimed the Brains Board.

The Hackers led by ten, 52 to 42.

"Sam did it!" Mona shouted, as she rose from her seat. "My boy did it!"

Fred yelled, "Thatsa way to go, Sam!"

Mona noticed Joe had been too busy flirting with the brunette in the next seat to see Sam's moment of glory. She slapped Joe on the side of the head. "Pay attention and quit trying to get in her pants. Then you might amount to something—like your brother!"

Red-faced, Joe slumped in his seat.

In the press section, Percy Smathers leaned over to whisper to Diane Mercross. "It's time. Tell your contact to put the video up on the Brains Board."

"If that's what you want." She left the press box and made her way to the arena's control room.

In an effort to put the game further out of reach, the Hackers' Jaycee Yancey called a Double It! as she faced Brian at centercourt for a popular arts question.

"For four points," said the referee. "Who won a Grammy in 1958 for singing 'Catch a Falling Star'?"

Jaycee swatted her buzzer and answered the question. "Perry Como!"

"A WINNER!" the Brains Board noted.

The Hackers led by fourteen, 56 to 42.

Jake Clayton looked as though he was having a rough flight when he returned to centercourt to face Chase later in the third quarter.

"There's a strong headwind, but I can ride it out," said Clayton. "I'm bringing this baby in for a landing! Have the emergency equipment ready!"

"Thank you for flying on Crazy Jake Airlines," Chase commented.

"Get back to your seat and fasten your seat belt!"

Lester Block hesitated before deciding it was safe to ask the question. Before he could say anything, a video appeared on the Brains Board. "What's going on?" Block asked his assistants.

A giant image of Percy Smathers filled the Brains Board's screen.

"I am Percy Smathers. I apologize for interrupting the Brains Bowl, but I feel it is my duty to show Brains officials and the billion people watching the Brains Bowl the following video. It reveals the type of person this man really is. He is a sinister influence who casts a long and evil shadow on the game and the values we all hold dear. After you watch this, I am sure you will understand why it was necessary to interrupt the game."

The film clip began.

Moments later, a video featuring Smathers—not Rock—appeared on the screen. The video consisted of a rambling outburst Smathers unleashed when he did not know he was being filmed. Diane had talked a film editor into giving it to her. Thus, the massive Brains Bowl audience was treated to a look at Smathers, not Rock, going berserk ...

"I'll expose Rock if it's the last thing I do. I don't care what lengths we go to, I want to destroy him."

An aide said, *"You can't use your show to attack your enemies!"*

"That's exactly what I'll do. When I'm finished, Rock will have no friends, no reputation, no place to hide. ... Hire a private detective. I want to uncover every unsavory aspect of his life. Lie if you need to. This is my mission in life!"

"You can't do that!"

"You're right. That's too much trouble. Maybe we should plant a bomb, blow Rock to kingdom come and be rid of him forever."

"You've gone off the deep end. You need help."

"You're right. I can't do it alone. I'll need someone to plant the bomb for me."

"That's not the kind of help I was talking about."

"What is this?" Percy hollered from the press area. "Who sabotaged me? What happened to the video on Rock? Where's Diane Mercross? I demand answers!"

"THAT'S THE STRANGEST THING I'VE EVER SEEN," Moose Harrison told his viewers. "I THINK WE ALL JUST WITNESSED PERCY SMATHERS COMMITTING PROFESSIONAL SUICIDE."

At centercourt, Jake Clayton mumbled, "And they call *me* Crazy."

Lester Block said, "Where was I? Oh, yes. For two points: Indiana University won six straight NCAA titles from 1968 to 1973 in what sport? a. soccer b. swimming c. basketball d. cross country."

Chase slammed the buzzer. "Swimming!" he roared.

The Hackers led by twelve.

At the end of the third quarter, the Hackers were in control, 61 to 46.

"ONE QUARTER TO GO AND FIFTEEN POINTS BEHIND," Moose

Harrison reported. "It LOOKS BLEAK FOR THE PHILS. THE PLAYERS ARE EXHAUSTED."

ON THE SIDELINES, ROCK FACED his weary troops.

"The game isn't going the way I hoped. It's going the way I feared. But let's pretend it was part of our strategy. We gave the Hackers the lead. We let them get overconfident. Now comes the hard part—turning it around. Digging out of this fifteen-point hole we're in.

"You are twelve minutes away from a horrible defeat, but you can still turn it around. *You can win this game!* Reach down in your souls and find the way to victory. You didn't work this hard to go belly up in the final game. There have been a lot of distractions, a lot of mistakes. It's time to put all that aside. Get your heads on straight and focus only on our goal. This is here, this is now. You've got twelve minutes to win this game—and a lifetime to regret it if you don't. *You can do it!* ... anything to add, Freud?"

"All season, I've been telling Rock to back off. To let up on the pressure. But now is not the time to back off. Like the coach says, this is the time to give it everything you've got. *Let's win this game!"*

"Couldn't have said it better myself," Rock commented.

AS THE FOURTH QUARTER OPENED and the world specialists met at centercourt, Wolfgang Heller was not pleased to discover his opponent was another Phils second-stringer—Annie.

He glared at Rock. "You send subs up against the highest scorer in the league? This is an insult to me! *I call a terminator!"*

Rock called a timeout and made a substitution, as he had the right to do under the rules. He yanked Annie out of the game and sent Edgar back in. The terminator would now pit Wolfgang against Edgar.

When the timeout was over and Wolfgang came face-to-face with Edgar, he was not upset. "Play all the games you want, Rock. Makes no difference to me."

"For three points," said Lester Block. "When Nikita Khrushchev was removed from power in 1964, who emerged as Russia's powerful party secretary and premier?"

Edgar, the former secretary of state, slammed his buzzer. "Leonid Brezhnev was the party secretary and Aleksei Kosygin was the premier."

"TERRIFIC, EDDIE!" bannered the Brains Board. "GOODBYE, WOLFGANG!"

Edgar grimaced. "Its *Edward!*"

"THE PHILS CUT THREE POIINTS OUT OF THE HACKER LEAD—IT'S 61 TO 49—AND WOLFGANG, THE LEAGUE'S LEADING SCORER, HAS BEEN SENT HOME," Moose Harrison commented. "THAT WAS A BRILLIANT PIECE OF STRATEGY ON ROCK'S PART."

Julie Howard and Maxwell Tweed returned to the Hot Zone for a quotations faceoff.

"For two points, name the author and the novel." said Lester Block. On the Brains Board appeared the quotation:

> "It was the whiteness of the whale that above all things appalled me."

"Oh, my Lord," Rock muttered on the sidelines.

Julie couldn't believe it. She slammed the buzzer first. "Herman Melville, *Moby Dick*!"

The Brains Board flashed: "JULIE IS A WINNER!"

The Phils trailed 61-51.

Brian and Jaycee Yancey faced off over a three pointer.

"What are you doing after the game?" Brian asked.

"Target practice. What did you have in mind, Tender-foot?"

"Nothing."

"I thought so."

Lester Block read the three-point question: "In 1968, this song was recorded by the man who wrote it, but it didn't have much success. Then, it was recorded the next year in Memphis by a popular singer and it became a number one hit. Name the song and the writer."

On the Brains Board, a video began to play. The music was very familiar. The vocalist was Elvis.

Brian and Yancey both slammed their buzzers, but Brian was first. "Mark James, 'Suspicious Minds'!"

Their lead cut to seven points, the Hackers called a time out, but the crowd was still on it feet, swaying to the music. The referees let the video continue playing. And they let the video continue throughout the timeout. The crowd loved it. And so did the players.

Rock was upset by the distraction. Freud was not. "This is just what the team needed, Rock! Look at their faces. They're full of life. Full of fire. This is their moment. They've cut the lead to seven and they're ready to roll!"

Rock watched the spectacle in amazement. "I hope you're right."

After the timeout, Leroy Hollinger outdueled Margaret Kramer and the Hacker lead was back to ten, 64 to 54.

Sam Winslow and Cynthia Medlow rendezvoused at centercourt.

"The good news is I'm paying for your flight home," Sam told Medlow. "The bad news is it's on Crazy Jake Airlines."

"Thanks, but I know Crazy Jake better than you do.

There's no way in creation I'll get on a plane he's piloting."

Lester Block read the two-point question as it appeared on the Brains Board:

> Some have called this man the father of radio. He invented the triple-electrode vacuum tube. Who was he?
> (a) George Porter
> (b) Lee Deforest
> (c) Otto Stern

Sam swatted his buzzer.

"Lee Deforest!"

"WAY TO GO, SAM!" raved the Brains Board. The Hackers led 64 to 56.

Chase and Crazy Jake Clayton met in the Hot Zone.

"I'm having a little trouble getting my landing gear down," Clayton said. "Prepare for a crash landing!"

Chase grumbled "I may never fly again."

"Me either," said Lester Block. "For two points, who is credited with saying 'baseball is ninety percent mental and the other half is physical'?"

Chase confidently swatted the buzzer. "C. Yogi Berra!"

"WAY TO GO, CHASE!" The Hackers led by six, 64 to 58.

Edgar and Rene Lacoir, Wolfman's replacement, faced off at centercourt for a world question.

"I want to be the next secretary of state," Lacoir remarked. "How hard can it be? You aren't that bright."

"You amateurs think it's easy to screw other countries and plan covert operations and launch wars. It isn't. Stick to Brains and leave diplomacy to the grownups."

The head referee read the question as it appeared on the Brains Board:

> For two points: what is the capital of the Cook Islands?
> (a) Avarua
> (b) Lincoln
> (c) Plymouth

Edgar slammed his buzzer.

"(a) Avarua."

"RIGHT ON, EDDIE!" declared the Brains Board. The Hackers led 64 to 60.

Margaret and Leroy Hollinger were transported to the Hot Zone for a renaissance faceoff.

"For two points," declared Lester Block. "COBOL is a computer programming language. What does COBOL—"

Hollinger hit the buzzer. "It stands for Common Business-Oriented Language."

"WAY TO GO, LEROY!" said the Brains Board.

Moose Harrison was beginning to fear the worst for Chicago fans. "THE HACKERS LEAD BY SIX, 66 TO 60, WITH TWO MINUTES AND EIGHT SECONDS REMAINING IN THE GAME!"

When the timeout ended, Julie and Maxwell Tweed met in the Hot Seat. Rock signaled Julie to call a "Double It". The two-point question was now worth four points.

"This could backfire on the Phils!" Moose Harrison pointed out. "If the Hackers get the points, they will be ten-points ahead and the game will be out of reach!"

Fans watched nervously as Lester Block declared, "For four points, name the source of this quotation:"

> "I loathe people who keep dogs. They are cowards who haven't got the guts to bite people themselves."

Julie punched her buzzer. Rock's eyes opened wide as she paused before answering. Finally, she said, "August Strindberg."

A roar erupted from Chicago fans as the Brains Board flashed "WAY TO GO, JULIE!"

"ELEVEN SECONDS REMAIN AND THE PHILS TRAIL THE HACKERS BY TWO POINTS, 66 TO 64." Moose Harrison exclaimed. "NOW, IT'S ALL UP TO THE HISTORY ACES—THE PHILS' UNTESTED RECRUIT, SAM WINSLOW, AND THE HACKERS' CYNTHIA MEDLOW. THEY WILL BATTLE OVER ONE FINAL THREE-POINT QUESTION. TALK ABOUT PRESSURE! ROCK JUST CALLED A TIMEOUT."

In the stands, Mona Winslow was a nervous wreck. "My heavens. Sometimes I didn't trust Sam to take out the garbage. Now everything depends on him?"

"That's right, ma," Joe said. "Pretty scary, isn't it."

Fred rose from his seat. "We should get out of here before all the taxis are taken."

Mona glared at him. "Don't you dare move! Sit down and wait till it's over!"

Fred reluctantly planted his butt on the bleachers.

With the Brains Bowl championship on the line, Sam and Cynthia Medlow rode to the Hot Zone.

Sam took a deep breath as noise in the stadium began to subside. Franklin, Indiana seemed a long way from the Emerald City Dome. What was he doing here, and who were all these people?

On the sidelines, Rock moaned. "So it all comes down to Winslow. ... Good Lord ... He probably thinks he's playing basketball. What did I do to deserve this?"

"Should I give him the list in alphabetical order?" Brian whispered to Margaret.

The crowd waited anxiously. Lester Block began reading the final question as it flashed on the Brains Board.

Sam nearly keeled over. It was about the Middle Ages. His Achilles heel. Everything was riding on his knowledge of the Middle Ages. Lord, was he in trouble. Sam recalled his terrifying dream about a dissertation on the Middle Ages: ... *Very poorly executed. Does not meet our standards. Beat it, kid.*

He focused on the question:

> Two of these statements about the Middle Ages are not true. Which ones are they?
>
> 1- Students in church schools were taught Latin.
>
> 2- Charlemagne's empire included much of what is now central Europe.
>
> 3- Oxford was founded by students who left Cambridge during violence between the university and townspeople.
>
> 4-Elizabeth de Clare paid for the education of many boys in England and provided help for thousands of people in need.
>
> 5- Geoffrey Chaucer wrote *The Canterbury Tales* in the fifteenth century.

Sam pushed his buzzer before he finished reading the question. He knew he had to answer it.

"Number three is incorrect. Cambridge was founded by students who left Oxford. And number five is incorrect. Chaucer wrote *The Canterbury Tales* in the fourteenth century."

Sam and the crowd waited .....

"That's correct!" proclaimed Lester Block as time ran out.

Ecstatic Chicago fans cheered and hugged each other as the Brains Board flashed "CHICAGO PHILS—BRAINS BOWL CHAMPIONS!" Fireworks exploded. Confetti floated down from the rafters.

Brian and Chase snuck up behind Rock and dumped a huge container of root beer on him.

"What the hell?" Rock muttered. Then he realized the team had drenched him, just like football players drenched their coaches when they won big games. Soaking wet, Rock grimaced. "Y'know, when players drench a coach, they generally don't use root beer."

"Sorry, coach," Brian said. "We're new at this."

Moose Harrison was ecstatic as he described the bedlam to fans watching across the country and around the world. "THE PHILS DID IT! AGAINST ALL ODDS, THE AMAZING CHICAGO PHILOSOPHERS HAVE WON THE BRAINS BOWL. AN INCREDIBLE FOURTH-QUARTER COMEBACK GAVE THEM THE CHAMPIONSHIP!"

Fans rushed onto the playing area and lifted Rock, Sam, Julie, Brian, T.J., Edgar, Annie and Juanita onto their shoulders. They were about to hoist Margaret when she growled, "don't even think about it!"

Freud's and Chase's celebrating was more subdued. They collapsed into seats and chugged down beers as they watched the pandemonium around him.

A short time later, Rock, soaking wet, pounded Freud on the back. "We did it! We really did it!"

Freud grinned. "It just shows what determination and a truckload of anti-depressant drugs can do!"

Rock congratulated team members and slapped them on the back as cameramen, reporters and photographers swarmed around him. Ben Sloan crowded in next to Rock so he could be in the pictures.

"I knew Rock could do it," Ben told reporters. "He's one in a million."

Ben looked around, sniffing. "What's that I smell? Root beer?"

"What about rumors that some of your starters won't be back next year?" someone shouted at Rock.

The voice sounded familiar. Rock turned toward the questioner and was stunned to see Henry.

"I thought you took a coaching job."

"I did. This reporting gig is temporary. So, are some of your starters leaving the team?"

"We'll be better than ever next season. Brian, Chase and Edgar are under contract for another year. We'll be talking to the others. I expect all of them back."

"Not me," Margaret grumbled a short distance away. "We fought our way through incredible obstacles and got the job done. Now, I'm going to rest my nerves for about twenty years."

"What about you?" a reporter asked Sam.

"I don't know. Too soon to say."

Irene finally found Edgar Woodford. "When we get back to the hotel," she said, "we'll need to tell Glory all about the game."

"She knows what happened," Edgar said. "I left the television on so she could watch it."

A reporter was interviewing Julie when Sam came up and pulled her away.

"Let's get away from all the pressure and have dinner alone tonight," Sam suggested.

"The Brains Bowl is over. There's no pressure."

"We need to talk about our future together."

"What future together?"

"That's one of the things we need to talk about. I love you, Julie, and I know you love me."

"I never said I loved you."

"I know, but you're such a klutz when it comes to relationships, I forgive you."

He kissed her.

Brian, watching from fifteen feet away, shook his head. "Well, that's just dandy. Half the team is making out and I'm stuck contemplating my naval."

Diane Mercross came up beside him. "What's the matter, Brian. Feeling left out?"

Brian smiled. "Not any more. Got anything planned for the next twelve hours?"

"Yes."

"Oh. Well have a good time." He started off.

"Not so fast, Brian! I thought we'd do it together."

She caught up with him.

As T.J. and Kathy headed to the locker room, Moose Harrison shoved a microphone in front of Rock. "YOU ACTUALLY DID IT, ROCK! AGAINST ALL ODDS, YOU PULLED IT OFF! HOW DO YOU FEEL NOW THAT YOU'RE THE CHAMPIONS?"

Rock took a deep breath. "TERRIFIC ... BUT IT'S NOT AS SAT-

ISFYING AS I THOUGHT IT WOULD BE. NEXT SEASON, THERE WILL BE ANOTHER WHALE TO SLAY, ANOTHER TITLE TO WIN. AND AFTER THAT, ANOTHER ONE. WHEN DOES IT END? WHEN CAN I STEP BACK AND SAY WE REALLY DID IT?"

Brian came up behind Rock. "NOW, COACH. WE CAN SAY IT NOW. YOU SPEARED THE WHALE. LET IT GO."

Rock glared at him. "THAT'S JUST THE KIND OF LAZY, GOOD-FOR-NOTHIN' ATTITUDE I'D EXPECT FROM A CALIFORNIA BEACH BUM. WELL, MISTER, ENJOY TONIGHT, BECAUSE TOMORROW WE START TRAINING FOR NEXT SEASON!"

As Brian wandered off with Diane, he muttered, "I've got to find a better job."

Mona, Fred and Joe pushed their way through the crowd and reached Sam.

"My boy, the hero!" Mona wailed.

"Way to go, little brother!" Joe shouted.

"Thanks," Sam said. "By the way, there's someone you should meet. This is Julie. Get used to having her around, because we'll be spending a lot of time together."

Mona looked shocked. "I thought the television said Julie was engaged to someone else."

"I was, but we broke up yesterday," Julie explained.

Mona felt faint. "Yesterday. And a day later, you and my son are together?" She fell into a seat and whispered to Fred, "I told you we shouldn't let Sam go to Chicago. First, it was Uncle Walter's lips freezing on the beer can. Then, Sam goes up there for four weeks and he's practically engaged. … Well, don't just stand there. Straighten him out!"

Fred nodded. "Welcome to the family," Fred told Julie. He turned to his son. "You did good, Sam. Congratulations. … So, what happened to the money you sent me?"